MARY

13

To the memory of John Attenborough
who inspired me to write this novel,
and to my wife Daisy for her patience and
fortitude in keeping me writing.

Acknowledgement

To my local library for having the manuals of
'The Times' covering the periods between 1930 and the 1960s.

MARY
An unusual vagrant

Robert Bennie

HALLMARK PRESS

Published by Hallmark Press International Ltd
34 Lambton Court,
Peterlee,
County Durham
SR8 1NG

Typeset by TW Typesetting, Plymouth, Devon

Printed by CPI Antony Rowe, Eastbourne

ISBN 978 1 906459 08 6

Suffolk County Council	
07436379	
Askews	Jun-2009
	£7.95

CONTENTS

SYNOPSIS

Mary was well known around the newspaper offices of Fleet Street, because she was very poorly clothed and was always seen carrying two bags that contained her belongings. She was a quiet lady who never spoke to anybody, but there were occasions when she was heard speaking in an educated tone of voice. Then following enquiries and researching by some newspaper workers, it was discovered that she had at one time been a qualified staff nurse, and this caused them to wonder how she could have descended into the life which she was living.

It was snowing just before Christmas Eve as Mary made herself comfortable in a doorway opposite the church of St Clement Danes in the Strand. Looking at the church and knowing that it was the church of the RAF it reminded her of her husband who had been shot down and killed during World War II, then as the peals of the church rang out their rhyming tune, it also reminded her of her childhood. Every day since she was a child she had written a diary of all the events that happened to her during that day. With the street lamps giving her light, and while the bells were ringing out their tune, she found her pencil and began to write the day's events. Afterwards she began reading the book and as she fell asleep, she dreamt of her family, her childhood and the traumas they had been through. It was Mr and Mrs Swinton, friends of her family who lived in the village of Hemelsham, who had given her the financial help which had enabled her to get her nursing qualifications. She relived the unfortunate meeting with a doctor, the lothario son of the Chairman of the General Medical Council, but it was a chance meeting with Shirley Withers, a feature writer with the *Daily Tribune*, who befriended her, who eventually managed to find out the reason why Mary is a vagrant.

The story also reveals how Mary's behaviour and character influenced many other people's lives.

1

MARY'S PARENTS

Joe Mummery was born in 1898. When he was a small lad at school his friends, who were 12 months older than him, because of his surname called him 'Mummy'. Joe left school in 1910 at the age of twelve, and one of his friends who was already working on a farm got him a job there as a farm labourer. In the evenings he and his friend met up with their other four friends and played games. It was in 1915, on a Saturday afternoon, when they were all together talking about the War with Germany and the big recruitment drive taking place throughout England, that suddenly one of them said, 'Why don't we all join the Army, and be together?' They agreed, and off they all went to Bembridge town market square where there was a tent with the Union Jack flag flying from a mast and a burly sergeant, looking very smart in his uniform, standing just outside the tent.

When the sergeant heard they all wanted to volunteer, he smiled and let them into the tent to sign the forms. However when he heard banter going on amongst them about Joe being 12 months younger than the rest, he said Joe couldn't join, but added that in twelve months time Joe could volunteer again and he would be accepted. On their return to the village when the news got round that they had volunteered, they had a small party and everyone was pleased they were enlisting to help the war effort. It was some time after they had joined the Army that they came home on leave in their new uniforms and told everyone they were in 1st Battalion of the Oxford/Bucks Light infantry and were going to France. Joe was sad that they were leaving, but told them to save a place for him because he would be joining them within twelve months.

It was some time later that Joe was told that four of his friends had been killed and one had been seriously injured and eventually died. This news made Joe more determined to join the Army to avenge their deaths, and in March 1916 he again volunteered and became a member of the Royal Welch Fusiliers.

Within a few months Joe was in France at Bethune, at first posted at the rear of the fighting to help with stretcher bearing the wounded to a field hospital. However because of a severe shortage of fit fighting men, Joe soon found himself on the front line in a machine gun unit. After a long time fighting and because of the noise of the heavy British guns and the German shells exploding all around them, he and the men in his unit had not had a decent night's sleep and his nerves, and the nerves of many men with him, were near breaking point. Luckily another machine unit was ordered to relieve them and this enabled them to move back to a rest area for some respite and sleep.

For several days it had been raining incessantly and by the time they had reached the rest area, he and his men were very wet and tired and they searched around for a dry place to make themselves as comfortable as possible. Joe and a few others found a barn damaged by shells that still had part of its roof in place. Inside the ruins Joe quickly scrambled underneath an old farm cart that had a load of farm waste and rubble on it, but being completely exhausted he hadn't noticed the smell of a several-day-old corpse lying on top of the cart.

After a short period of rest they were sent back to another sector of the front line, and it was on the journey through Etaples he noticed on a board in bold letters the following words:

A wise old owl lived in an oak,
The more he saw the less he spoke,
The less he spoke the more he heard,
Soldiers should imitate that wise old bird

Joe realised it was a very wise old adage and proceeded to commit it to memory, hoping to remember it after the war. They had travelled via Dranoutre and Vlamertinghe and then somewhere to the east of the Menin Gate, where they were told to dig in. After days of fighting and heavy shelling, a shell burst close to him and he was badly injured by its fragments and by the poisonous fumes of Bromine gas, which culminated in him being transferred back to England. He eventually recovered from the shell injuries, but because he had trouble with his breathing he was discharged and invalided out of the Army. Joe thought it a dishonour to be invalided out of the Army, and it was only after seeking advice from an Army Chaplain, who explained to him the correct way to look at his discharge, that he eventually accepted it.

On arriving home, though his parents knew he had been wounded and had been medically discharged, he never told them how bad his injuries were, but he did tell them that he was never going to work on a farm again because he wanted to use his army training and experience to get a better paid job.

A short while later he heard of a job requiring someone with the knowledge of explosives to work in an iron ore quarry. This quarry was 40 miles away near the village of Hemelsham, and being determined to get the job and not having any mechanised transport, he knew that he had to be totally reliant on his bicycle and pedal all the way.

Before leaving home he told his parents that if he got the job he would write to them and let them know where he was lodging.

At night he slept out in the open, using his army training to keep himself warm and dry. The journey took him two days. After stopping to rest on the banks of the river Witham and eat the sandwiches he had brought with him, he eventually arrived at the village of Hemelsham, still very tired and hungry. Putting his bicycle against the wall of the village grocery shop, he wearily went inside and there he met Millie Doran, a young girl who sold him some bread and cheese, and in answer to his questioning she explained exactly where the quarry was situated.

At the quarry, Joe went into a hut where he was interviewed by the manager who said he was looking for a person with experience in explosives. Joe told him of his army experience, and immediately was told that he was just the person they wanted in the quarry. Joe decided not to tell the manager about his injuries or his breathing problems, and was told to start work on Monday morning. On leaving the quarry Joe went back to the village grocery shop and asked Millie if she knew of a place to stay. A lady came into the shop just as Millie was telling him that she could not offer him accommodation and didn't know of anywhere else he could stay.

He came out of the store feeling very dejected and despondent, knowing that without lodgings he would be unable to start work on Monday. He was slowly pushing his bike along the road, when the lady who had been in the shop came hurrying along and walked beside him saying, 'I do apologise for overhearing your conversation with Millie just now about wanting somewhere to stay, but can I suggest you go to the vicarage?' and began to point and show him where the vicarage was situated.

Joe noticed she was a strikingly good looking woman and all the time she was talking to him and pointing to the vicarage, he was noticing her beautiful hazel eyes and slim body. Just as she was about to depart, she smiled at him and said, 'I feel sure that the vicar, who is a very nice and considerate person, will be able to assist you.'

With gratefulness showing in the tone of his voice, Joe said, 'Thank you very much.' As she walked away he felt a surge of emotions within himself and a feeling of longing, that if only he could have met her under other circumstances, he would be asking her to go out with him. He stood there watching her for a few more moments, then turned his gazed to the vicarage and began to walk towards it, with mixed emotions because he was very apprehensive about meeting the vicar, and his thoughts were still on the young lady who appeared so nice and good looking. Yet he had the feeling that the vicar would be able to help him. When the Reverend Newham opened the door, having listened to Joe's difficulties he invited him into the house, where he proceeded to ask Joe many questions about himself and what had he done during the war.

Joe described how had joined the Army and some of his lighter wartime experiences in France, then he explained he had cycled 40 miles to obtain work at the quarry, and that unless he could find accommodation he would not be able to start on Monday. When Joe had finished speaking, the Rev. Newham looked at him very intently and to his embarrassment closely examined his features. Then saying 'I will not be moment,' he rose and left the room, to return within a few moments with Mrs Newham who, when she heard the reason for Joe's visit, looking at Joe, she nodded her head to her husband and then left the room.

While his wife was out of the room, the Rev. Newham and Joe continued to talk to each other, particularly about the church and its role in society. About ten minutes had gone by when there was a knock on the front door, and Mrs Newham came into the room followed by another woman in her early twenties, whom Joe immediately recognised as the lady who had shown him the way to the vicarage. Mrs Newham introduced her to Joe as Miss Ethel Kyte and proceeded to tell him that Miss Kyte's brother and father had been killed in France during the war and the shock of their deaths had caused Miss Kyte's mother to have a serious heart attack and she had died, leaving Miss Kyte all alone in her cottage. Joe was then asked again to explain his position to Miss Kyte.

Having heard his explanation, Ethel Kyte looked at Rev. Newham, who was nodding his head, and she said to Joe, 'I need someone to help me pay the rent of the cottage I live in, and if you promise to pay me money towards the rent and not come home drunk, or interfere with my way of life, then I can offer you a room.' Joe was delighted to hear this news and gave his promises to her, at the same time thanking Rev. and Mrs Newham for their kindness and understanding. After another short talk with the vicar, Joe and Miss Kyte left the vicarage together and walked down the lane towards her cottage. Being summertime, the hedges were in full bloom and it made a picturesque sight with the grass verge full of wild bluebells and daffodils. The sight of it enthralled Joe and he began to talk to Ethel about it, until after a few more paces they reached the cottage where she lived, and Ethel invited Joe inside.

The time simply flew by and after a short talk they reached a solution and an agreement on where he was going to sleep. With this solved Joe was able to start work at the quarry on Monday morning.

Three weeks later Joe and Ethel walked past the vicarage as Mrs Newham was changing the front room curtains. She saw them go by, and because of the manner in which they were acting towards each other, she felt very pleased because it appeared that they were getting romantically involved with each other.

A few Saturdays later, Mrs Newham invited Ethel and Joe to afternoon tea and while Joe and Rev. Newham were in the garden Ethel, who was with Mrs Newham in the kitchen making the sandwiches, very suddenly said, 'Joe has asked me to marry him! I feel sure that I love him, but I'm not sure what to say, because I feel maybe we should wait a few more months . . .' Mrs Newham looked at Ethel and said very sincerely, 'Ethel, I am very delighted to hear this news. If you feel that Joe will make you happy and treat you with respect, and I'm sure he will, why wait? Now if you do decide to get married, would you like my husband to conduct the marriage service for you?' Ethel's face was very red as she said, 'Oh yes please I would like that very much.'

Exactly one month later Ethel and Joe were married in the village church of Hemelsham, with Joe's parents and a number of the villagers being present to see the wedding.

Ethel's cottage was rented from the local village Squire, and the day after their wedding, Ethel and Joe decided to visit him. The Rev. Newham, being very friendly with the Squire, had told him all about Joe's wartime exploits and about him marrying Ethel. The Squire, who knew Ethel from a small child, also knew how much she had to endure to overcome the traumas of the death of her father, brother and then of her mother, and when he met and talked with them, he decided to give them a wedding present of some money to buy some personal things, as well as four weeks free rent.

Joe and Ethel always worked together to make their home comfortable and appeared to be a happy couple, and it was no surprise to Mrs Newham that within ten months Ethel gave birth to a baby girl. It was she who recommended to Ethel that the Rev. Newham christen the baby, whom Ethel called Margery. Because of their close relationship, as well as all the help they had received from the Newham family, Ethel asked Mrs Newham to be a Godmother.

The sun always shone in the rear garden of Joe and Ethel's cottage and as they looked over the small hedge they had a lovely view of the cows and sheep in the fields. There was a small copse of trees about a mile away, that partially hid an Royal Air Force flying school, and when Margery was in the garden she was able to see the aeroplanes flying very low over the fields, then zoom up into the sky before twisting round and diving down to fly very low over the fields and the copse.

Joe and Ethel were well thought of by the villagers and regarded as one of the respectable families who went to church regularly. Joe worked very hard in the quarry and, poorly paid like all the other workers, after paying the rent of the cottage they only had enough money to buy essential food. Although they did not have many clothes, they always made sure Margery looked clean and tidy in the pram when they were out with her and they were always pleasing to talk to and never moaned.

Everyone knew that Ethel worked hard to keep the cottage looking nice and they knew that Joe loved his garden, where he had a small neatly cut lawn with a colourful border of geraniums, roses and red pansies, which Joe always told everyone reminded him of the red poppies in the battlefields of France.

In 1923 the small airfield was enlarged, now having a housing estate for officers and three brick buildings for the airmen. Having all this extra accommodation meant that the village was doing more trade in the pubs and the village shops. One day the owner of the grocery store died and Mr and Mrs Swinton became the new owners.

Joe loved Ethel very much and he adored his little girl who, as she became older, skipped every day along the lane to meet him coming home from work. One day after he had finished his evening meal he was sitting on the grass in the rear garden when Ethel came up to him and asked him to listen to Margery sing. She was four and half years old, and standing before him in a lovely childish way she lisped her way through the rhymes of 'Ring a ring of Roses' and 'Oranges and Lemons'. She could not pronounce some of the words properly, which made Joe smile and clap his hands, which made Margery very excited, and Ethel had a hard job getting her to sleep that night.

One day, during his summer work break, Joe decided to take Ethel and Margery to see his parents. As they lived 40 miles away in a large village called Wisham, this meant going by bus, which they had to change four times. As they were going over one of the many bridges the buses had to cross, Margery became very excited when she saw people on the river in punts and small boats, and wanted to know why they were wearing straw hats. Ethel told her that they were young people studying at a big school called a university and the hats were part of their school uniform.

Margery was asleep when they reached Wisham and when they arrived at his parents' cottage they put her in the same bedroom where they were going to sleep. Joe's parents, George and Maude, were excited to see them and felt happy that Joe had settled down and married Ethel. Knowing that Joe was working and had such a good wife and a lovely little daughter, made George and Maude feel very contented.

Not having seen each other for a long time, after a quick meal the four of them sat in the small rear garden and chatted very late before going to bed. The following morning Joe and his father decided to go to Medhurst farm, where Joe used to work, to see the cattle being sold. At the farm, Joe noticed his father was limping. 'What's up Pop?' he asked, why are you limping?' His father sharply replied, 'Nothing's the matter with me, stop worrying. It's only a touch of rheumatics.' Joe was shaken by his father's sharp retort, but he put it down to his dad going to bed late the night before.

While Joe and his father were at the farm, Ethel and Maude had taken Margery to the village shops, which were set in a semicircle around a large pond, with a wide expanse of grass running down to its edge. All the villagers came to this spot, both to do their shopping and, with the village pubs being nearby, it was also the ideal place where they could meet for a good chat and have a lovely picnic. The pond was fed from a small culvert that contained rainwater from the adjacent hills, and therefore the water was always fresh and had plenty of wildlife in and around it. It also had another culvert that went under the main road into the village, thereby enabling the water from both culverts to gently flow into the river Witham. It was an ideal place in the summertime to bring children, because after shopping, most of the villagers sat on the grass or outside the 'Wheatsheaf' and the 'Goose and Gridiron' pubs.

Being a beautiful sunny day, Ethel and Maude had bought some lovely newly baked bread from the local baker's shop, fresh out of the oven and still warm, and from the grocery shop they had bought cheese and tomatoes. When Joe and his father appeared the men immediately suggested that they go to the 'Wheatsheaf' and buy beer and soft drinks so that they could stay by the pond and have a picnic. With the sun shining Ethel and Maude agreed and soon they were all eating sandwiches, drinking beer and soft drinks and looking at the little pea moorhens running in and out of the reeds and long grass at the water's edge, whilst swans, ducks and other wildlife swam around on the pond. With other people sitting on the grass nearby also drinking and eating, Ethel and Joe felt happy having their picnic with his parents and watching Margery playing happily with a little girl whose brother was sailing his boat. Joe told Ethel that he loved this spot because in the summertime when he was a little boy, he built and had sailed his home-made wooden sailing boats on the pond, and in the wintertime when the pond was frozen, he and some of the lads from the village used to play and slide about on the frozen pond playing hockey with home-made hockey sticks.

The sun shone every day from cloudless skies, and being on his firm's annual week's holiday, Joe and Ethel took Margery every day to feed the ducks and other wildlife on the pond, and soon they were suntanned and looking very healthy. At the end of the week George and Maude, both now in their late sixties, were sorry to see Joe and Ethel go home. They had not told Joe and Ethel that prior to their visit they had both been unwell, and they felt that this might be the last time they would see them. When Joe with Ethel and little Margery were leaving the cottage, Maude gave Margery a porcelain clock that had small porcelain yellow flowers decorating it. 'My Luv,' she told Margery as she gave it to her, 'every time you look at this clock it will remind you of your Nanny and Granddad.' After kissing each other goodbye, Joe promised he would try and visit them again before Christmas. On the bus on the way home, Margery was showing Ethel and Joe the clock her Nanny had given her.

Two months later Joe received a letter from his mother saying that his father was ill in hospital. He was unable to get leave of absence from work during the week, and it was the weekend when he left Ethel and Margery at home, while he rather anxiously travelled to the hospital near Wisham. As he entered the ward corridor he could see his mother at his father's bedside, and as he walked past the Sister's office, she came out and asked him whom he was visiting. Hearing his reply, she invited him into her office and sent for the doctor who was attending to his father. When the doctor arrived he explained to Joe that his father was suffering from acute blood poisoning and his condition was worsening. The doctor then asked Joe if he knew whether his father had cut and cleaned the corns of his feet with an open-ended razor which he used for shaving. Joe thought for a moment, before saying 'No'.

The doctor said, 'Your father told me that a short while ago that he had cut his toe while he was cutting a corn and it had bled, then without cleaning the razor he later shaved with it and he cut his face.' The doctor paused for a moment before saying, 'I'm sorry to say, your father didn't take care of the cut on his toe, nor the cut on his face, and I am sorry to inform you that severe blood poisoning has set in.'

'During the summer I noticed my father was limping', said Joe, 'and he told me that, though his leg was red and hot, it was caused through rheumatism.'

'That must have been the start of his illness,' replied the doctor, 'because the foot and leg are now in an advanced stage of gangrene and if we had been able to see your father at an earlier stage, we could have amputated his leg to try and stop the gangrene from spreading. Unfortunately not having any competent drugs it is too late to combat the gangrene. I'm sorry to tell you that he has only a few months to live, and therefore we are going to keep him in hospital.'

Seeing the shock on Joe's face the doctor said to him, 'Would you like to sit down and wait a few moments before visiting your father, and would you also like me to inform your mother of the serious condition your father is in?'

Joe thought for a few seconds before he said, 'Yes please, but break it to her gently, because recently she too has not been in the best of health and the news of this will certainly shake her.'

Due to the severe economic recession throughout the country, Joe was unable to obtain days off to visit his father again for a number of weeks and when he did manage to get time off from work, on arrival at the hospital and going straight to his father's bedside he saw his father's features were ashen and he had his eyes shut. Joe felt that his father was very near to death and he reached forward and held his hand. As he did so, George opened his eyes and gave Joe a weak smile and mouthed a thank you. Then giving a big sigh and a slight murmur, he died. It was then that Joe noticed that his father's face had lost its look of pain and a look of peacefulness appeared in its place.

Joe walked very sadly away from the hospital. When he reached his mother's cottage he thought how old she looked. Seeing the expression on Joe's face and hearing of George's death, she cried out loud, 'Oh no, not my George!' and started to cry. A few moments later she began gasping for breath, her face went deathly white and suddenly she collapsed into Joe's arms. Very gently he seated and settled her into a chair and hurried to the neighbour next door. On hearing of George's death and the collapse of Maude, she told Joe to go back to his mother while she rushed to fetch Mrs Spence, the lady whom the villagers called upon to attend to their needs at the time of births, illnesses or deaths. Because many of the villagers were unable to pay medical fees, Mrs Spence was well known by the local village doctor as the person who helped the villagers at such times.

Directly Mrs Spence reached the cottage, seeing Maude with her eyes shut and her face beginning to sag, with her left arm hanging limply by her side and her head resting on her left shoulder, she knew that Maude had suffered a severe stroke and was lapsing into unconsciousness. She told Joe to get Dr Brevin to come quickly to his mother. When Joe returned he helped Mrs Spence put his Mother into a more comfortable position and shortly afterwards the doctor arrived, but as he went to examine her, Maude's body gave two mighty convulsive jerks and went entirely limp. The doctor tested and examined Maude and said she had died.

To Joe, the shock of losing both parents within three hours was very severe, but he managed to control his innermost feelings until he arrived home, where in the quietness and sanctity of his own home, and with Ethel by his side, he let his emotions burst forth.

A week later, Ethel and Joe returned to Wisham. Ethel took Margery to one of Maude's neighbours and left her there, while she and Joe attended to the funeral of his parents, who were buried together in a small corner plot in the village churchyard. The day after the funeral, as George and Maude had only rented their cottage, Joe began clearing it of his parents' possessions. After packing a couple of small boxes containing personal items that he was taking home with him, he managed to dispose of the small amount of furniture his parents had, by giving it to some of the neighbours living nearby.

The Christmas of 1925 for Ethel and Joe was a quiet one, however they did try to make sure that Margery had a nice time, because Joe had managed to get a very small Christmas tree and he had put it in a garden bucket containing earth, and putting a little tinsel on the branches, and with red berries from the bushes growing nearby to decorate it, he placed it in the corner of the room.

When they put Margery to bed on Christmas Eve, they gave her a pillowcase to hang at the end of the bed, telling her that Father Christmas might call and leave her some presents. When she woke up in the morning she found inside the pillowcase some home-made dolls and some sweets and fruit.

In the afternoon, Margery stood in the middle of the room near the open fire which was burning logs, and the flames were making shadows on the wall behind the Christmas tree. She sang her party piece of 'Oranges and Lemons' without making a single mistake and watching the shadows on the wall and listening to her, for a few moments Ethel and Joe forgot their money troubles. They felt proud of Margery and realised she was beginning to grow up and developing her own lively personality.

As the weeks went by, Joe and Ethel were worrying about the state of their finances. They had heard and noticed that the country's economy was very bad, and it was not only affecting them, but also many others in the villages, towns and firms around the country. Joe and Ethel knew the people's mood in the country had changed, because they were hearing of more and more people who were being made redundant and everyone was getting angry at not being able to find work. Everyone had an air of discontentment about themselves and at Joe's firm, though some people had been made redundant, Joe had still managed to keep his job, but he was made to work more hours each week for less pay, which meant he was working longer and harder and seeing less of Margery and Ethel.

It was because of lack of investment in the quarry and due to bad working conditions that Joe could foresee an accident occurring, and although everything appeared normal, the work was being performed on a very tight and stringent budget. This meant that because of the fear of losing jobs, the last thing anyone was thinking of was safety. During this period, Joe was also worried how he was going to keep his family well fed, because events were taking place during the year throughout the country that had a marked effect upon his life, and he had been told that because of the economic recession he would have to work a three-day week with a good deal less money coming in for the household.

On a very sunny day very shortly afterwards, Ethel was walking past the shops in the village with Margery by her side, when she met the Rev. and Mrs Newham. During her conversation with them she told them of Joe's problems at work and how they were having difficulties making ends meet due to their lack of money. It was after listening to Ethel that Mrs Newham told her of a position that Ethel might like to do which might help them with their money problem.

Mrs Newham asked her if she would be willing to work at the Squire's manor, because she had heard that the girl who was working as a chambermaid was leaving to get married and going to live in Norwich.

Without consulting Joe, Ethel readily agreed because she knew that she had only enough money left in her purse to buy a few meat bones and vegetables and she felt she had to take the job. But she also knew Joe would be very upset. Because of his concern for Margery, when Joe heard of what she had done he was against her working, but due to Ethel's common sense and perseverance, he relented and thanks to Mrs Newham speaking to the Squire, she started work as a chambermaid at the village manor.

Just after Ethel had started work, Joe's firm stopped trading. It was shortly afterwards that Joe heard that the miners of Jarrow were protesting about their working conditions and were marching to London. He said to Ethel that when those miners walked past Kirkbridge he was going to join them, but due to Ethel's protestations he was persuaded to stay at home. It turn out to be good advice, because a short while later the whole country was caught up in a general strike, and together with the turmoil of the strife and disturbance, a number of people were arrested.

When the strike was over and the troubles subsided, it took businesses a long time to reopen, and it was two months before the management could reopen the quarry and Joe was able to start work again. During the general strike the quarry was closed, but when it reopened Joe found the working equipment and the conditions at the quarry had deteriorated very badly. But because of their fear of losing their jobs, none of the workers would listen, or assist him, with his complaints on safety. However within eighteen months of reopening there was an accident, two men were killed and several men were badly injured, including Joe.

Ethel was still working at the manor and Margery, who was now eleven years old, loved going to the village school, and particularly she loved singing in the school choir, but she had been told by Ethel that after school she must run home to help Joe, who was slowly recovering from his injuries and recuperating at home.

One day after staying behind singing in the choir, she and her friend Susan came home and found Joe asleep in a chair in the garden, and on the grass beside him was the morning newspaper whose headlines read:

Calamitous end to a great British airship – Empire appalled by the loss of the R101 with 46 lives – Among the dead was Lord Thomson the Air Minister, and Sir Sexton Branker, Director of Civil Aviation.

After Margery had said goodbye to Susan, she began reading those headlines again, because she remembered seeing that airship when it flew over the village of Hemelsham. At that time she thought it looked so lovely and was amazed how it stayed up in the air just floating quietly along. Suddenly Joe awoke and seeing her standing beside him he said, 'Hello sweetheart, what have you been doing today? Have you had a nice day at school?' While Margery was answering him telling him about the school choir, he reached down beside his chair and picked up a book. When Margery had finished talking to him, he said to her, 'Margery, there is something I have been meaning to say to you for a long time and it is in this book,' then pointing to it he said, 'and I want you to always remember it. This is the Holy Bible, and there is a passage I would like to read to you.' He opened the bible and Margery sat on the grass while he read from it. After he had finished he said, 'That reading was from the book of St Luke, and the reason for me reading that to you, is that if ever you are lonely and in need of help, I want you always to remember that passage of scripture because it will always give you great comfort and guidance.'

She had been enthralled listening to him reading the passage, and she was equally pleased as he again related to her the verse of poetry he had seen in France about the wise old owl who lived in an oak tree, and she asked him to repeat the poetry again while she wrote it down in her school book she used as her diary. She felt sure that from the way he had spoken about the verse in the bible and the story of the old owl, her father must have been feeling very lonely and sorry for himself, because he began to give her more advice saying, 'You must learn to listen, observe and be silent, because only then will you be able to understand and learn what other people are actually saying'.

After he had spoken to her, Joe asked her if she understood what he meant and she replied, 'No Daddy, not quite, but I am certain it will become clearer to me one day, later on.'

Everyday after school, she went to the grocery shop to buy some groceries, but as she didn't have any money to pay for them, Mrs Swinton would put it on the 'Slate'.

Margery knew that this was a method of paying for the things at the end of the week and she also knew that most of the villagers used this method for purchasing their groceries. It was while Ethel was working at the manor earning the extra money to help them with their expenses that Margery was also acting as a nurse to her father while he recuperated from his terrible injuries, and with Mrs Swinton having great sympathy for Ethel and Margery she would sometimes not put the full amount they owed her on the 'Slate'.

One day, being alone in the dining room, Joe noticed soot falling down the chimney into the fireplace and he realised that the chimney needed sweeping. The next day he walked, with the aid of walking sticks, to where the village chimneysweep lived and arranged for him to sweep their chimney. Joe was on his own as he watched the chimneysweep connect the brush on to the rods and put them through a hole in a sack which he had put against the wall of the fireplace as he swept the chimney. Because so much soot had come down behind the sacking the coal dust began affecting Joe's lungs.

Having lost his job at the quarry, Joe began to look for other work and sometimes he managed to get some occasional work with local farmers. One day he arrived home, and as he was eating his evening meal, he said to Ethel in a rather strong manner, 'Do you know what some silly idiotic journalist wrote in the newspaper today?' Before Ethel could say a word, Joe continued, 'that idiot of a journalist wrote that Herr Hitler's hopes of ruling Germany were dashed forever. Do you know Ethel, I do believe Hitler is a dangerous person, because when he was in prison, he wrote a book called *My Struggle*, and I believe that when he and his Nazi party get into power, he is going to do an awful lot of harm to many people, including us, the British.'

Ethel looked at Joe in amazement because she had never heard him speak of that book before, and she had never before heard Joe speak so vehemently. Margery who was sitting nearby heard her father continue, 'There was also another article in the paper where the writer said he had visited a prison camp at a place called Dachau in Germany, which had formerly been a munitions factory, and the Germans had erected two rows of electrified fencing around the camp to keep the prisoners penned in. The prisoners were mainly Jews, Gypsies and political enemies of the Nazi party. Now Ethel, do you realise what I am saying? This is a dangerous period and Hitler and his political party are also dangerous, because if Hitler, and those people who are running that prison camp, take over Germany, we could be in for another war. I firmly believe we should be listening to what that Winston Churchill fellow in Parliament is saying.' Joe paused for another moment then said, 'Another thing Ethel, look at us here in this country, it's 1933, all we have is paraffin lighting and an outside lavatory, yet at that prison camp in Germany, they have electrified fencing around that camp. We were supposed to have won the Great War, but this just goes to show how far we are behind them in this country compared to Germany's standards.'

Margery was sitting nearby listening to her father talk about electrified fencing and was wondering what electricity was, but it was Ethel who began to see that what Joe had said to her a few weeks ago was becoming a reality, because she realised the events in Europe were beginning to have some serious effects in this country. Nearly all the newspapers had headlines that a war was coming, and many firms were asking their employees to work longer hours.

One day when she was in the village, Ethel heard that workmen were required for work to expand RAF Hemelsham Manor, the aerodrome near to their village. Ethel went home and told Joe, who was very excited about this news, and knew that if he could go to work he would earn some money. The next day he reported at the airfield and to his surprise he was given full time employment. He was told by the contractors that they had a lot of work, because they were going to expand the airfield runways and build large hangers to house aircraft and also to build a new bomb storage plant, together with a number of buildings for the accommodation of more airmen. He was told to start work the following day, and when he reached home, Joe said to Ethel, 'I am sure I will have work for at least the next two or three years and now I feel very contented, because I can look forward to some regular money coming into our household, which should ease our worries.'

Over the next twelve months due to the pressure by the construction company trying to complete certain projects on time, Joe found his working days were becoming longer and harder and he was earning more money, but he also knew his health was not as good as it should be. He also knew that recently he had been experiencing bad bouts of coughing, together with severe pains in his chest. At first he thought the pain was caused by a bad cold and he didn't tell Ethel anything about it, because he knew she would worry over him. But one evening as he was resting at home, whilst he was having one of those very bad coughing bouts, he collapsed and after being seen by the doctor was taken to Kirkbridge town hospital. Three weeks later he died.

The doctors told Ethel that Joe's lungs had been severely affected during the war and it was this deterioration and the injuries he had received at the quarry that had brought his life to an end. Joe's death had a marked effect on Margery, because she had just left school and being very close to him she was at an impressionable age and felt that not having a father figure around, she would be unable to achieve her ambition of becoming a nurse.

In 1935 and in order to celebrate the Jubilee of King George V and Queen Mary, the government gave permission for a chain of 2000 beacons to be lit on every hill across England, also for parties to be held in every town and village throughout the country, and to mark this great event, the local council gave permission for a big village party to be held in the village hall. That evening, while everyone was enjoying the festivities that were taking place inside the village hall, Mrs Swinton went outside and saw Margery a forlorn figure standing all alone gazing into the distance.

Margery was feeling very lonely thinking of her father's death, as she stared at a beacon that she could see burning on a hilltop in the distance. On being asked why she was looking so sad, she told Mrs Swinton of her disappointment at not being able to train as a nurse, because she was unable to support herself financially. Mrs Swinton did not hesitate and immediately offered Margery a paid position in her village grocery shop. Margery paused and thought for one moment before she eagerly said, 'Oh thank you. I accept, yes please!'

Shortly afterwards the Squire, who was 85 years of age and in ill health, sold the cottages where Margery and her mother were living to a private company. He also sold part of his farmland to the Air Ministry for further development and he bequeathed his household manor to the National Trust, who allowed him to live in it until he died. Shortly after this, the Squire died, and this meant that Ethel had lost part of her weekly income, but luckily she knew that with Margery going to work, whatever money she brought home would help them with the rent to their cottage.

Margery was 17 years of age when she spoke to Mrs Swinton of her longing to be a nurse. Mrs Swinton knew that Margery had always shown a keen interest in nursing because when the St John Ambulance Brigade held their meetings in the village hall, Margery always attended their meetings. Unbeknown to Margery, Mrs Swinton, who was a voluntary worker at the hospital in the nearby town of Kirkbridge, spoke to a Dr Longmuir there and asked him if he would interview Margery to see if she was suitable for training to be a nurse.

Being the son of a poorly paid Scottish miner he had studied hard to overcome the many difficulties in his desire to become a doctor, and therefore he knew the meaning of hardship and had developed personal radical and socialist views. It was because of those views that certain wealthy members of the local parish council did not consider him to be good enough to be consulting doctor in their hospital. He knew of their discontent with him, but this did not deter him from agreeing to see Margery.

Margery went on her own to the interview with Dr Longmuir, where he learned of how Ethel had managed to look after Margery on her five shillings a week widow's pension, and how Margery had found time to attend the meetings of the St John Ambulance Brigade every week in the village hall. Despite knowing that Margery had only a limited knowledge of medical matters, after he had asked her a numerous questions, especially the question of whether she would be willing to study hard and then seeing her enthusiasm, he told her he would be willing to help her.

Margery knew that to be a nurse, the one person, besides Dr Longmuir, she had to convince she was good enough was herself. She knew that Mrs Swinton and Dr Longmuir wanted her to succeed, and this made her very nervous. She began to study very hard and she hoped that by trying hard and following Dr Longmuir's advice and tutelage that she would succeed.

Mrs Swinton was unable to have children, but she felt that if she had had a child, she hoped it would have been a daughter like Margery. She allowed Margery plenty of time off to study, as well as assisting her to purchase her study books, and also paying for her tuition fees. She was also paying Margery a weekly wage for working in the village store. Although Margery's hours of training were very long and arduous, she had to stay late at night studying at the hospital.

One evening after finishing one of her evening studies, whilst waiting for the country bus that was supposed to leave the bus terminal at 9.00 p.m., she met Gerry Rothwell, whom she knew from her school days. Gerry was a ginger haired lad who lived in the same village, but being one year older he had been in the school class one year ahead of her. She was pleased to see him because as it was very dark, she knew she would have company walking home with him in the village, and also he would be someone she could talk to on the bus on their way home.

She began to tell him of her desire to be a nurse and that at moment she was being taught anatomy and was interested in the entrails of the human body. He laughed and replied he was training to be a butcher and had just killed three pigs with a humane gun and had to disembowel them. The manner by which he told her of his horror at doing such a thing made both of them laugh together, so that by the time the bus had reached the village, they were like old school friends again.

As they got off the bus, he said, 'Would you like me to walk you to your cottage?' She replied, 'If you want to.' When they reached the cottage, which still had the roses that her father had planted growing up the walls, as she went to go down the path to the front door, to her surprise he quickly kissed her on the side of her cheek.

The following evening after finishing her studies, she found Gerry waiting for her again at the bus terminal in Kirkbridge, and later when they arrived in the village, Gerry again walked her home, but when she said goodnight to him, he leaned forward and held her and gave her a lingering kiss on her lips, then as he walked away he called out rather cheekily, 'Goodnight Margery, I'll see you again tomorrow night.' She began to look forward to Gerry meeting her every evening, however when she told Ethel and Mrs Swinton about him, both of them warned her to be careful and to concentrate hard on her studies.

Two weeks later, in order to try and stop her seeing too much of Gerry, Ethel went to see Mrs Swinton and they had a good chat about the relationship between Gerry and Margery and decided that they would take Margery to Kirkbridge to see the film *Showboat*. It was the first film Margery had ever seen and she was amazed at the scenery and the wonderful voices of Paul Robeson and Alan Jones who sang the lovely tunes, especially Paul Robeson singing 'Old Man River'. Because Margery loved singing, on the bus going home she began humming the tunes to herself rather loudly, and Mrs Swinton thought that at any moment Margery was going to burst out singing. Ethel and Mrs Swinton were very pleased after seeing the film that for a short while Margery appeared to be concentrating more on her studies, and they had noticed that Gerry only met Margery at the weekends.

It was on one of those weekends when Gerry called to take her out that they walked beyond the village towards the airfield, and they could see a large twin-engined plane. At that moment an airman was walking by and Margery stopped and asked him what type of aeroplane it was. He replied, 'Why that's a new plane and what we call a Wimpy, but its real name is the Vickers Wellington and it's a bomber aircraft, and a lovely plane to fly.'

Leaving the aerodrome they walked on and turned into Spratts Lane, where they came to the quarry where Margery's father had had his accident. On seeing the quarry, she said to Gerry, 'Years ago my father worked in this old quarry and there was an explosion and a very serious accident and he was injured. After he recovered from his injuries he never worked in that quarry again.'

Then pointing towards the aerodrome in the distant she said, 'but he also worked for another company that enlarged that aerodrome and built those large hangers over there where those aeroplanes are standing.' They had now reached a spot that was out of sight of the aerodrome and village. It was a secluded spot, with a large grass verge and plenty of trees growing along the edge of the lane, and they both knew it was where the local couples came to do their courting, because nearby was a small stream that eventually meandered its way through the various fields to the river Witham. Gerry stopped walking and turning towards Margery. He surprised her by putting his arms around her and as kissed her passionately on her lips, she could feel his hands gently moving over her body.

Pulling herself away from him she told him that though she liked him she did not want to get too serious with him because she wanted to finish her studies to become a nurse. Gerry looked downhearted, whereupon she took hold of his hands and held them and said, 'Gerry, we can still be good friends and still meet and go out together, but we don't have to get too emotional about our friendship do we?' They stayed there for a few moments holding, occasionally kissing and talking about their future. On their way home they were laughing and joking together and Margery felt as though a stronger, newer, and nicer feeling had grown between them.

When they were nearly at the end of Spratts Lane, they noticed the wild watercress growing in the water of the small brook that ran lazily down beside grass verge of the lane. They stopped and Margery said, 'Gerry wouldn't it be nice if we could take some of that lovely looking watercress home to my mother. I bet she would think a lot of you for doing that'. Hearing Margery say that, Gerry took off his shoes and socks stepped into the brook and picked a large bunch of water-cress which they took back to Ethel. She was so pleased that she made them some lovely sandwiches of salmon fish paste with the fresh water-cress and she also gave them a cup of tea and they told Ethel how lovely the sandwiches tasted.

2

LONDON & WORLD WAR II

With Margery studying hard at the hospital, Gerry found it difficult to see her and with the rumours of war spreading in Europe, he joined the Territorial Army, which meant he couldn't see her very often because he was always going away on weekend manoeuvres. However they continued to meet occasionally and see each other as often as they could and this situation remained the same until the summer of 1939, when Gerry, like many other young men in the Territorial Army, received his 'calling up papers' and was told to report to Catterick army barracks for mobilisation. Margery felt very upset knowing that Gerry was going to be away for some time, that on the day when Gerry left to go to Catterick, she went with him to Kirkbridge railway station and as she kissed him goodbye he promised he would keep in touch and write to her.

With Gerry being away, she concentrated even harder in the process of taking her final examinations. A short while later she was informed and became very excited to know that she had passed all her examinations with credit, and very shortly afterwards she began working as full-time nurse at the hospital.

It was 11.15 a.m. on Sunday, 3 September 1939, and Margery was off duty and coming out of church with her mother and Mrs Swinton when they, with some other congregation walking beside them, heard in the distance that strange, haunting, wailing sound of an air raid warning floating across the fields. Mrs Swinton suddenly exclaimed, 'That sounds like the air raid warning from Staunton village . . .' and before anyone said anything she added, 'Surely they must be testing it. We can't be at war?' Whilst she was talking the siren in their own village began making the same sound and everyone looked at each other and began to wonder what was happening.

PC Maxwell, who was near retirement age, had cycled all the way to the church and was breathing heavily. Taking a deep breath he said, 'Ladies and Gentlemen, the Prime Minister has just announced that

England has declared war on Germany, and as the Germans have very fast flying machines which could bomb us, I advise all of you to hurry home and take shelter immediately.'

Some of the villagers had prepared for the war by digging Anderson air raid shelters in their gardens and covering the roof and sides with earth, whilst others had internal shelters which, when not used as a shelter, became a household metal table that had a thick metal square top and thick metal legs all made of heavy steel, sides covered with heavy metal mesh, and a small hinged metal mesh entrance. These were called Morrison shelters.

Margery and her mother had one of these, and after hurrying home from church and going in their cottage, they quickly bent down and scrambled through the mesh entrance and lay down on the floor beneath the table metal top. After waiting about 30 minutes and realising nothing appeared to be happening they cautiously ventured out from the shelter and went outside their cottage to see if any of their neighbours were about. In the distance they could see a number of people had con-gregated around the grass square in front of the police station. Margery told her mother to wait by the cottage while she went to see what was happening.

When she arrived at the square she could see inside the police station, where poor old PC Maxwell was in a terrible state, with the telephone ringing continuously and many of the village people calling out to him, some saying, 'Are the Germans coming?' others, 'If the Germans are not coming, why don't you sound the all-clear siren?'

Seeing all the commotion and feeling sorry for PC Maxwell, Margery decided to ride on her old bicycle to the nearby RAF airfield to try and get some information. As she was cycling up the lane she could see RAF lorries laden with sand bags and airmen putting them across the lane to make barricades. She went up to an airman who appeared in charge and asked what was happening. He replied, 'It's all right Miss, cos now we're at war we've got orders to close and barricade all roads leading to the airfield.' Then he, rather heartily, said, 'But I wouldn't worry Miss, cos we've also been told that it will be all over by Christmas.' She thanked the airman, who wished her good luck, and hurriedly cycled back to the village and told the villagers what the airman had told her. When she had finished they began cheering and, laughing, and they dispersed, the men going to 'Wheatsheaf' and 'Goose and Gridiron' and the women going home to get the dinner ready.

Within a short period the army units came to the aerodrome and put their guns around its perimeter. The village began to have an unusual look about it, because the bank and the police station had sand bags all around the front of their windows and the bank had sand bags placed close to its entrance doors. All the village shops looked peculiar because they had 2-inch-wide tape bandage across their windows to prevent them breaking from the blast from bombs.

As time went by, Ethel began to feel less nervous, because once some of the lanes were closed around the airfield and buildings barricaded, everything appeared to remain the same. But every now and again the siren would wail out its sorrowful notes of warning and there would be a flurry of excitement about the German aircraft that were flying near the airfield. What frightened Ethel most of all was the noise of the anti-aircraft guns when they began firing out their deadly spiteful message and would not stop firing at the German aircraft until some British fighters appeared and chased them away.

One day Margery was on duty at the hospital when a German aircraft, later identified as a Heinkel 111, was shot down by the Army gunners and crashed on a golf course near Kirkbridge, killing two of the crew, with two members being badly injured and taken to Kirkbridge hospital under an armed guard. That day Margery was on duty, and when she first heard that German airmen had been brought to the hospital for treatment she thought it was a rumour, but it was only when she was walking along one of the hospital corridors and saw soldiers armed with rifles standing in the corridor outside a private ward door that she realised it was true.

In March 1940 as she was going to work she met Gerry's parents, and she had a bad shock from them, because they told her that Gerry was getting married to a girl from Darlington who was expecting his child. This news was quite unexpected and hurt her very much, because from the letters she had recently received from him, he had written to say how much he loved her and was looking forward to seeing her again. Within a short time however she began recovering from her initial shock and was determined not to let anyone know how she felt, or to know of her innermost feelings of sadness and distress at being so badly let down by him, though she wrote in her diary how sad she was. With the evacuation of Dunkirk taking place, together with the tremendous number of wounded soldiers coming into the hospitals, notices began appearing on the hospital notice boards appealing for volunteers of experienced nursing staff being required in hospitals around the London area. After the notice appeared Margery read it several times and waited until the following day to give it plenty of thought, then she decided to volunteer. Much to her surprise she was accepted. She prepared herself for her mother's reaction at the news of her departure to London, and to help her cope with this, she had informed Mrs Swinton of her intentions and invited Mrs Swinton to be present when she told her mother that she would soon be leaving to help the wounded soldiers and people in London area. On hearing the news, Ethel began to cry and began putting forward all manner of excuses as to why Margery should stay at home with her in Hemelsham, but Mrs Swinton explained why it was important for Margery and other nurses to offer this help.

When Ethel heard Mrs Swinton saying, 'Now Ethel, do stop making a fuss, it is very important for Margery to help the soldiers, nursing is her job,she stopped crying. At the end of May, Margery received a letter informing her to report to Charing Cross Hospital in London, and although she felt sorry she was leaving her mother she became very excited of the prospect of what lay ahead of her, but at the same time apprehensive about the dangers of the bombing from the expected air-raids. When she arrived in London and alighted from the train she was carrying her suitcase and walked along the platform concourse with her gas mask in a small cardboard box with a piece of string attached to it to enable her to carry it.

Observing a policeman with his gas mask in a pack with a steel helmet on his shoulder, she went up to him and asked him the way to Charing Cross Hospital, whereupon he directed her to the underground station. This form of travel was very new and strange to her and she was amazed at what she saw. It was while she was waiting for the underground train to arrive that she noticed that along the platform were two-tiered iron framed bunks against the walls. As her train passing through the stations there were more bunks of this kind placed along the platforms and also in the corridors leading from the plat-forms. Suddenly the war and all her fears of terror and its implications came upon her. However, looking around at some of her fellow travellers, she noticed that as they were talking they appeared to have a calm air of defiance about them.

The hospital she was reporting to, Charing Cross Hospital, was in the centre of London and quite close to Trafalgar Square. When Margery emerged from the underground station into the daylight, she noticed the statues and the church of St Martin in the Fields nearby. She stood there just looking around at Nelson's Column, and suddenly remembered those sailors who had marched through London on their way to receive the Freedom of London and she felt very proud that she would, if she was needed, to be able to support them in her duties. She was startled when she noticed that the statues around the square, together with those at the base of Nelson's column, were all heavily sandbagged to stop the blast of bombs damaging them and she realised that war was very frightening.

On entering the hospital she met the Matron who introduced her to another nurse called Helen Stuart, who was to be her room-mate. Both being of the same age, and having similar personalities and temperaments, they soon became very good friends. Helen told Margery that her parents lived in Reigate in Surrey and that her father was an accountant, her mother was a teacher of English at a local Grammar school in Reigate and her older sister had recently married.

Helen was good looking with a bubbly vivacious nature, and because of her ability to make people feel at ease Margery soon found that she was captivated by Helen. The fact that Helen had an older sister, Margery thought, made Helen have a more outgoing personality. In their off duty moments, Helen was always encouraging Margery to meet people and go out and see London and it was soon after the government had lifted the ban on the closure of all cinemas throughout England, that they decided to see a film. On entering a cinema near Victoria Station, as they went to their seat Margery saw the vast size and great expanse of the cinema, and seeing a man sitting at a large electric organ she was struck with amazement when the man started to play and the organ began to rise out of the floor. Helen burst out laughing at Margery's look of astonishment.

Another day, when they had a few hours off from work, they decided to go to Hyde Park, and it was while they were walking around the park looking at the underground shelters and the trenches that had been dug in the ground, and admiring all the lovely arrangement of the flowers growing there, they heard in the distance the warning sound of the siren. They didn't worry, and because they appeared not to be worrying or hurrying, a policeman, who had an air raid warden by his side, came hurrying over to them and began to admonish them for not going to the nearest air raid shelter. 'Didn't you hear my three long blasts on my whistle?' shouted the warden to them, then before they could answer, he exclaimed as he saw other people slowly walking past, 'Oh my goodness, look at that lot over there! I'll have to hurry over and get them quickly into a shelter.' He hurried off, at the same time blowing three more long blasts on his whistle, leaving Helen and Margery with the policeman. Margery said to the policeman, 'Why is that warden blowing three long blasts on his whistle?' the Policeman, before replying, looked quizzically at Margery then said, 'Miss, if you are being silly and trying to be clever, I will charge you, but if you don't know, I will tell you, it is because after the warning siren has sounded, the warden gives three long blasts on his whistle to warn everyone that an air raid is imminent and enemy aircraft will be shortly overhead, and they could start dropping bombs at any time.'

He asked them if they had heard the warning sound of the siren, and when they answered 'Yes,' he told them to look towards the east of London. Looking in that direction they could see many dark specks moving in and out of the white fluffy clouds, and high above the clouds were more dark specks, and they could also see the other planes looking like specks of silver, as they moved and weaved about the sky.

The policeman began speaking very quickly. 'Can you see those dark specks? Well they are the German bombers, and those tiny silver ones above them, they are the British planes having a fight with the German fighters in what is called a dogfight.'

Suddenly they saw one of the silver planes with smoke pouring from it dive straight downwards from its high position towards the earth, and then they saw a parachute opening and watched it slowly floating down to the ground. Then they began to hear the firing of the anti aircraft guns and the explosion of falling bombs, and the policeman was saying to them, 'Come on girls. hurry up. I've got to get you both to a shelter.' But when they excitedly told him they were nurses from the Charing Cross Hospital and they should really be at work now that an air raid was taking place, much to their surprise he stopped a bus, which was going in the direction of Charing Cross, and he told the driver they were nurses who had to get to the hospital at Charing Cross very urgently. The bus driver, who was a cheery and talkative person, told them rather saucily, that due to the air raid he may have to take them on a more sexy scenic route, but not to worry because he would soon get them to their destination. After much laughter with the bus driver, they eventually arrived at Charing Cross and after thanking the driver they went inside the hospital, where Matron, walking quickly towards them, gently scolded them for not taking shelter. But after listening to their story, she said she was very pleased to see them, because everyone was very busy taking the patients from the wards to a place of safety and others were caring for those patients who were too ill to be moved from the wards to the shelter and so their assistance would be very much appreciated.

A few days after their visit to Hyde Park, the daylight raids began in earnest, and by September many of the staff in the hospital were beginning to feel exhausted, because they had not been able to have time off, except to go to bed and try to sleep, and they found that the bombing at night also kept them awake. All the nursing staff had been kept very busy, working non-stop. Every day of the week it had been the same routine, work – sleep, work – sleep. Some days the air raids were so severe that no sooner had the all-clear siren sounded and everyone had begun to relax and take things easy, and were beginning to make their way out of the shelters to start work with the patients, than the warning siren sounded again and it was all rush and tear to get the patients back into the shelters.

One day Margery heard the drone of the many enemy bombers flying overhead, then she heard the sound of the bombs making a noise like screaming children as they fell through the air before exploding on the ground and the hospital was shaken by some other bombs exploding nearby. Very shortly afterwards news began filtering through the hospital that Buckingham Palace had again been damaged by bombs. The following morning someone showed them a copy of the headlines of the *Daily Tribune*, which read:

175 Shot Down. Another bomb on the Palace
5 Raiders Crash on London – 5th Hospital Bombed

Shortly afterwards, during a short tea break, she was told how an army bomb disposal section, under the leadership of Lt R. Read, had taken three days to defuse a one-ton unexploded bomb that had been dropped not far from them, and the soldiers had taken it to Hackney Marshes where they exploded it. What brave men they were, she thought, because all the time they were trying to defuse the bomb, other bombs had been falling around them. She was quite shocked when she looked up at the calendar on the wall and saw that it was Monday 16 September 1940, and realised what a short time she had been in London, and so much had happened around her, and she began to write all that had happened in her diary.

A few weeks later, because of the tremendous devastation and destruction to the attacking German air force by RAF fighter planes during the past summer months, the German High command decided to switch from daylight bombing to heavy night-time bombing. This soon became evident as the air raids during the day became lighter and less frequent, while the bombing raids at night was getting more prolonged and heavier.

One night when Margery awoke she knew the bombing during the night had been bad, and even though she and Helen had been in the air raid shelter, they had been kept awake most of the night and had only managed to get a few hours sleep and as they went to go on duty. 'We didn't get much sleep last night did we?' she said to Helen. 'I wonder what type of harrowing day will be in store for us?' The following morning, when they awoke in the air raid shelter, an extremely heavy night raid had left many buildings around the Charing Cross area either destroyed or badly damaged. Further down the Strand towards Fleet

Street, buildings were devastated or badly burnt, and St Bride's Church had been reduced to ruins except for its spire, which now stood surrounded by devastation. Because of the heavy bombing Margery and Helen had again not been able to get much sleep and were feeling very tired, when this was the sight that greeted them on that morning of 1st January 1941 when they, and some other nurses, accompanied doctors to the badly bombed buildings near St Paul's Cathedral. A number of people were badly injured, and they had to help the rescue teams extract those who were trapped in the bombed ruins.

Having dealt with that emergency, they were called upon many times to go to similar situations. On 18 April 1941, when they were both on night duty working together, the noise of the falling bombs, which sounded like screaming children as they came down before exploding on the ground, plus the sound of breaking glass and masonry falling down nearby, scared both women and terrified most of the patients. When the morning came, they both felt very tired by the hard work of attending to the patients and moving them from one place to another, and they knew they looked a dreadful sight, but it was when they went outside they were amazed to see that their hospital had not been badly damaged. They could see it only had some windows shattered and some indentation where the shrapnel had smashed into the brickwork, but when they looked further around and saw the full amount of damage in the buildings nearby they were again shaken. Someone told them that eight other hospitals had been badly damaged by bombs and many of the staff and patients killed and injured, and they nervously laughed and their bodies begin to shake with emotion and fear, as they realised how lucky they had been. Due to the severe bomb damage to the adjacent buildings and the unexploded bombs lying buried in some of the ruins, many roads nearby were closed, which was causing great interference to the movement of traffic in and around Trafalgar Square and also considerable inconvenience to the ambulances going to fetch some of the injured people and bring them to hospital.

Having worked very hard without a break during the long summer raids and during the period of heavy night bombing, she and Helen, together with the other nurses, began to feel the strain of the heavy work. Then one day they were both called into Matron's office and informed that due to the exemplary conduct they had shown during the bombing, they were both being recommended to the hospital authorities for the words 'Highly commended' to be registered and put into their personal records. Hearing the news, they came away from Matron's office laughing, and excitedly exclaiming to each other, 'I wonder what is going to happen to us next?'

It was on one of those rare days when they were both able to get time off, that they went to the Odeon cinema at Marble Arch to see *Gone with the Wind* starring Clark Gable and Vivien Leigh. While they were queuing and having to wait a long time to go in, two airmen with RAAF on their shoulders and wearing sergeant strips and with the brevet of an Air Gunner on their breasts were standing behind them and began to talk. One of the airmen asked them where they worked. Helen rather flirtatiously replied, 'We're nurses from Charing Cross Hospital, near Trafalgar Square.'

Very quickly one of the airmen, pulling up his sleeve and holding out his arm to her said, 'Oh dear, I've been standing here for such a long time, I think I'm going to faint. Quick! Do you think you could feel my pulse? I think I'm going to fall down through exhaustion . . .' Helen could see he was smiling so she took hold of his arm, and they all began laughing at each other, after which the same airman laughingly said, 'Would you mind if we sit with you, because when the film is over, we would like both of you to show me and my pal Kevin, the way to Trafalgar Square, because without our pilot and our navigator to guide us and show us the way home, we always seem to get lost in the dark?'

Before Margery could say anything, Helen winked at her, at the same time gesticulating to her to stand closer to the other airman as she replied, 'Yes, that will be all right with us, and afterwards we'll be delighted to show you the best way to Trafalgar Square. We will guide you and I'm sure we won't get you lost, will we Margery?'

Margery hesitantly answered 'No,' but being embarrassed at the way Helen was talking and being told what to do, the other airman, who appeared to be a little quieter than his companion, made her feel more at ease with him, standing quite still where he was, at the same time saying, 'It's all right, Miss, you don't have stand close to me.'

She nervously looked towards Helen, but Helen was too busy snuggling up to her airman and was paying no attention to her, and this made Margery feel uneasy. However, because Margery was hesitating to talk, the airman next to her said, 'Look, it's daft me standing here calling you Miss. If I tell you my name is Kevin, I know your name is Margery because your friend has just called you that, so don't be afraid I won't bite you, and will you let me call you Margery?'

Margery was fascinated by his Australian accent and the polite way he pronounced his words that she felt obliged to speak to him, so she rather tentatively replied, 'Yes Kevin, that's all right,' and because she liked his polite manner she said, 'By the way, what part of Australia do you come from?' He replied very proudly and cheerfully, 'Why it's Geelong, which is 20 miles outside of Melbourne, and in case you don't know, Melbourne is the capital of Victoria, which is the finest state in Australia!' She felt at ease in his company and began to feel very excited, together with his cheerful answers, and when he enquired where she lived, she laughingly replied, 'Oh! I doubt you will have ever heard of it, or know where it is, because it is a little village in the Midlands called Hemelsham.' His face had a big smile on it as he said, 'Oh! the Midlands is it? Well let me see, isn't there a small pub called the 'Wheatsheaf' and another pub called 'Goose and the Gridiron' in that village that are near a pond?'

Hearing him mentioned the names of those pubs, her face reddened and she quickly looked around to see that no one could hear her as she quickly and quietly said, 'There's a large aerodrome there and it's quite close to Mother's home and my dad, before he died, worked there. Then you must be stationed there?'

It was his calm manner and the way he quietly answered her saying, 'Yes you are right,' and then because of his Australian accent and the way he was speaking to her as he answered each of her other questions, she suddenly felt an affinity between them and felt herself being attracted towards him. This feeling made her feel more relaxed and when the time came for them to go inside the cinema it seemed only natural for Helen to sit with her airman, whilst she sat beside Kevin.

During the film that she noticed that Helen and the airman she was with were cuddling and kissing each other throughout the film, and when it finished and they came out into the darkness of the night sky they were holding hands. On the bus on their way to Trafalgar Square, she and Kevin sat together. Soon they were talking to each other about the film, then he suddenly changed the subject and said how he would like to see her again when she was visiting her mother in the village of Hemelsham.

When they arrived at Trafalgar Square, Kevin was still asking her if he could meet her tomorrow, but she replied, 'I would love to, but I doubt if I can get the time off,' and then for some inexplicable reason she wrote her name and address on a piece of paper and gave it to him saying, 'Perhaps you might like to see me on your next leave when you are in London. If so, you can write to me at the hospital and let me know and I will try and get some time off to be with you.' Then seeing Helen was kissing her airman passionately, it made her look at Kevin, but he was already walking towards her and she was amazed when he put his hands on her shoulders and he gently kissed her on her lips. After they had said a few more things to each other, they said their goodbyes and Helen, pointing the direction they had to go and waving her hand, called out, 'Bye, boys, it's been nice being with you, and don't forget Australia House is in that direction on this side of the road.' The airmen began to walk away and after watching them walk slowly up the Strand, Margery and Helen went into the hospital laughing and talking very excitedly about the airmen they had just met.

A week later Margery received a letter from Mrs Swinton informing her that her mother was very ill in hospital, and she immediately went to see the Matron showing her the letter. After reading it, Matron gave Margery permission to have leave of absence for three days. When she arrived at Kirkbridge hospital she found her mother gravely ill, suffering from pneumoconiosis. Seeing the serious condition her mother was in, she immediately left her mother's bedside and telephoned Charing Cross Hospital to inform the Matron of her mother's serious condition. On hearing that Margery's mother had no other relatives, the Matron granted Margery an extended compassionate leave. Because Margery wanted to visit her mother every day and did not want to sleep in her mother's house alone, she asked Mrs Swinton if she could stay with her in the village shop in Hemelsham.

After visiting her mother on the third day, while she was waiting at the town's covered bus terminal for the bus to take her back to Hemelsham village, deep in thought about her mother's illness, an airman standing in front of her turned and faced her. Suddenly she saw it was Kevin. They both laughed, but she was so startled she started to blush and her face went red with embarrassment. Kevin immediately began talking to her, saying, 'Why hello, isn't that lovely young lady called Margery who I met in London?' and when she nodded, and before she could answer him, he continued, 'I'm so glad you're here, because I was just about to go back to my billet and write you a letter, to ask you to meet me on my next leave in London.' He paused for moment and said, 'but now that you are here, perhaps we could meet and go to the cinema one evening? By the way I have heard there's a good film at the Savoy called *The Women*, starring Rosalind Russell, Norma Shearer and Joan Fontaine.'

She was feeling very tense with the worry about her mother, but listening to the easy manner in which he was talking to her she began to relax, so that by the time their bus had left the depot, they were talking as though they had known each other for ages. He became very concerned when he heard of her mother's illness and how serious it was, and when she told him that was the real reason why she couldn't go to the cinema with him in Kirkbridge, he wanted to know where she was staying in the village. When she told him she was staying with her good friend called Mrs Swinton, who owned the grocery shop in the village, he replied, 'That's good, because I can now walk you home.'

It was very dark when the bus eventually reached Hemelsham, and because of the blackout regulations there was no street lighting, and as he had decided to escort her to Mrs Swinton's shop, he held on to her hand as they walked along. On passing the 'Goose and Gridiron' pub and hearing singing voices, he laughingly said, 'I know that's some of my mates in there singing, I can recognise some of their voices.' She immediately said, 'I will be all right, Kevin, if you want to go inside with them. I can see my own way home.' He replied, 'Look here, I said I will walk you home, because I'm not letting you walk home alone in the dark.'

When they were near the shop, they could see in the distance the small beam of a torch coming towards them, and then Mrs Swinton came into view. Soon she was close to them and she was surprised to see Margery with a man in uniform standing there beside her. Margery introduced Kevin to Mrs Swinton, who told them she had been to the village hall to attend a meeting of the WVS. It was a cold evening and when they had finished talking she invited them to go inside for a warm drink.

In the bright light of her lounge, Mrs Swinton could see Kevin more clearly and was very impressed by his appearance, especially by the way he spoke to her. Whilst she was making cocoa for the three of them in her small kitchen, she was quietly looking into the lounge, through a crack beside the door.

She could see how Margery and Kevin were looking at each other and she was pleased that Mr Swinton was out drinking at the 'Wheatsheaf', because this gave her plenty of time to encourage the relationship between the two of them.

When Kevin said he had to get back to the aerodrome, Mrs Swinton made an excuse to leave them together by going into another room at the rear of the shop. As Kevin said goodnight to Margery she stood up and he leaned forward and gently brushed his lips against hers, saying, 'I will try and accompany you tomorrow evening to the hospital, when you visit your mother.'

This made Margery feel very happy, and over the next four days, Kevin was able to be with her every time she visited her mother. On the fourth visit to the hospital that she said to him, 'Kevin, this time would you come with me to the bedside? I know I'm asking a lot of you, because my mother is very ill, but I would be very grateful if you would come with me, and even though she is so ill I'm sure she will be very pleased to see you.' At the bedside Kevin spoke quietly to Ethel and held her hand, and it was as if she knew something, because she squeezed his hand and as she did so winked at him, while at the same time she gave him a nice smile. Then Ethel began looking at Margery. While her mother was holding Kevin's hand, Margery was looking at them and she saw her mother was nodding her head and smiling as if to say she liked what she had seen and was in agreement with Margery's choice.

Seven days later Ethel died and Margery was very grateful that Kevin had not been flying, because he was able to have some time off to help her with the funeral arrangements. After the funeral Margery went back to the hospital in London, but before doing so she arranged to meet Kevin and told him that she would be coming back to Hemelsham within a few days to dispose of her mother's personal belongings, because the cottage where she and her mother lived was a rented one, and was being repossessed. She told him that she was going to live with Mrs Swinton and would have to move some of her own things into the spare bedroom above the village shop.

A week later, Kevin managed to get a few hours off duty to help Margery move her belongings, and afterwards they went into Kirkbridge where they managed to find a table for two in the tea-rooms in the High Street. Whilst Margery was pouring the tea, Kevin began to tell her that he was being posted to another aerodrome, but he couldn't tell her where as he did not know himself. Then he said, 'I know you may think I'm being childish and talking silly, but I'm an only child, and for really personal reasons, I can't explain to you at this moment about my family. However I want to keep in touch with you, because you do mean something special to me.'

When she put the teapot down, he gently held her hands in his, and as she was looking directly into his eyes, she could somehow tell he was speaking from his heart. From the way she was looking at him, it was easy for him to say, 'All right, I've got to tell you this. Ever since I first met you, I cannot get you out of my mind and I haven't thought of anyone else, not that I even wanted to, because I do really believe I have fallen in love with you. I know I am being silly and romantic, but do you think you could fall in love with me and be my girlfriend? You may think I'm being foolish, but with me flying around like I do, I am rather scared of the future because I'm going on operational flying duties, and in those odd few moments when I'm flying, I usually have no one to think about, and I would like to think there is someone who loves me and is waiting for me to come back to them.'

She started to blush and to hide her embarrassment she smiled as she replied, 'Kevin I do like you very much but it is too early for me to talk about loving you, because I don't know what love really is, but I would like to be your girlfriend. You say you have no one to think of when you're flying, but what about your parents, don't you ever think about them? You see, I do know what it is like being an only child, because as you know until recently, I only had my mother and now she has gone, all I have left is Mr and Mrs Swinton, and they are only good friends and they are getting old, so I would like to be your girlfriend, because like you, I don't want to be lonely.'

He looked crestfallen as she was talking but then he smiled when she said, 'But if you let me have your new address, I do promise you I will write to you and we can keep in touch with each other, and perhaps meet again in London when you are on leave again.'

Kevin had a big grin on his face as he replied, 'Great, and I promise you I will write and give you my new address as soon as I know where my posting will be, and then I can tell you all about my so called family. Now let's drink our tea and go to the pictures.'

Outside the café, they set off towards the cinema and he held her hand as they walked through the market stalls in the square. Not liking the choice of films at the 'Exchange' cinema, they walked further on to the 'Savoy', that was showing a film called *The Thief of Baghdad*, starring Conrad Veidt, Sabu, and June Duprez.

Being double British Summertime, it was still daylight when they came out of the cinema, and they walked slowly along the road holding hands, each deep in their own thoughts. Margery could feel him holding her hand very tightly, suddenly she felt as though a strong electric shock had passed between them and somehow she knew that he meant everything he had said to her. They both knew that he had to be back at his base before 11.30 p.m. so they ran very fast to the bus depot to catch the last bus to Hemelsham. When they arrived at the village and reached the shop it was 10.00 p.m. and she invited Kevin in for a cup of tea and to meet Mr Swinton.

Mr Swinton he was very impressed with the way Kevin spoke and his smart appearance in his dark blue Australian uniform, and while they were drinking their tea Mrs Swinton noticed how Kevin kept smiling and looking at Margery, and she felt he seemed to have an expression in his eyes that said he needed Margery very much.

Having finished their drink Kevin looked at his watch and said he had to go, otherwise he would be late. When Margery went to the front door with him, and before he said goodnight to her, he whispered, 'I will write to you at Charing Cross Hospital and whenever possible I will come and visit you.' He held both her hands in his, and as their lips met, she felt a great surge of emotion go through her body and her heart again began to beat very fast, then as he went through the doorway he whispered to her, 'I love you,' and quickly disappeared into the darkness. When Margery returned to the lounge Mrs Swinton noticed that Margery's face was flushed and that her eyes were bright and glistening, as if she was ready to cry.

The following morning after she had said her farewells to Mr and Mrs Swinton, Margery was sitting in the bus taking her to Kirkbridge railway station thinking of Kevin, and as it left the village and climbed a small hill, through the bus window she could see, across the fields, the buildings of the aerodrome, and a plane taking off. As it was climbing up into the sky, she suddenly thought of Kevin being in that plane and it worried her, because she remembered what he had said to her yesterday about thinking that there was someone who loved him and was waiting for him to land and to be with them again, and she whispered a short prayer.

The thoughts of Kevin brought to her a new and wonderful sensation of being desired and of being needed and of belonging to someone. At the railway station she was thinking about all those things and didn't remember changing buses at Kirkbridge, or managing to get a seat on the train to London. Suddenly the movement of the train stopped and she realised the train had stopped moving. Looking out of the window she knew it had stopped between Peterborough and Huntington, then looking around she saw the corridor of the train was packed with servicemen. When she heard someone shouting outside the window of the train, she opened the window and put her head out and she could see the train guard walking along the track and heard him calling out very loudly, 'There's an air raid in progress in London and property near Euston station has been damaged, and this is going to cause a delay, and the train may be diverted to St Pancras.'

It was late in the afternoon when the train eventually arrived at St Pancras station, and a very kind railway porter advised her to get a taxi because the underground rail tracks had been damaged by bombs and the underground trains were being cancelled.

Outside the railway station she was surprised and very delighted to see two army officers getting out of a taxi with their suitcases. She ran to the taxi and gasping for breath asked the taxi driver to take her Charing Cross Hospital. While they driving along, the taxi driver enquired, 'Are you going into hospital, I hope it's nothing serious miss?' She was shaken by the question and said, 'Oh no it's nothing like that. I'm a nurse at the hospital.' While driving along the taxi driver was talking to her and just before they arrived at the hospital he said, 'My wife was taken ill the other day and you nurses have been doing a wonderful job looking after her and the other patients, especially in these trying conditions.' On arriving at the hospital he said, 'Now I don't want you taking offence at this, but I would rather you not pay me any money for your fare. Please take it as a small repayment as a debt of gratitude for the wonderful work you nurses are doing.'

She felt embarrassed by his remarks and was pleased to have arrived at the hospital, but she became even more embarrassed when the he got out of his cab and helped her with her suitcase. Whilst she was thanking him for his kindness and as she went to pick up her suitcase, her face reddened as he tenderly kissed her on the side of her face and heard him saying, 'Good luck, love, and thank you very much for all that you are doing for everyone.'

At the hospital, as she was going to the room she shared with Helen, she met her. Helen looked surprised to see her and said rather hurriedly, 'I'm so glad you're back. It's lovely seeing you Margery, because it has been so lonely without you! I'm sorry that I have to rush but I'm late for duty. You can tell me all the news when I come off duty later tonight.' Helen hurried away leaving Margery bewildered but she did find time to write in her diary all the events that happened to her.

Later that evening just as they were about to go to bed, Margery told Helen about the death of her mother, but when Helen offered Margery her condolences she noticed that Margery quickly carried on talking, as though she wanted to shut from her mind the thoughts of the loneliness she was experiencing, because she said, 'I'm sorry Helen, I'd rather not talk about my mother just now. But I can tell you how I met Kevin.'

Helen sat up in amazement saying, 'Do what? You met who? Who's Kevin?'

Margery replied, 'Do you remember those two Australian airmen we met when we went to the Marble Arch Odeon to see *Gone with the Wind*? Well, in Kirkbridge I met the one called Kevin and it was after visiting my mother in hospital and while I was waiting for the bus to take me to Hemelsham he was waiting for the same bus to take him to the aerodrome, which is near the village.'

She went on to explain how Kevin had accompanied her several times to visit her mother in hospital and after the funeral how he had helped to move her things into Mrs Swinton's shop, and how he had said he missed her and told her he was in love with her.

Margery said, 'Helen, I know I'm being silly but I am worried over a number of things. Firstly, I am not sure I am really in love with him because I don't really know him. Secondly, I'm all mixed up because I miss him being around me, and thirdly, I am worried over his new posting because he told me he will be flying on operations, and I don't know how I will feel if something serious happened to him.'

Helen quickly interrupted. 'Oh! Margery don't be a daft fool all of your life! All you have to do is to start thinking positively. You will soon know when you are in love, because subconsciously you will always be thinking of that person and when you're alone you are still constantly thinking of him and wondering where he is and what is he doing and hoping he is also thinking of you. Then you get that longing feeling for him to be with you, and also for him to hold you in his arms and to feel his lips upon yours.'

Helen paused to get her breath, then carried on speaking. 'Margery, I don't know whether that is love or lust, but I do know that is how I feel about the person I have just met. So don't just think you are the only one who may be unsure of themselves, and don't sit there feeling sorry for yourself, because you have to think positively and remember that old adage my mother said to me, which is: we all have faults, and if you think your man is the right one for you, then grab him, because there are many men in this world who don't have many faults, but there are many more who have lots of faults.'

Margery was amazed at the strong feelings that Helen had put into those words and then she suddenly realised that she didn't quite understand what Helen had said about her meeting someone, so she said to her, 'Hey! What was that you said about you recently meeting somebody? Who is he, and do I know him?'

Helen replied, 'Well. While you were away, we had a patient brought in here, a badly burnt airman whose plane had been shot down and he had parachuted into the sea off of Southend. Mr McIndoe, a Canadian surgeon, came to see him, but because of the heavy night air raids, he asked for the airman to be transferred to the Queen Victoria Cottage hospital at East Grinstead. Because I had been the nurse who had been on constant duty with him all the time the airman was here and had helped to change the bandages after he'd been placed in a bath of saline water. I was asked to accompany him to East Grinstead. When we got there I was amazed, because our hospital is fairly modern and up to date, but at Queen Victoria Hospital that poor pilot was put into an old brown wooden hut which they called Ward 3. When I came back here I spoke to Sister about it, she told me that Mr McIndoe is a fantastic surgeon because he is performing skin graft operations on all those badly burnt airmen and other service personnel, that have never been done on anybody before, and he is the talk of the medical profession.'

Helen eyes began to have laughter in them as she paused and said, 'Mind you, it was also a gift from heaven for me. You see, Margery, by going to East Grinstead I was able to stay overnight at my parents' home and it was while we were having our evening meal that one of our neighbours came in to see my parents, and they brought with them their son, Ian, who was home on leave from the army. Ian and I had been to the same school and knew each other very well. Then during the evening meal Ian said he would be in London for a few days and asked if he could meet me. My parents were looking at me with expectation on their faces, so I agreed, and a few days later Ian was waiting for me outside this hospital and we had a great time together. By the way, you have only just missed him because he went back to his unit yesterday. However he did say before he left that he was going to write to me because I had agreed to be his girlfriend. Isn't that great?'

Helen was really excited, but they heard the air raid warning, which meant they had to leave their room immediately and help take the patients to the hospital air raid shelter. In the air raid shelter they sat there on their bunks and told each other nearly everything about their respective boyfriends. When they awoke in the morning it was a dark dismal day and they were due to go on duty and both feeling very tired, because, as well as going to sleep late through talking to each other, the noise of the heavy noisy bombing had kept them awake most of the night.

Ten days later found them both sitting on their beds reading the letters they had each received. Suddenly Helen jumped up and flinging her arms high in the air, she gleefully shouted out, 'Yippee! Ian has been promoted and is now a 2nd Lieutenant, a "one-pipper" as he calls it, and he is coming here to London and wants me to meet him.'

Looking at Margery who was sitting there with a letter in her hand just staring into space, Helen stopped jumping around and anxiously asked, 'What's the matter, Margery, has something happened to Kevin?'

Margery who was looking a little absentminded, replied, 'Oh! I am sorry, I should have congratulated you on Ian's promotion. No! It's nothing as bad as that, nothing has happened to Kevin, it's just that he is insisting he is in love with me and wants me to return his love. The funny thing is that I don't know what love is and yet I do miss him.'

Helen looked at Margery and then sat beside her saying, 'Margery, I haven't told you the full story yet because I didn't know how you would take it after the loss of your mother. On Ian's last leave, we discussed the war and all the events happening around us and we realised that at this moment in time, things look very bad and bleak around the world. So Ian and I agreed that we would live for today and hope and pray that there is going to be a tomorrow, because no one knows what the future holds, or what tomorrow will be like, or if there will be another tomorrow.'

Margery felt a great sorrow on hearing Helen talk that way and was just about to say so, but Helen carried on speaking. 'Somewhere, everyday, someone is being severely injured, maimed or killed. Why even the other day, I heard from my mother about one of our neighbour's sons, called Alan Warburton, whom Ian and I knew and went to school with. His parents had just received a telegram from the War Office informing them that he was lost at sea in his submarine. It was because of his death that Ian and I discussed the bombing of the hospitals where eight nurses had been killed, so we decided to grab whatever happiness that comes along, because the way things are at present, we don't know what is going to happen next.'

Margery looked at her as Helen said, 'Now I have to go to work and I'll see you later. Bye Margery,' and Margery realised that in that one moment of explanation, Helen had grown from a youthful, sensuous, captivating and exciting type of person, into a very attractive, mature, sensible woman. With a big smile and laughter in her voice Helen left Margery all alone to think and ponder on what she had just said to her.

Almost immediately Margery's thoughts turned to Kevin, and slowly she read his letter again until at the end of it she began to realise how much he loved her, and also realised how much she missed him. Suddenly she remembered what he had said to her, that when he was on a flying mission she was the person he was longing to get back to, because she was the person who was always in his thoughts.

She thought of Helen's words of grabbing whatever happiness one could because there may be no tomorrow and she realised those words seem to make a lot of sense. Then taking a piece of writing paper, she immediately wrote Kevin a letter saying how much he meant to her and how much she missed him, and at the bottom of the letter she wrote, I love you. She addressed the envelope to Sgt K. Hopkins RAAF, c/o RAF Breighton, Yorkshire, and she put the envelope on the table.

When Helen's duties had finished and she came into the room and saw the envelope on the table she wondered what Margery had said in it. She didn't have to wait too long because Margery was sitting on her bed and on seeing Helen, Margery spoke to her. 'Helen, having listened to you and re-read Kevin's letter, I have written to him and told him how I feel and how much I miss him.'

Helen started to laugh and giggle and became very excited as she said, 'Oh! that's wonderful news because now I've have some more good news for you. I didn't want to tell you everything earlier on because I knew how worried you were about your feelings towards Kevin, but now I know you have him to think about, I want to tell you my good news before you hear it from someone else.'

Helen had a big smile on her face as she said, 'As you know, Ian and I went to the same school and our parents are very good friends. We belong to the same church and we went to the same youth club and he used to see me home every time I went there, therefore it was only natural that we would go out with each other, but when he joined the army and asked me to be his regular girlfriend I refused him at first, but I did say I would write to him, which I have done. However when I saw him again at East Grinstead, I fell in love with him. Then he came to London and we went out together, and being in his company was sheer heaven to me. Then the day before he was due to go back to his unit, he told me he had always loved me and asked me to marry him, and I accepted, and we're going to be married very shortly. Isn't that marvellous, Margery?'

Margery put her arms around Helen and gave her a big hug, congratulating her on her engagement. As they drew apart Helen said, 'I telephoned my parents and told them the news and they were delighted. They later wrote to me telling me that Ian and I can get married in the same church that we went to when we were in the church choir, and they have been to see the vicar, who is still there, and he will be marrying us. It is going to be a real family affair, and Margery, I would love you to be there, and perhaps Kevin may be able to get leave to escort you.'

Two weeks after she had posted her letter to Kevin, Margery received a letter from him saying that he was hoping to get a few days leave in three weeks' time and asked her to make arrangements to have a few days off to be with him. He also thanked her for her letter and said he was pleased to know how she felt about him, because he loved her very much and he was also looking forward to being with her again.

Margery was kept very busy in the hospital and it was only in her spare moments that she was able to concentrate and think about Kevin, then she received another letter from him saying he would be in London on Tuesday the 15th. On casually looking at the calendar she saw it was already the 14th, and she began to fret and worry because she had not been to see Matron about having the time off. At that moment Helen walked into their room and could see that Margery was very upset. 'Margery, what the dickens is the matter with you?' She asked. 'Have you heard something awful about Kevin?'

When Helen heard what the trouble was she said, 'Margery, stop worrying. I know that Matron comes in very early every day, and as you are on early shift tomorrow I'm sure if you go and see her today she will give you time off, because she can always get someone to cover the early shift.' Margery began to calm down and went to bed feeling much better. The next morning she went to see the Matron and explained her reasons for wanting time off, and after listening to her, the Matron, who had always thought very highly of Margery, told her that she could have five days' leave, starting from the end of her shift.

The next day at 12.30 the hall porter telephoned her ward to say that there was an airman waiting to see her in the hall. She rushed downstairs to see him and when she went up to him she was so excited she could hardly speak. Kevin made her calm down and when he heard that her shift finished at 2.00 p.m. and she had to change her clothes, he said would go and have a drink somewhere nearby and come back for her at 2.30 p.m.

He met her at the hospital main doors and before they even left the hospital, he told her that he had managed to obtain two tickets for the evening's performance at the Piccadilly Theatre, to see Noel Coward's *Blithe Spirit*, starring Cecil Parker, Fay Compton, Kay Hammond as the ghostly Elvira and Margaret Rutherford as the lovely eccentric medium, Madame Arcati.

Knowing that other nurses had been to see the play and had told her they thought it was good, she became so excited to be going that Kevin had a hard job trying to quieten her down, until he said, 'Now look here young lady . . . shut up!'

After the show they were slowly walking hand in hand along the road in the direction of Trafalgar Square and laughingly discussing the supernatural and whether there was life after death. Neither could agree to reach a definite answer to that question, and Kevin said, 'Well, I hope you die first because then you can be waiting for me, because you always make me wait for you.' They both burst out laughing, especially when Margery said, 'Oh! So you expect me to die first do you, and meet you with a cup of tea in my hand?'

While they were walking towards Trafalgar Square they were still laughing at each other as he replied, 'Yes, and I also expect you to show me the way.'

When they had reached Trafalgar Square, she noticed on his chest coat under his A/G brevet he had a small piece of blue and white ribbon, and pointing to it she asked, 'Kevin, what is that?' He said in a rather casual way, 'Oh! it's a medal they gave to me called the DFM.'

Margery, who was not happy with his casual answer, demanded, 'What were you given it for?' He looked at her a little nonplussed because he was thinking how could explain what actually happened without making her worry over him. He reached inside his pocket and withdrew an envelope. After a little more coaxing from Margery he looked away from her dispassionately and he handed it to her a piece of paper saying, 'We had a little trouble on a recent bombing mission.'

Taking the letter out of the envelope he had given her she read:

Headquarters, Bomber Command, Royal Air Force.
Command Routine Orders by Air Chief Marshal Sir Richard Pierce

1. The Commander-in-Chief wishes to bring to the notice of all ranks of the Command the commendable conduct of the under-mentioned members of crew of No. 196 Squadron
   J.21020 P/O.M.K.Ospring   Pilot
   J.20963 Sgt K.Hopkins   Wireless Operator

2. On the night of 21st June 1941 the above named officer and NCO were members of a crew detailed to cover an attack on Gelsenkirchen. At a point approximately 10 minutes before the attack, the aircraft was attacked by a ME-110 and in the ensuring engagement the rear gunner was badly wounded and rendered unconscious, the starboard engine set on fire and the inter-com system rendered u/s.

3. Following the timely aid of the wireless operator, (Sgt K.Hopkins) who helped to restore the intercom system, when another enemy plane attacked the aircraft, it was the through the coolness and skill of the wireless operator in operating the rear turret guns, that he managed to shoot the enemy plane down.

4. With one engine still on fire, the Captain, although being injured, set course for home and displaying great ability he successfully brought the damaged aircraft to reach Woodbridge, and despite a crash on landing due to having a tyre shot away, he saved the crew from further injury.

5. The coolness and initiative displayed by the members of the crew, is a fine example of captaincy and co-operation under very trying circumstances, and their conduct is worthy of high praise.

Air Vice Marshal
i/c Administration
Bomber Command

Margery sat there amazed at his air of indifferent lack of emotion, especially his the off-hand way when asked by her to describe the incident, and she started to question him about it. All he said was his pilot was awarded the DFC as well.

He countered her questioning by saying, 'If I thought of these things emotionally, or even started to look at it morally, I can tell you I would never fly again. Now listen to me. The gunner, who was my friend, was the one you met in London when we first met you and your friend. He died on the flight back to this country, and if you ask me whether I intend to carry on flying, the answer is yes, because it is my job to fly and fight.'

He could see that she was looking very worried by what he had just said and carried on speaking. 'When I joined the air force those good old

Australian instructors taught us an old saying – that the fear of death is worse than death itself. Sure I'm scared, we are all scared, but don't you worry about me because I'm in a good crew and it is because we are all scared that we are all looking after each other.' Hearing him say that with such firmness in his voice, she decided not to ask him any more questions about the medal.

With Charing Cross Hospital being quite near to the Union Jack Club where Kevin was staying, which was just across the river near Waterloo station, it meant that he did not have far to walk after leaving Margery at the hospital. It also meant they could stay out later and spend more time together.

He had asked her if she would like to go dancing as he knew she loved it, and as it was raining the next day and he didn't want them to get wet just walking around, he thought he would take her to the Covent Garden Opera House, where servicemen were able to take their girlfriends. When they went inside, it was a lovely surprise for him to see some other members of his crew dancing and some more airmen from his squadron standing close by drinking.

Sometime during the evening, after introducing her to his mates, they were told the warning siren had sounded and they all had to leave the dance hall to go down into the air raid shelter. It was while they were down in the shelter, she was surprised to hear Kevin and his friends laughing and saying that they would rather be up there flying than down in the shelter on the receiving end of the bombing.

Being wartime, the Tower of London was guarded by soldiers, and the next day they were walking round the outside of the castle when Kevin suddenly stopped and asked her to sit down on a seat. Looking at her he said, 'Margery, I've got something important to say to you. I have asked my CO for permission to marry you, and it has been granted. Is that all right?' She was in absolute amazement because she replied, 'Is this supposed to be a proposal of marriage?' With a big smile on his face he said, 'Yes!'

She had her eyes fixed rigidly upon his and she could see that his eyes were genuinely pleading with her to say yes. She thought for a moment and asked, 'I wonder what your parents will say when they hear that their son is getting married to an English girl?'

He replied rather dispassionately, 'Oh don't worry about them. When I was about three years old my parents parted and my mother left me with my aunt, her older sister. I never saw my mother again and it was my aunt who looked after me and made sure that I went to a proper school.' Before she could ask another question, he carried on, 'My aunt and uncle lived in a small bungalow in Auborne Street in Geelong, which is 20 miles outside of Melbourne, and they were very good and made a great fuss over me, but as they were much older than my parents and they didn't have any children of their own, I always felt lonely. It wasn't because they were unkind, or anything like that, it was because all the other children had a relationship with their younger parents, which I didn't have with my aunt and uncle. Really and truthfully I ought to be very grateful to them, and I am, because of all that they did for me, and I will always love, respect and remember them for that. They were not rich and they always did their utmost to give me everything they could afford to give, but I suppose the resentment I have within me is against my parents for abandoning me.'

He paused for moment and she asked him, 'Have you ever tried to find your parents, or have they ever contacted you?'

With great venom in his voice he said, 'No! And I don't want to,' he carried on, 'because in 1937 my Aunt and Uncle were involved in a road accident and my uncle was killed and my aunt was seriously injured, which left her bedridden. She was left paralysed down one side of her body and had to be put into a nursing home, and in order to pay for my uncle's funeral expenses and the nursing home fees, the bungalow was sold and I had nowhere to live, so I had to go into a home for destitute children. I didn't like it in there, and when I was able I volunteered for the Australian Air Force and was accepted as ground crew, where I trained as a wireless mechanic and telegraphist.' For a moment Kevin appeared to be reminiscing over his childhood.

At the same time Margery was thinking of his unfortunate childhood and she thought how lucky she had been to have had a mother and father to help her. Kevin continued, 'About a year after I had joined the airforce, because the Station Commander was very strict, and he ordered the ground crew to fly in the planes to test the repaired equipment they had fitted into the aircraft. I love flying and I always volunteered to fly on the test flights. Then one day when I was flying and testing the equipment, the pilot asked me why I was always volunteering to fly, and I told him I love flying.' He paused for a moment before continuing. 'The pilot said that now Great Britain had declared war, why didn't I apply for re-training as air crew, because the airforce will be needing more men like me who love flying. I was very lucky because after I had my medical, I went for my preliminary aptitude tests and I found I knew most of the examiners, which made it easier for me. Shortly afterwards I was informed I had passed the exams and I was posted to a gunnery and wireless telegraphy course, where I met a couple of nice lads, and luckily ever since we passed our exams on the course and since we came to England we have managed to stay together. In fact they were some of my mates you met the other day when we went dancing in the Covent Garden Opera House.'

'Are you flying in big planes, or small ones?' she asked. He replied, 'I was flying in a plane called a "Wimpy" that had only two engines, but now we have been given a short rest and hopefully we will all be staying together as a crew and soon going training to fly bigger planes with four engines.'

Margery, hopeful and naïve, said, 'Having two more engines, does that mean it will be safer for you now?' He was laughing and nodding his head as he looked at her. They began to walk away from the Tower of London and walk towards Trafalgar Square and he suddenly noticed a worried frown on her face and he asked, 'Now what's the trouble?'

She replied, 'I'm scared, because I don't know what love is, but if it is a very deep feeling that one has within oneself about a person, and that feeling is still very strong even when that person is not around, then I am very much in love with you. I know I'm being silly but I need and want you to be around me all the time. I want to be married to you, but I am very worried over you flying and having an accident.'

When she had finished speaking Kevin laughed out loud and said, 'Oh! You are wonderful and I am so happy you want to get married to me. Let me assure you, I do love you very much, but you are as daft as a soft haired brush, because you don't have to fly to have an accident. Don't you realise that anyone can have an accident, anywhere and at any time, even walking across this road?' As he finished speaking he put his arms round her and gave her a big kiss and just as he did, the sirens started sounding the warning of an impending air raid. 'There you are,' he said, 'how's that for timing? I told you anything could happen to anyone at any time! Now the air raid warning has sounded, but let's hope it was an accident and someone has put their finger on the wrong button.'

They were laughing together as they went down the entrance to Trafalgar Square underground station, which was being used as an underground shelter.

As they went down the second stairway the lights went out and the emergency dimmer lighting came on. Kevin looked at her, 'Don't worry. It is only because there is an air raid and all the main electricity is switched off.' He held her hands as they slowly made their way further down, then on reaching the bottom of the stairs he held her against the wall with his hands on her shoulders and very solemnly said,' I don't know what fate has in store for us, and like many of my friends we all think it is a good idea to grab whatever happiness comes along. I want you to know that I want that happiness now, because I love you very much and I am praying very hard that the war does not go on too long.'

She looked into his grey/blue eyes and she felt they were silently speaking and yearning for her, then she heard Kevin saying, 'Don't worry I'll always be near and around you.' She could feel his hands on her shoulders and she leaned forward to put her arms around him and when her cheek touched his face she whispered in his ear, 'I love you and I want to marry you.' Kevin was kissing her when two sailors ambled by, one of them calling out, 'Trust the Brylcream boys to get all the luck!' Margery didn't care what they said because she knew that she and Kevin had each other and they were looking forward to a lifetime together. Very shortly afterwards they heard people saying the all-clear siren had sounded, then the main lights came on. On arriving at ground level they were pleasantly surprised to find the sun was still shining and people hurrying back to work. Kevin suggested they went into the Lyons Corner House nearby.

They went upstairs to the main restaurant where a musical trio was playing. A waiter escorted them to a table and while they were ordering their meal, Kevin casually said to the waiter, 'We are celebrating our engagement – what do you suggest we order?'

After recommending the meal they should have, the waiter hurried away and a few moments later another waiter came to their table with two wine glasses and a bottle of wine. 'I'm sorry', said Kevin, 'I didn't order that.' To which the waiter replied, 'We know sir, it is from the management and staff, with all their best wishes to you and your bride to be.'

Hearing from the waiters the news of the engagement and noticing Kevin's A/G brevet with his medal ribbon beneath, seemed to engender in the other diners a warm feeling of gratitude and thankfulness for the work he was doing. Some even raised their glasses and cups in a toast to them, whilst others shouted out, 'Congratulations and thanks, Cobber, for all the help you give us.' Others when they passed Kevin and Margery's table stopped and wished them the best of luck.

All this attention made Margery feel very self-conscious and her face reddened and her heart began to beat faster. Feeling embarrassed, she said, 'Kevin, I think everybody appears to be laughing at us.'

He leaned across the table and held her hands, saying, 'Don't worry about anything, because we know our engagement and our wedding is for life and we will only be able to enjoy one engagement day because all the rest will be anniversaries, so let us say thank you and enjoy their congratulations and best wishes to us.'

Hearing his strong and manly voice, she realised just how much she was relying on him and how strong his love was for her. After they had finished their meal, Kevin asked for the bill, but was politely told by the waiter that the waitresses and waiters had clubbed together to pay for it. This shocked him and he was astounded by their generosity. At that moment the floor manager was passing by and Kevin called to him and told him of the generous gift the staff had made, and said he couldn't accept it. The manager responded by saying, 'One of the waiters' brothers is in the RAF and was shot down and badly wounded, and this is his and the other waiters' way of thanking you for the job you are doing and asking you to accept the meal as a wedding present from them. And,' he laughingly added, 'if you like I will increase the cost of the meal!'

The manager shook hands with both of them and wished them luck and as they headed for the exit doors of the restaurant, the musical trio started to play 'Wedding Bells' in their own inimitable fashion, which made the rest of the diners look up and, seeing them leaving, began to clap their hands and sing in time with the music. It was 6.30 p.m. when they walked out of the restaurant, but due to double British Summertime they had lots of time to stroll around, hand in hand, in the lovely warm evening sunshine.

The following day, Kevin took Margery to a jewellers shop and asked to see the engagement rings. She chose one with a large single diamond within a square, with smaller diamonds on each side of the square. On looking at the tab attached to it, however, she saw the price and exclaimed, 'Well we will not be able to afford that one,' and was in the process of putting it down, when the sales assistant said, 'Oh! I can reduce that by £10.00, madam, because that tray of rings has been partially damaged by the bombing.'

All the time he was speaking the sales assistant was winking an eye at her, and suddenly she began to understand he was being very generous towards them. Kevin also saw what was happening and immediately said, 'Thank you very much indeed, you are very kind.' Margery was looking in amazement at Kevin as he handed the assistant £30.00. When they were outside the shop he explained to her that he received extra money for flying and had managed to save a few pounds, and he said, 'Now don't you start worrying because I wouldn't have bought for you if I could not have afforded it and remember, you are to me worth every penny.'

It was a nice day with a light wind blowing, making the clouds move slowly across the sky. They were strolling along just enjoying being together, Margery with the blissful feeling of wearing the engagement ring on her finger and knowing that she was going to be married. She was also thinking of how much Kevin loved her and how happy she was, when suddenly he broke the silence by saying, 'I see the barrage balloons are flying low, so I assume there will not be an air raid just yet.' Margery was taken back by that remark and said to him in an unbelievingly way, 'You must be psychic, how can you be so sure of that?'

With his eyes smiling at her, he replied in a simple yet confident manner, 'When the people in the listening posts near our coast hear the noise and see the enemy planes approaching, they relay that information to various people around the country and to those people who are in charge of the barrage balloons flying here and at the south coast. When they hear the news that the planes are heading towards London, it is them who give the order to raise the balloons to their operating height. It is so simple to understand isn't it!' She didn't know whether to believe him, but hearing his explanation gave her a great sense of security and she decided she would.

The next few days seemed like heaven and the days simply flew by, because she was having a great time going to such places as the Nuffield Club, the Windmill Theatre, and Covent Garden Opera House where, because she loved dancing, they joined in with the other servicemen and their girlfriends and wives, dancing to a live dance band.

When the time came for Kevin to return to his aerodrome, she went with him to Kings Cross Railway Station, and just before he kissed her goodbye he said, 'Now don't you start worrying about me, or about our wedding, because everything will be just right. Stop sending out those negative vibes and only have the positive ones, and always remember that the positive vibes are the ones that give you the strength and the energy to carry on. Don't forget we will soon be married in that little church in Hemelsham.' On her way back to the hospital, she began to realise Kevin had taken over her life completely and her mind was going over the events that had happened to her during the past few days, and thinking about them caused her to hum one of the tunes she had heard whilst dancing. Suddenly she stopped humming the tune and stood quite still and thought, 'What would I do if anything happened to Kevin?' For a moment her heart stopped beating and tears filled her eyes, but immediately she scolded herself and began to pull herself together because she remembered what Kevin had just said to her.

3

MARGERY'S WEDDING

Margery was in a calmer frame of mind by the time she reached the hospital, and she immediately went to tell Matron her plans. Matron was delighted. She had always liked Margery, and knowing of her family position and of her loneliness, had taken it upon herself to watch over the girl's nursing abilities and to take a motherly interest in her welfare. It was because of that interest that Matron looked intently at Margery and asked her if she was sure and knew of the responsibilities she was taking on.

Matron was extremely pleased from the tone and manner of Margery's reply, because she felt that standing before her stood a strikingly good looking petite young woman with an unusually quiet yet resolute personality, who, from the manner in which she had conducted herself throughout the recent air raids and her general work in the hospital, had proved to be a dedicated person to the profession she had chosen. Matron congratulated Margery and after wishing her good luck said, 'Are you intending to retire from the nursing profession after you are married?' Margery replied hurriedly, 'Oh no, Matron! I will seek Kevin's advice on whether he has any objections to me remaining as a nurse when the war is over.'

Later on, in the quietness of their room, Margery told Helen of her engagement to Kevin and of her visit to the Matron. Helen jumped up from her bed and excitedly exclaimed, 'Great! I told you so. Did you get engaged because of what I said about grabbing at what happiness you could before it was too late?' But before Margery could say anything Helen sat down beside her and demanded, 'Right, now tell me all about it.' She sat perfectly still and enthralled listening while Margery explained the circumstances about her engagement and saying, 'It was all Kevin's insistence, but I want you to know that I love him very much, I already miss him being around telling me what to do, and by the way, we are hoping to be married shortly after your wedding. Isn't that wonderful?'

When Margery had finished talking, Helen said, 'Yes it is wonderful and I am so glad for you and Kevin, and I wish both of you every happiness. I am so pleased you mentioned my wedding, because I want both of you to be there, you will try and attend won't you?'

Margery replied, 'Of course we will, but it will be up to Kevin and his flying duties whether he attends. But whatever happens, I will be there.' They were both giggling and teasing each other about their respective weddings when they climbed into bed.

A few days later Margery received a letter from Kevin informing her that he was unable to get leave for Christmas. Later that evening, when Helen came into their room Margery told her that Kevin was unable to get leave and they both decided to volunteer to work over the Christmas period. Fortunately on Christmas Eve night there were no air raids and this enabled them, with the other nurses who were on duty, to walk round the darkened wards with their lamps aglow, singing Christmas carols to the patients.

While they were standing in one of the wards, the patients noticed it was snowing, and what with snow falling and with the nurses wearing their capes, and swinging their lighted glowing lamps whilst singing carols, the patients told the nurses it was one of the most beautiful sights they had ever seen, such a typical Christmas scene.

The year of 1942 began with very heavy air raids on London and in the surrounding districts. This meant that Margery and Helen were both very busy tending to those people with the usual illnesses, as well the air raid casualties. In the meantime Margery had written to Kevin about the invitation to Helen's wedding and she received a reply saying he was unable to attend it. He also added that he would like her to go to Hemelsham and arrange for their wedding banns to be read, because when his course finished, he had arranged for leave to get married. Having read the letter twice, she was delighted to know he wanted them to be married in the same church where her mother and father had been married. She hurried off to see the Matron to explain to her the reason why she wanted the time off. That evening when Helen came off duty she told Helen why Kevin couldn't go to her wedding, then she told her that she was going to Hemelsham soon to arrange for her own wedding banns to be read.

A few days later Margery left London by train to the Midlands, and there she changed from the main line on to the small country line. As the train ambled along to Kirkbridge along a single line track through the lovely rolling countryside of the fields of tulips and daffodils, flowers she knew so well, she was looking out of the window at that lovely sight and thinking of her own wedding and the bouquet of flowers she might be holding, and how her life had altered since she had met Kevin. She was pleased when she arrived at Kirkbridge and managed to get a bus for Hemelsham without having to wait.

Arriving at the village she went to the village shop, where she found Mr and Mrs Swinton in the process of cleaning the shelves. They were very surprised to see her. While having a cup of tea with them, Margery was soon explaining the reason of her visit and when she had finished telling them about her forthcoming marriage, they asked her to stay with them for a few days.

'I am awfully sorry,' said Margery, 'you know I would love to, but I was only given one day's leave to see the vicar about the reading of the wedding banns.' Then as she started to leave the shop she suddenly said to them, 'Oh! by the way, do you think you could be so kind as to hear the banns read for me?'

Mrs Swinton replied, 'Of course we will. It will be our pleasure.'

Walking up the path towards the vicarage, she had mixed feelings of apprehension and joy because she knew there was a new vicar and was unsure what he would be like. Nearer to the vicarage door, she felt an inner glow and her nervousness and apprehension just disappeared. When the door of the vicarage opened, she was pleasantly surprised to see that the vicar was a relatively young person, and inviting into his lounge he made her feel most welcome. She explained the reason for her visit and told him, 'I was born in this village, baptised and christened in the church, and when my parents died they were buried in the cemetery of this church, and my husband to be was stationed at the airfield not far from here.'

After listening to her, the vicar said, 'I know you are a local girl and I know the history of your family, because Mrs Swinton is always telling me how well you have progressed in your desire to be a nurse in London. I also know you have a bedroom above her shop, so technically you are a local girl living here in this village, and therefore I can see no reason why you cannot be married in this church and I will be delighted to perform the wedding ceremony for you.'

Laughing nervously she said, 'Thank you very much indeed, I am ever so pleased and very grateful to you. Directly I hear from Kevin, I will let you know the date of the wedding.'

Leaving the vicarage she was feeling very pleased with herself and glowing with excitement, and was hurrying along anxious to let Mrs Swinton know of the good news, when suddenly she came to a halt. In her excitement she had forgotten that she had no one to escort her up the aisle at her wedding, and now doubts began to filter into her mind as she continued her walk. Seeing Margery's downcast expression as she entered the shop, Mrs Swinton immediately exclaimed, 'Margery, won't the vicar let you get married in our church?'

Margery mournfully replied, 'Oh no, it is nothing like that. The vicar was ever so nice to me and said I can be married in the church, but when I was coming back, I suddenly realised that with my father being dead I have no one to escort me down the aisle.'

Mrs Swinton's broke into a big smile. 'Oh! Is that all, don't you worry, because how would you like Arthur to be your escort? I know he would be delighted if you were to ask him and it would make him a very proud man.'

Margery's face broke into a smile. 'I think that is a wonderful idea and I would be more than happy if he would.' When Mr Swinton was asked, all three of them burst into tears of happiness and they still had tears in their eyes as Margery left on the bus for Kirkbridge.

At the main line station she went into the buffet bar and although there was a big queue, she still managed to obtain a cup of tea. Much to her surprise she also managed to get a seat on the train. Making herself comfortable, she began to think how lucky she had been to get a seat and how fortunate she was to be getting married in Hemelsham church. She was thinking of all those things as she closed her eyes and fell into a deep sleep, only to wake up when the train reached Kings Cross Station.

With Kevin not coming home on leave, and Helen's wedding day not being far away, and everyone in the hospital being very busy, the days simply flew by. Margery went to see the Matron about having time off to attend Helen's wedding. Entering Matron's office she nervously pleaded, 'Matron, I know that everyone is extremely busy, but please could I have some time off to go to see Nurse Helen Stuart married? Helen and I share a room together and we are the best of friends. If you do agree, I could swap my early shift for night duty that day, and I promise that I will be back immediately after the church service and in good time for it.'

Being so short staffed, Matron appreciated Margery's offer to swap shifts, and having complete trust in her to keep to her promise she said, 'Of course you can. And I would like you to tell me all about the church service and what Nurse Helen was wearing.'

In the church at Reigate, Margery watched Helen walk very serenely down the aisle holding on to her father's arm with him looking very proud beside her, she thought how beautiful Helen looked as she carried the small bouquet of red flowers that complemented her white wedding dress, and how smart Ian was in his army officer's uniform.

After the wedding service, Margery went to the reception hall and looking around she saw the top table had a two-tier wedding cake upon it with all the other round tables set individually apart and decorated with flowers. She commented to a waitress how lovely it all looked. Just before the wedding reception began, Margery managed to talk very briefly to Helen and Ian, telling them how wonderful the service had been and how beautiful the reception hall looked. 'I must go now,' she said, 'because I promised Matron I would be back in time for the night shift. I do congratulate you both and wish you a very happy and long life together.'

On the train going back to London, Margery was thinking of Helen's wedding and where Helen and Ian were going to spend their honeymoon in Cornwall, and she began to compare Helen's wedding with her own wedding, and said out loud to herself that she and Kevin would never be able to afford a sumptuous wedding like that. Fortunately there was no one else in the train compartment with her, because tears began to run down her face as she again said out loud, 'I can't even afford a white dress, so how can I afford to have a reception?' When she looked down at the dress she was wearing, she sobbed even louder, saying, 'Why, I haven't even got a decent dress to wear!' Suddenly she could hear Kevin's voice saying to her, 'Always think positively . . .' and she said, 'Pull yourself together, at least you have Kevin and there isn't another couple in the world who love each other as much as we do. I will have to manage somehow.'

One month later, when Helen returned to work at the hospital after her honeymoon, she told Margery she had applied to join a hospital near to her parent's home in Redhill. Margery was upset hearing of Helen's decision to leave Charing Cross Hospital, but fully understood her reasons for doing so.

Margery received a letter from Kevin, and she told Helen that he was hoping to be home on leave in three weeks time to make arrangements for their wedding. However just before she received the letter from Kevin, she told Helen she had previously written to Mrs Swinton about her worries over the dress to wear at her wedding, and Mrs Swinton had sent her a letter and some money to buy a dress.

Helen replied, 'Why that's great, because I know of a place where you can buy a nice wedding dress and it's not far from here, but I must warn you the area has been badly bombed, and it looks in a bad shape, but I do know the dresses are relatively cheap and the shopkeepers are still very good dressmakers. I'm sure you will find a dress there that you will like and at the price you want to pay.'

The next day they went see Matron and arranged to have a few hours off. When they were on a bus going to Stepney, Helen said to Margery, 'Don't worry about the state of the place I'm taking you to, because it has been pretty badly bombed, but it will be well worth your visit going there.' When they arrived and Margery saw the devastated area with all the bomb damage to the buildings, she exclaimed, 'Oh Helen! How could you build my hopes up and bring me to this place. I'm certainly not wasting my precious little money and time on a place like this.'

Helen was annoyed at hearing Margery's words and stopped walking, grabbed Margery by the arms, swung her round to face her and looking at Margery, exclaimed, 'What did you think of my wedding dress then? Did you think it was that horrible?'

Margery was surprised to be held by Helen in a firm grip and could see that Helen was upset and very annoyed. 'I told you at your wedding that I thought it was a lovely dress and you looked very beautiful in it,' she said, 'and I still think that, but I don't see what your wedding dress has to do with me not liking this place.'

'Well,' said Helen petulantly, 'my parents brought me here because they knew of a shop, which even though it has been badly damaged by bombs, it still has, and does sell, good quality dresses, and the people here do not ask awkward questions about the correct number of clothing coupons required, and I can also assure you the prices are much cheaper here than for a similar dress in the West End shops.'

Margery could feel the force of Helen's anger and could also see the logic of her reply. 'Oh Helen, I am sorry for my outburst, but you know I am very worried about my money problem and the small number of clothing coupons I have. I should have trusted you, so please forgive me and let us go on to the shop.'

The shop from the outside looked a complete wreck, with all its windows covered with odd pieces of wooden panels, but when they went inside, it was very clean and very bright from the electric lights. Helen said to a small bald-headed man, with glasses on the end of his nose, 'Hello Mr Rabonovitch, do you remember me? I came in here with my parents not so long ago.'

Mr Rabonovitch looked quizzically at Helen, then his face broke into a big grin. 'Vhy of course I remember you. You had the dress I recommended, but your Mother at first vos unsure. Vos everybody pleased vith it?' Helen replied, 'Yes, and I know I looked superb in it. Thank you for helping me to choose it.'

'Good!' he said. 'Now vot can I do for you?'

Helen replied, 'Oh! My visit here is not for me, it's for my friend here, because she is the one who is getting married and she would like to choose a dress. Is that all right?' Mr. Rabonovitch turned to look at Margery. 'Hello my girl! Vot are you looking for – but before you tell me, let me tell you I vill not sell you anything you do not like, or more specifically, I vill not sell you anything I feel does not suits you, all right?'

While he was speaking, Margery was warming towards him, and for some unknown reason she said, 'My boyfriend is in the RAF and is an Australian, flying at the moment in Bomber Command, and he has asked me to choose a decent dress, but before I do, let me tell you; both my parents are dead and I haven't a lot of money, and most of all, I haven't many clothing coupons. All I want is a decent dress, one that is not too costly and one I can afford.'

Without waiting to hear if she wanted a white bridal dress, Mr Rabonovitch disappeared behind a large draped curtain, which was shielding an opening to another room, then reappeared with some lovely two-piece suits and he selected a beautiful peach coloured one with a pleated skirt. He was holding it against her when Helen said, 'Margery, it certainly looks lovely against you, why not try it on?'

While Helen and Mr Rabonovitch remained talking to each other, Margery went into a very small room at the rear of the shop. When she reappeared dressed in the peach two-piece, he looked at Margery, pursed his lips, then throwing his hands outwards and upwards as only a person of Cockney/Jewish origin can do, he exclaimed, 'My Gawd! My girl! vhat a beautiful sight you look.'

Margery looked embarrassingly at him, then looked at Helen who was nodding and smiling at her, and she knew that she must look nice. She felt very snug and comfortable in it, and knowing the outfit fitted her slim figure perfectly she felt very happy.

However she knew she wanted a white wedding dress and asked Mr Rabonovitch if she could try one on. He began shaking his head and said, 'I vill sell you a vhite vedding dress, but vhy vaste money on a vhite dress, vhen you look so perfect in that one; My girl! All you need is a pair of peach coloured stockings and shoes to match and you have the complete vedding and going away outfit.'

Seeing a look of sorrow come into her eyes and face he said, 'Vell, are you vorried about the vhite dress, or are you vorried vot this is going to cost you? Don't you vorry because if you choose to have the peach suit, I know you vill have enough money and clothing coupons in your purse to pay for the suit, stockings and shoes.'

Without waiting to hear what Margery said, he said to Helen, 'Take your friend down the road to Mrs Jacob's shop. By the vay that shop is also badly bomb damaged, but not to vorry, Mrs Jacob is a good voman and her gear is also very good. Just tell her I have sent you and she must help this beautiful young lady to have peach coloured shoes and stockings. Oh yes – I very nearly forgot – and mention the name of Ronnie Orton to her.'

Helen was curious and said, 'Why Ronnie Orton?' Mr Rabonovitch with a twinkle in his eyes and with a mischievous smile on his face replied, 'Miracles take a moment to happen, but the miraculous takes just a little longer. Ronnie Orton takes a moment to provide some things, but sometimes he can do the miraculous, but it takes a little longer.'

Three hours later, Margery had everything she required for her wedding, including a small peach coloured handbag, peach stockings and peach coloured shoes. Returning to Mr Rabonovitch shop, she thanked him most sincerely for all his help and guidance, then as she went to leave he laughingly said, 'Vell didn't I tell you, you had enough coupons and money to pay for all your vedding gear.' then he leaned forward, kissed her and wished her good luck and every success for the future.

They were both carrying the bags and walking back towards the main road to catch the bus and Margery was busy talking about how nice Mr Rabonovitch was, when suddenly Helen apprehensively interrupted and remarked, 'We had better hurry – I see that the barrage balloons are flying high, and we will be very lucky if we get back to the hospital before the next air raid begins.'

They were just walking through the hospital main entrance when they heard the warning sounds of air raid sirens, and soon they heard the sound of the engines of the enemy planes coming over, as they rushed into the shelter.

As the days went by, Margery began to worry because she had not heard from Kevin, but suddenly a letter arrived informing her that he had finished his course and the wedding could take place, and that he had received his Commanding Officer's written consent to get married. He also added that after their wedding service he had arranged a small reception in the 'Red Lion' hotel in Kirkbridge, booked a room for them, and was also going to take her for few days on honeymoon to the Lake District. Having read the letter three times and knowing the 'Red Lion' hotel was the biggest hotel in Kirkbridge, with large rooms with big chandeliers hanging from very highly decorated ceilings, she began to worry how they were going to pay for the reception and the honeymoon.

Later that day when Helen had finished her day shift she went into their room and found Margery crying. Thinking something had happened to Kevin, Helen immediately said, 'Oh my God what's happened? Why are you crying, has something happened to Kevin?'

Margery began to wipe the tears from her eyes and saying, 'No! Nothing like that. Kevin is all right, but I've had a letter from him saying he has hired a banqueting suite and a room for the night at the 'Red Lion' hotel and he is also taking me on honeymoon to the Lake District, and I don't know how we are going to pay for it.'

She began crying again when she heard Helen laughingly saying, 'You daft fool. I'm sure that if Kevin says he can afford to pay for it, he will. All you have to remember is that he loves you and he wants to give you the best he can afford.' Hearing Helen say those words seemed to calm Margery down, because she went to see the Matron and explained that not having any close relatives she would like Helen to be at her wedding as she was going to be the matron of honour. Matron knew they were good friends and agreed for them both to have a few days off.

On the eve of the wedding, Helen accompanied Margery to Hemelsham village where they stayed and slept at Mrs Swinton's shop. When they awoke in the morning, Helen looked out of the bedroom window and seeing the clear sky said, 'You are a lucky girl Margery! It's a beautiful morning, the sun is shining and there are no clouds in the sky and no breeze. It looks as though it is going to be a lovely day with sunshine all day.'

As the morning went on Mr and Mrs Swinton fussed around, which made Margery feel very nervous, but Helen, always close on hand, made sure that Margery remained calm.

While they were having a mid morning cup of tea Mrs Swinton said to Margery, 'Arthur and I have a little surprise for you. We have ordered a pony and trap to take you and Arthur to the church, and afterwards a car to take you and Kevin to Kirkbridge for the reception.' She added, 'To keep Arthur and me company, would you mind if Tom and Betty Reynolds, our friends from next door, came to the reception afterwards?'

Margery could hardly hold back her emotions as she replied, 'Of course they can, and thank you very much for that lovely surprise; I think now is the time for me to thank you and Arthur for all the love and support, as well as the financial help you have given to me. You have been like a mother and father to me and I appreciate it very much.' Margery began to wipe tears from her eyes and Arthur, who had heard everything Margery had said, walked into the room in his dark suit with a white carnation in his lapel, saying, 'And it has been worth every penny. Anyway I never thought I would be so lucky as to be escorting a lovely bride like you to her wedding in a pony and trap.' Whereupon they all burst out loud laughing.

At the church when the time came for Margery to begin her walk down the aisle, she looked at Arthur, and as a gesture of encouragement to him gave his arm a big squeeze and took a deep breath. Looking into the church she saw a number of Kevin's friends, as well as a large number of villagers, were present.

As she slowly began her dignified walk down the aisle, she felt Arthur straighten his shoulders and she knew then that he was a very proud man. Hearing the church organ playing, Kevin and his best man stood up, and he looked over his shoulder towards her. He felt a lump in his throat, because she looked so radiant and beautiful carrying the small spray of flowers that complemented and blended with the smart peach ensemble she was wearing.

Halfway down the aisle, the sunlight rays, shining through the ornamented stained glass window, formed an incandescent aura all around her. At that moment, as everyone in the church looked at her, they could see this bright colourful glow all around her, though strangely the radiance of the aura didn't cover Mr Swinton. Walking behind them Helen, who also saw this glow, knew that something special had occurred, and felt a huge surge of emotion within herself, which caused her to shiver. On looking around she noticed that everyone else appeared to be experiencing the same feeling, and it made her realise that whatever her own wedding had cost, no money on earth could have bought this sensational emotional experience, which she knew everyone else appeared to be sharing. Somehow she felt that everyone who had witnessed that bright glow that had shone on Margery knew that something very special had happened and they could also sense and feel the great love which Kevin and Margery showed in their gestures and looks to each other.

At the end of the marriage ceremony, when the bridal couple came out of the church into the bright sunshine, Kevin's airforce friends had formed an arch with brooms, and as the bridal pair began their walk beneath the arch of brooms, they were calling out to them and making them laugh. Throughout all the joviality which was now taking place between Kevin and his friends, most of the wedding guests had noticed that all the airmen, who were looking very smartly dressed in their best blue airforce uniforms, all looked very young and were probably in their late teens or early twenties, and that some of them even had medal ribbons sewn on the breast of their jackets.

After everyone had come out of the church, Margery and Kevin went by car to Kirkbridge, whilst Mr and Mrs Swinton and all the other guests climbed into two RAF lorries that Kevin's friends had borrowed for the occasion. Helen was squashed between the driver and an airman wearing a pilot's brevet and with the letters RCAF sewn on his shoulder.

Because of their closeness in the confined space in the cabin in the front of the lorry, to make more room, the airman put his arm around Helen's shoulder.

Due to the fast and erratic way the driver was driving the lorry along the country lanes, it made Helen and the pilot come into physical contact and she knew from the manner in which his arm kept pulling her to him, and the laughing intimate conversation they were having, as well as the way certain emphasis were being made on some of the words, that a flirtation was taking place, and she was enjoying every moment of it.

In the car, Margery was very worried and kept asking Kevin how they were going to pay for the wedding reception. He held her hands in his, gave her a big kiss and said, 'Sweetheart, you do worry don't you? The chaps in my crew and a few of my mates in the squadron have clubbed together to pay for our wedding as a wedding gift, and because of that, a few of them will be coming to the hotel for a drink later this evening.'

On reaching the 'Red Lion', they entered the highly polished cherry-wood panelled hallway and went into the large dining room with its ornate chandeliers. Margery's eyes shone with joy as she looked in amazement at the layout of the tables. When she saw a large two tiered wedding cake covered in white and blue icing, she took a deep breath and in an incredulous and trembling voice enquired, 'Oh Kevin it's beautiful, how on earth did you manage to get a cake made like that?'

With a voice full of great confidence and pride, Kevin replied, 'My mates in the cook-house made that for you; and you can thank them yourself, because they are coming here this evening to meet and have a drink with you.' While waiting for their guests to arrive, Kevin and Margery stood by the doors that divided the hallway from the dining room and they heard hoots of laughter and shouting coming from outside the hotel. It was the airmen who had brought some girls with them, and after congratulating Kevin and Margery they headed straight for the bar that was conveniently placed at the other end of the room.

Everyone was soon drinking, laughing, relaxing and enjoying themselves and on looking around Margery noticed that Helen and the pilot who had travelled with in the lorry were holding hands and were laughing and talking to each other, and it was the way Helen was looking at the pilot that made Margery to ask Kevin who he was.

Kevin replied, 'Why that's Mark, our pilot and captain of our aircraft, who in the opinion of our crew is the best pilot in the squadron. Now don't start worrying about Helen, she is old enough to look after herself, and knowing Mark, I am sure he will look after her.'

As the afternoon and evening went on and the late arrivals came and joined in the fun, the party became a more joyous occasion. Some of the airmen were getting quite merry and although they appeared slightly drunk, they entered into the games and proceedings with great gusto. Seeing the look of concern on Margery's face at some of the antics taking place, Kevin whispered to her, 'Don't worry, they are letting their hair down and having a good time, it's been a terrible strain they have been under these last few days.'

Later on during the evening, Margery noticed Helen was in an alcove, being very attentive and amorous towards Mark, and hoped that Helen was not getting too involved with him. Then Kevin came to her and and told her to watch the next dance. A jovial chap, who was the navigator in his crew, he said, began leading everyone off in a dance around the room, which Kevin said had originated in the officers' mess a few days ago. It was such an uproarious dance that made everyone laugh and it got everyone into such a muddle, that it made the whole evening became a very joyous and lively occasion.

It was 11.30 p.m. and the party was still going very strongly. Margery suggested to Kevin that they say goodnight to their guests, but with Kevin being slightly drunk, much to the delight of the members of his crew, she had to assist him to depart with a little dignity, by holding tightly on to his arm to keep him in an upright position.

Going from a very warm room into the cooler air of the corridor leading to the bedrooms appeared to have an effect on Kevin, because by the time he had managed to climb the stairs to reach their room, his legs were beginning to fold under him and she was having great difficulty holding him upright. On entering the bedroom, as they staggered towards the bed, he stumbled and fell face downwards onto it. She turned him over onto his back and as she looked at him and heard his snoring, and seeing his eyes shut with his fair hair falling over his forehead, she noticed how young he looked. She knew then that she loved him very much and whatever fate had in store for them no one else would ever be able to take his place. With those thoughts going through her mind, she carefully removed his shoes, socks, jacket, tie and shirt, then as though she was dealing with a patient, she rolled him one way then the other to remove his trousers and then covered him with the bedclothes.

Looking at Kevin sleeping as she undressed and put on her night-dress, she felt great love for him and when she lay beside him in bed, she thanked God for a lovely wedding and a beautiful sunny day, and said how grateful she was for all the lovely things that had happened. Then very gently she held Kevin's hand in hers and fell asleep. It was 4.00 a.m. when Kevin awoke and went to the toilet, and she was awakened by his movements. When he eventually came back into the room, he looked out of the window and then as he snuggled back into bed, she whispered to him, 'Are you all right?'

Kevin, startled by her whisper, turned on his side to face her. As he did so he laid his arm across her chest and gently kissed her on her lips, whispered, 'Thank you for putting me to bed last night. I am sorry for the condition I was in. I don't know how it happened, please believe me.

I think it must have one of my pals who mixed my drinks just before we started to say goodnight to everyone, because up until then I had hardly been drinking.' All the time he was whispering, he was snuggling closer and closer to her while his hand was discreetly undoing the buttons on her nightdress. Then he lowered his face onto her breasts and very gently he started to kiss and caress them. As she put her arms around him, she could feel his erect manhood against her thighs.

Very slowly he removed her nightdress and at the same time he was kissing her on the lips, face and breasts. When he gently entered her, she knew from that moment they would always be as one person, not joined together as they were at that moment by their bodies, but together in their love and affection for each other.

Their lovemaking was not a mad passionate affair, but a gentle lasting emotional experience and this feeling was to remain with them throughout the whole of their honeymoon.

They were staying at a small quiet boarding house on the edge of Kendal and one day they were quietly walking hand in hand along the lanes nearby, admiring the stark beauty of the rambling countryside, when suddenly their thoughts were shattered by the noise of low flying aeroplanes, a savage reminder of the war and the trauma and dangers that went with it.

The next morning at breakfast, Margery heard two people talking about Beatrix Potter, the author, who lived in the Lake District, and she remembered that when she had been at school she had read her book *The Tale of Peter Rabbit*, and they talked about the story later that day while they were out walking. Margery was also thrilled when they came to an old castle overlooking the river. The castle was in ruins and close by was a notice on a board, which she read out loud: 'This is the birthplace of Catherine Parr the sixth wife of King Henry VIII.' She turned to Kevin and said, 'Kevin, promise me that after the war, you will bring me back here, and possibly with our children, to see this beautiful historical place again!'

That evening after they had eaten their evening meal they went to the nearby local pub, had a couple of drinks and played darts with a some of the local people, after which they went back to the boarding house and retired to their room where their love for each other seemed to grow stronger and stronger. The day before their honeymoon ended and they were due to leave, Kevin made a strange remark to her: 'Margery, I want you to know I love you very much and I will never let you down, and I want you to always remember that whatever happens to me, I will always be near and around you.'

Margery was bewildered by that remark and with a surprised expression her face said, 'That is a very sad, poignant thing to say. Are you expecting something bad is going to happen to you?' Realising what he had said, he very hastily replied, 'No! No of course not. I only want you to understand that all the time I am away from you, I will always be with you in my thoughts.'

The following day they travelled to Preston together, where they parted, with Kevin having the long journey to Breighton, knowing he was going to be posted to an HCU aerodrome. Margery travelled straight back to London and to Charing Cross Hospital.

Twelve weeks after returning from her honeymoon, she was in her room in the hospital writing a letter to Kevin, when Helen came in and, seeing Margery, stopped quite still then rather dramatically grabbed her arm. 'Margery I must talk to you very urgently!' Margery looked up rather amazed and was quite stunned because when she looked at Helen's very worried face she could see she was ready to cry. She immediately put down her pen, saying, 'What's the matter Helen? Has something terrible happened to Ian?'

Wiping her eyes Helen replied, 'No it is not anything like that thank goodness, it's me. I need your advice, as well as your help, I know you are good at these things and it's a rather long story, so please be patient with me.' She sat on a stool facing Margery and began.

'At your wedding, I became very friendly with an airman called Mark, who is, as you know, a pilot. We seemed to hit it off from the first moment we saw each other in the church and then when we were in the airforce lorry taking us to Kirkbridge we became attracted to each other. At your reception in the hotel we stayed very close together and we both had plenty to drink and were quite merry, though I must add, that neither of us was drunk. After you and Kevin had said your goodnights to everyone and went to bed, Mark and I were having a final drink when he asked me where I was going to sleep that night. I told him that I was going back with Mr and Mrs Swinton to Hemelsham.'

Helen stopped talking for a moment then she said, 'Mark and I were in the alcove at the end of the room and when I looked around I found that Mr and Mrs Swinton had left without me. I told Mark I was worried about how I was going to get to Hemelsham so he went to the booking desk and when he came back he said the two RAF vans had left a few moments before and there was no transport. Mark said he had asked if there were any rooms vacant and was told there was only one room left and asked me if I wanted him to book it. I thought for a moment and I still do not know why, but I said yes. It was a large room at the rear of the hotel. Well Mark and I slept together and as you can guess, yes, we made love, and now I am all mixed up, because I now find that I love Mark as much as I love my husband Ian.'

Helen began to cry again and with the tears running down her face she said, 'Margery I am very worried because I've missed one of my periods and I am overdue for my second, and I am quite sure I am expecting a baby. What can I do?'

Margery was momentarily shaken but before she could say anything, Helen was talking again. 'Oh, Margery, suppose I do have a baby . . . I am quite sure that I am pregnant and I am also certain that Mark is the father, what am I going to do and what am I going to tell Ian?' Margery could see the anguish on Helen's face and the distress she was suffering. She kept quiet for a moment and was thinking very hard.

Then Margery said quite sternly, 'Now look here Helen. If you are quite sure you are going to have a baby and you think Mark is the father, then you cannot erase what has happened between you and Mark, because what happened, happened and there is no argument to that, so your first priority must be to the baby you are expecting, and then to your future, and I feel that your future is with your husband, Ian.' Margery paused for a moment then said, 'By the way, I know I shouldn't be asking you this question, so do forgive me, but when was the last time you saw Ian and made love to him?'

Helen blushed and her face went red as she said, 'Just over three months ago, just before your wedding.' Then trying hard to remember, Helen shyly said, 'Yes that's right. I remember now, Ian had couple of days leave and he called for me here and we spent the night together in the Strand Palace Hotel.'

Margery was smiling when she said, 'Good! That helps, because at the moment you feel you are expecting a baby and you believe Mark is the father, and you may at this moment believe you are in love with him and no doubt you are . . .' Margery stopped talking for a moment holding her hand to her head, and then with a big smile on her face said, '. . . but you are a married woman and you haven't given your marriage a chance. The night you stayed at the Strand Palace Hotel you could have been made pregnant by Ian, so why not accept you are pregnant and accept it as your husband's? Then if it is a girl why not call it Margery after me or if it is a boy you can call it Mark.' Helen had a frown on her face, but Margery continued talking. 'Both names begin with the letter M, and if any questions are asked, you could say you named the baby after the first letter of my name.'

Understanding the wisdom of what Margery was saying, Helen's expression changed and her face broke into a big smile. But suddenly it changed again into a solemn look, as she said, 'What do you think would happen if Mark was to write to me? What should I say?'

Margery asked apprehensively, 'How could he write to you unless you have given him an address to write to? You didn't give him one, did you?'

Helen was shaking her head at the same time saying, 'No all I said to him was, that I would be soon leaving Charing Cross Hospital and going to another hospital, and I would write to him when I knew where that hospital would be.'

'Good,' said Margery, 'because if a letter from Mark does eventually find you, you can always cross that bridge of trouble when it arrives. Promise me Helen, you won't write to Mark, to even tell him of your condition, will you?' Margery paused to look at Helen, then began speaking again. 'I know I am being very selfish asking you not to write, but you must realise that Kevin is in the same aeroplane as him, and I am sure that Mark would start worrying if he knew you were expecting his baby, he would want to see you, and I don't want Mark worrying over anything, I want Kevin safely home with me. If you do as I have suggested, it will be helping both of us.'

Helen again burst into tears as she put her arms around Margery, saying, 'Oh! Margery, I will always be grateful and remember you for all your help, guidance, wisdom, and of course your common sense, and when I send you the new address where Ian and I are hoping to live, I will be ever so pleased if you would come and visit us. Then we could chat over old times and you could discreetly let me know how things are with Mark.'

On the day that Helen left the hospital to start work elsewhere, she laughingly said to Margery, 'Now don't forget, keep in touch and please write and let me know how you are progressing, and I will write and let you know the good news when it arrives. Good luck. Bye.' Then waving her arm she walked away from the hospital for the last time.

Margery watched Helen depart in a taxi, and a few moments later when back in her room she felt that lonesome feeling come upon her. It was then she realised that since she had arrived at the hospital the only person she had ever been friendly with was Helen and she didn't really know any one else, except the Matron.

As time went by and with the air raids continuing, and not managing to make new friends amongst the rest of the staff, she began to work harder and became more dependent upon Kevin's letters. Shortly afterwards she and Kevin spent five wonderful days of his leave together in London, going to theatres, dancing and visiting the 'Overseas' Club. When Kevin's leave had ended and he had returned to his base, she felt the loneliness even more, because not only did she miss Kevin, but when she returned to her room that she missed Helen not being there to laugh and talk with. It was then that she wished she could obtain a position in a hospital nearer to Kevin.

Just before Christmas she received a letter from Kevin saying he would be unable to be home for Christmas, and because she was lonely, she again immediately volunteered to work over the Christmas holiday period of two days, and the early period in the New Year. Then she received a letter from Mrs Swinton informing her that Mr Swinton had died of a heart attack When she came back to the hospital after attending his funeral, the effect of losing someone to whom she had grown very fond of, and who had escorted her at her wedding, together with the departure of Helen and missing her company, made Margery want to work even harder, because she felt lonelier and more isolated than ever.

She had been very busy working hard and was beginning to feel the strain when sitting her room during one of her rest periods, that she received two letters, one from Kevin and the other one from Helen.

Having read Kevin's letter first, she then read Helen's letter, who told her that she had given birth to a baby boy weighing 7 lbs. 8 ozs with a birthmark on the left side of his hip. She had the baby in the local hospital, where they had treated her very well, and when Ian came home on leave and saw the baby, he was overjoyed and very proud at becoming a father of such a beautiful baby boy. Helen also wrote that she knew of someone else, whom they both knew, who had a similar birthmark in the same place, and she was pleased and grateful that Ian had agreed to call the baby Mark.

After reading Helen's letter and thinking how she missed Helen's company, Margery realised how lonely she was without her being around. She became more autonomous and disinterested in anything not connected with her work, and by keeping herself to herself she never had close friends among her working colleagues, or became involved with anyone within the hospital, either male or female.

Shortly after receiving the letters, she was able to get a couple of days off and travelled to the Midlands to meet Kevin, where they managed to spend some time together in a small hotel in the country not too far away from his aerodrome. However it was when they were in the small hotel that she noticed a subtle difference in his behaviour. He appeared to be more solicitous towards her, and he had a nervous twitch in his face, which she had noticed was more noticeable when he was resting, especially with his eyes closed.

That night when they were in bed, she was suddenly awakened from her sleep by Kevin shouting out in a rather tense sleepy voice, 'Skipper that last burst of gunfire has badly damaged the hydraulics and the radio is dead,' then Kevin started shaking and mumbling about other things in the plane.

Looking at the bedside clock she saw it was only 1 a.m, and she realised that he was having a bad dream. She put her arm under his shoulders and gently pulled him towards her. As she did so he partially opened his eyes, and rather sleepily said, 'That feels better . . .' and he fell into a deep sleep again. Very shortly afterwards she fell asleep with her arm still around him. When she awoke in the morning, her arm was still around Kevin's shoulders and it had no feeling in it. Very gently removing it, and getting out of bed, she was standing by the window rubbing her arm trying to get the circulation and feeling back into it when Kevin opened his eyes. He watched her rubbing her arm, and laughing and appearing more relaxed he said, 'Why are you rubbing your arm? What has happened to it?' 'Oh it's nothing,' she replied, 'it's just a bit sore because I had it wrapped round your shoulders all night.' Then she said, 'Kevin, do you know you had a bad dream last night?'

He immediately sat straight up in bed and stared blankly at the wallpaper on the opposite wall. That look, together with the nervous twitch in his face, made Margery realise he had a bad time flying on operations.

He turned to look at her and said, 'Yes! I am sorry. I thought I did, and it wasn't a nice dream, anyway it is nothing to worry about.' Then, noticing the worried look on her face he said, 'Well you might as well know, it happened on our last flight a few nights ago when we had to go to a place called Gelsenkirchen, which is near Dortmund in Germany. We had a good flight out and everything was going lovely, when suddenly we got caught by gunfire and our plane was damaged. Being so near to the target we carried on, but the gunfire was so intense that our plane received more damage and one of the engines was on fire and put out of action and we had to limp home. Let me assure you, it was only due to the great skill of Mark, our pilot, that got us safely back to England.'

Visibly shocked by what he had just told her, she said quickly and rather nervously, 'If it was that badly damaged, how did he manage to land the plane?'

'With most of the hydraulics damaged we couldn't land at our airfield,' said Kevin, 'so Mark flew to the emergency airfield near the coast, where we knew there was a long runway. Mark made a wheels-up landing on the grass within the airfield perimeter and we all managed to scramble out with just a few cuts and bruises before the whole plane caught fire. When we arrived back at our airfield, because we have been doing a lot of flying recently and I believe, also because of our little mishap, the CO said that our crew could have five days leave. Now I do not want you to start worrying over me because of this. I keep telling you that I am in a good crew and we have the best pilot looking after us. All you have to do is to stop worrying and think positively towards our future life together.'

With that, he jumped out of bed, put his arms around her and began to kiss her tenderly on the lips. The day before he was due to return from leave, they were walking down a country lane saying to each other how lovely the countryside looked when Kevin suddenly said to her, 'Margery, do you think you could get a transfer to a hospital near the aerodrome? If you could, it would save me travelling down to London every time I get leave, and also being near to the airfield we could spend more time together and perhaps find a small place for us to be in.' She looked towards him and knew from the expression on his face and in his eyes, that he was pleading with her to say yes.

4

MIDLAND HOSPITAL

The following day Kevin accompanied her to the railway station to catch the train to London and as he said goodbye, he held her tightly by the shoulders and looking very intently into her eyes he said, 'Please try and get that transfer'. Not caring about the other passengers standing close by he kissed her passionately on her lips. On the journey back to London, Margery was thinking intently about the transfer and what she could say to the Matron, but because an air raid was in progress, she hadn't noticed the train had stopped outside London and was waiting for the all-clear siren. Arriving at the hospital, she was surprised to meet the Matron and whilst she was talking to her Margery told her about her desire to be with Kevin. Matron who was listening intently, very quietly said, 'I would like you to come to my office tomorrow morning before you go on duty.'

The following morning Margery reported to the Matron, who, being a very understanding person said, 'I have two things to tell you, Nurse Hopkins. Firstly I fully understand your position and your desire to be near your husband, and I will try very hard to find you a suitable transfer, but I want to inform you that when I do manage to find one, I will be very sorry to see you leave. Secondly I have some good news for you. I am pleased to inform you that you have passed your exams and you are now a fully qualified staff nurse.' Margery was delighted to hear that news.

It was late springtime and she received a letter from Kevin saying he was coming to London for three days, and she managed to have a few days off to be with him. It was Thursday 20 May when Kevin arrived in London and they went into Trafalgar Square and saw the many posters that had been placed around the square stating it was 'Wings for Victory Week – Buy War Bonds'. On looking at the posters Kevin said, 'That's a good publicity drive to get the public to buy war bonds to help us win this war.' Then he saw an aeroplane standing in the square and exclaimed, 'Why that's a Lancaster bomber, just like the one I fly in, and like the one that bombed the German dams a few nights ago.' Straightaway she excitedly asked, 'Is it really? Please can we go look over it?' He replied in a rather dispassionate manner, 'Yes. If you want to.'

She was very nervous when they joined the queue waiting to climb up the steps of the scaffolding which had been placed on one side of the aeroplane, and pointing towards the aeroplane she said to Kevin, 'What do those letters stand for on the side of the plane?'

He replied, 'Every plane has its own identification marks for a call sign, and those letters JD represent a call sign, so when the plane is coming in to land at its aerodrome, the pilot repeats the call sign and its identification names to the ground controller and the ground controller knows what plane is going to land. You might like to know that our plane has the name of "Phantom of Delight" painted on its fuselage, because I asked Mark if we could have that name.'

Being very curious she asked, 'Why the "Phantom of Delight"?'

'Because,' Kevin replied, 'when I had a few moments to spare, I was reading a book by William Wordsworth where he had written a poem called "She was a phantom of delight", which reminded me of you, and because like a nurse that glides around the wards looking after the patients, our plane is a beauty and glides quietly through the night like a phantom.'

She was intrigued and asked, 'Can you remember any of the poem?'

Kevin paused for a moment and began laughing before replying, 'I think I can, but if I get any of it wrong you won't scold me will you?' Then he very quietly said

> She was a phantom of delight
> When first she gleamed upon my sight
> A lovely apparition sent,
> To be a moment's ornament
> Her eyes as stars of twilight fair
> Like twilight's too her dusky hair

She was very excited they had named the plane after her and was enthralled listening to Kevin saying the poem, also slightly mystified as to why it should remind him of her. As soon as he had finished speaking she said, 'Kevin I don't understand why that poem should remind you of me. What is the connection?'

He replied, 'That day when I was sitting in the sergeants' mess and I picked up that book by Wordsworth, just before I came to that poem, I was thinking of you and the type of work you do, and after I had read the poem, I put the book down then thought how, because of the work you are doing, I think you are an angel of mercy. Then I saw the connection between you and the title of Phantom of Delight. You are a Phantom of Delight to the patients as well as to me. Because our plane is such a beauty to be in, I asked Mark if we could have that name for it. The rest of the crew agreed with me, and he said yes.'

'Oh you are wonderful,' she exclaimed. 'Thank you for having that name on your plane!' Soon they were climbing the scaffolding steps and Kevin began showing Margery where his wireless operator position was situated. He added, 'And that's a very safe place to be.' Looking through the closed window of the cockpit Kevin said to her, 'That's where Mark sits, and see that small seat just behind him? That's where I sit, so you know that I am perfectly safe sitting there.' After they had finished looking into the cockpit, and to ensure that everyone could view the Lancaster, an airman who was standing on the scaffold platform behind them gently hurried them to go down the scaffolding.

On reaching the ground, she said to Kevin, 'Do you think this plane has ever taken part in any bombing raids over Germany?' At that moment a uniformed officer was walking by and after Kevin saluted him he stopped, came over to them and nodding towards Margery, said to Kevin, 'I could not help overhearing the question this young lady put to you, Sergeant, and I thought she might like to know that this plane HAS recently bombed Berlin, and as you can see, it has come back unscathed.' Then looking at the breast of Kevin's A/G brevet and pointing to his medal ribbon beneath it, said, 'Congratulations on your award. By the way, are you still on active flying duties?'

'Yes Sir,' replied Kevin. 'I'm in 5 group.' The officer grinned as he said, 'So am I, but I won't ask you where you are stationed because there could be a very good chance that we might be meeting and flying with each other again! By the way, wasn't it a brilliant trip the boys did on the Mohne Dam?' Without waiting for Kevin to reply, he shook hands with each of them and said, 'I must be off now, and I do wish you both the best of luck.'

After the officer had left them, Margery said, 'Kevin, that was a piece of luck! Fancy him telling us that this plane has bombed Berlin and come back unscathed!' And with a big sigh of relief she said, 'Oh! I'm so pleased he told us that, because now I feel much easier in my mind, knowing where you sit and knowing how big the plane is and that it can bomb Berlin and other places and get back safely. I now feel much happier knowing that you fly in one these planes, especially if you are flying with lovely airmen like that officer and Mark, and now I think I know why you think so much of the airmen who fly with you.'

At the end of his leave, when he was saying his goodbye to her, Kevin said, 'Now don't forget. Go and ask the Matron to get you that transfer and get a hospital that is nearer to me. Ok?'

It was fortunate that soon after that leave, Matron called Margery into her office and said, 'Nurse Hopkins, I have just heard of a vacancy for a staff nurse at a hospital near Grantham. If that is anywhere near where your husband is stationed, would you like me to arrange a transfer for you?' Margery was so excited she could hardly speak, but managed to blurt out, 'Yes please, Matron. It's ideal, Kevin is stationed quite near there.'

Matron was looking at Margery's eager and excited face as she said, 'I am very sorry to lose you, because you have been a credit to us here at the Charing Cross, and to the nursing profession in particular, and I feel sure you will never let our profession down.' Matron then rose and said, 'Do you think you will keep to nursing after the war is over?'

Margery thought a moment then said, 'Matron I do hope so, and thank you very much for what you have done for me.' Matron shook Margery's hand as she said, 'Well Nurse Hopkins, I wish you every happiness with your husband and good luck in your new position.'

It was August when Margery began her new duties as a sister in charge of a ward in a hospital near Grantham, and she was now able to see Kevin more often. They found a small cottage to live in, and she began to take a greater care and interest in her general appearance, and because of this, her whole behaviour and attitude changed.

Early in December Kevin came home very excited and said, 'Margery, I have some very good news for you. You know Mark, my pilot and the skipper of our crew – well he has been promoted to Flight Lieutenant, and Jimmy Etheridge our navigator has been promoted to Flying Officer, and, would you believe it, I have been promoted to Flight Sergeant! Isn't that great, because this means we will be able to save more money towards the house we are going to buy after the war.'

During the next two weeks the weather deteriorated, it snowed and continued to snow all over Christmas, right up to New Year's Day, and because the snow was so thick on the ground, flying was cancelled. This enabled Margery and Kevin to spend a quiet Christmas together in the small cottage they were renting, where they were able to have a log fire and candles, making it a truly romantic idyllic time for them.

It was early in March, when after a very heavy day in the hospital, she arrived home and was thinking of Kevin, whom she had not seen for three days. After cooking herself a meal, she felt very tired and looking at the clock, saw that it was 9 p.m. she decided to go to bed early. At that precise moment, Kevin was sitting in his usual W/O seat in the Lancaster bomber, whilst Mark, his pilot, was getting the plane into position on the runway ready for take off.

Earlier in the day, when they were in the briefing room, listening to the Squadron planners explaining the target for bombing and the weather forecast for their flight to and from Saarbrucken, Mark had noticed that everyone in the room appeared rather edgy about the way the Briefing Officers were describing and making this trip look an easy target. This appeared to upset many of the experienced aircrews. Afterwards outside the briefing room Mark said to his crew, 'OK lads, don't worry about what some of the others have said in there, once the Pathfinders have marked the target, as we are in the first wave we'll go straight in, bomb the target and get the hell out of it.' Then turning to their bomb aimer he said, 'Do you hear that, Jimmy, it's straight in and no hanging about, we don't want to go round again.'

With that remark sounding in their ears, with a few nervous laughs they did their pre-flight inspection and climbed into their aircraft. As the plane gathering speed down the runway, and rose into the night sky, Kevin was sitting in his usual Wireless Operator's position, praying that Mark's words would be true.

Their outward flight went according to plan and they reached the target area just after the Pathfinders had dropped their Target Indicators. Just as they were dropping their bombs, they were coned by the blue haze of the master searchlight and within seconds all the other searchlights were on to them, making it look like daylight within the aircraft. The gunfire began reaching their altitude and shells were bursting all around them, with the shrapnel peppering against the aircraft. Mark immediately threw the plane into a steep corkscrewing dive, managing to break free from the beams of the searchlights and into the darkness.

They were now well off-course, and flying at a much lower altitude, and while they were hastily sorting themselves from the mess they were in, gunfire again began bursting all around them, badly damaging the aircraft, causing one of the engines to catch fire. The Flight Engineer managed to feather the engine, thereby partially putting the fire out, and they began to fly home. Mark was told that some of the crew had been hurt, though not seriously. He asked Kevin to assist the mid-upper gunner to help the wounded and called to everyone to be extremely vigilant and to be aware of night fighters.

He asked Jimmy, the navigator, where they were, but because some instruments had been badly damaged, Jimmy had to take an astro fix then gave Mark a course to fly. When they had been flying for about 35 minutes, the rear gunner shouted out a warning of a night fighter coming in, but before Mark could take evasive action the JU-88 night fighter racked the plane with machine and rocket gun fire, causing the Lancaster to catch fire again. Mark tried very hard to control the burning plane but it was very badly damaged and it crashed near a small French town, killing everyone on board.

When the plane crashed Margery was in a deep sleep, and was suddenly awakened from her sleep by a sudden snapping pain in her back and a severe aching pain within herself. It made her sit upright in bed, then suddenly a depressing feeling of loneliness came within her and she felt cold. She began to worry and felt something dreadful had happened. She tried to go back to sleep again, but the pain and her worrying thoughts kept her awake.

She lay there with her eyes closed, worrying and thinking, but then she remembered what Kevin had always told her to have positive thoughts, and she began to look forward to him coming home and said a silent prayer hoping that her fears were wrong.

In the morning, she got up feeling very tired, worried and drained of all energy, and as she went to work she began saying to herself, 'I am sure that if anything has happened to Kevin and his crew, I will soon receive a call telling me so.' At the end of the day, not having had a telephone call, she began to think her thoughts of the drama of last night must have been a bad dream.

5

AMERICAN AIRMEN

During the next few days, not hearing anything from Kevin and because she had not heard any aeroplanes flying during the past three nights, Margery again began to start worrying. Then realising there had been bad storms over the area for the past three days and nights, she kept telling herself not to worry and praying that Kevin could be delayed for various reasons. But the doubts still began to take shape in her mind.

It was later in the day as she was going about her duties in the ward that she received a telephone call from the hospital enquiry desk saying there was an airman waiting to see her. She immediately thought of Kevin. Going down the stairway towards the front hall, she could see the back of the person in RAF uniform, about the same height and build as Kevin. As she got closer to him she thought to herself, 'Kevin has had a haircut.' Tapping him on the shoulder she said, 'Kevin?'

The airman turned to face her and immediately she saw it wasn't her husband. 'Mrs Hopkins?' he said, hesitantly.

'Yes . . .'

'I am in the same squadron as Kevin, and one of his friends – I have met you before in London. I have been asked by the squadron adjutant to let you know that Kevin's plane is seven days overdue.

'This could be due to a number of things and there is every hope that the plane came down in unoccupied country, or in occupied territory, because no news had been received to say what has happened to it. So please don't give up hope, Kevin and his crew could be prisoners of war. I have been told to inform you, that if you do not hear from the War Department within one month; please contact Squadron Leader John MacAvory, the squadron adjutant, who is willing and may be able to help you with any further news.'

Margery, who had remained impassive, silent, with a drawn expression on her face, whispered, 'Thank you,' to the airman as he gave her a piece of paper with the adjutant's name on it.

Then he left. She turned and walked up the stairs in a confused and stupefied trance, neither hearing nor seeing anyone around her. Making her way to the Matron's office, she knocked on the door and went in and told her the sad news. The Matron immediately made Margery sit down and gave her a cup of tea. Whilst Margery was drinking the tea, Matron suggested that she be relieved of her duties for the day and have someone stay with her for a short while, but she declined the offer and tearfully said, 'Matron, I do thank you for relieving me of my duties for the rest of the day, but I would rather be alone. I don't want to be with anyone at this moment.'

On reaching her room in the cottage, she closed the door behind her and gave vent to her feelings by bursting into a flood of tears. Still crying, she staggered over to her bed and throwing herself upon it, cried and cried until she eventually cried herself to sleep. When she awoke the room was in complete darkness, and for a moment she wondered where she was.

Her eyes felt sore and it was only when she closed the curtains, switched on the light, and looked in the mirror, and saw how red and sore her eyes were, that she remembered what happened. She looked at the clock and realised she had been asleep four hours. Taking off her creased nurse's uniform, she washed her face, bathed her eyes, put on a clean plain dress and her heavy topcoat, then putting her purse in her pocket she went out into the evening darkness. To shield her neck from the cold night air she pulled up the collar of her topcoat and walked from the cottage, past the hospital and the closed shops, which were situated nearby. It was a clear night, with the moon and stars shining brightly in the sky. As she was walking past the shops, she could hear the planes leaving the aerodrome for another raid on the Continent. She felt the tears course down her face as she whispered a silent prayer for those men in the aircraft.

She felt that walking around the area would help her adjust to what had happened, and she let her thoughts dwell on Kevin. In doing so she became oblivious to everything around her. It was only the smell of fish and chips that brought her back to reality, and suddenly she felt quite hungry. Realising she had not eaten since early morning and looking around she saw the fish and chip shop was open. Passing through the blackout curtains hanging inside the door, she found she was the only person in the shop. After she had quietly asked for fish and chips, the owner said, 'I've only got snoek left, I assure you it's nice, will that be all right luv?'

She didn't really hear him speaking and was on the point of crying again, but managed a 'Yes please,' then heard him say, 'Where's your ration book luv? I must have your coupons.' Realising she had made a mistake and feeling very embarrassed she said, 'I'm sorry, I don't know what I am doing. I work in the hospital and live in the little cottage nearby and my ration book is there,' she went to leave the shop. The owner, who had seen her recently walking around with an airman, could see from the redness of her eyes that she had been crying, and sensing something was wrong, he said, 'Look, you might as well take these fish and chips with you. As you can see I haven't had many customers tonight.'

He began to salt and vinegar them and wrapped them in clean white paper, then to her surprise he said, 'I won't charge you, you can have them. Anyway I'm going to close the shop now because I don't think I'll have any more customers.'

Outside in the darkness she unwrapped the paper and began eagerly to eat the hot fish and chips. She hadn't realised how hungry she was. After she had finished eating, she began to walk away, but suddenly stopped because she could hear voices. Looking around she noticed she had stopped outside the 'Lord Kitchener' public house and on a sudden impulse she decided she needed a drink.

Opening the outer door, she parted the heavy blackout curtains on the inside and entered the saloon bar. Through the tobacco smoke haze she could see airmen and other people at the bar. She opened her purse, took some money from it and on approaching the bar, one of the airmen asked her if she would like a drink. Giving him some money she replied, 'Yes would you get me a gin and tonic, please?' She sat down at a table nearby and when the airman brought the drink to her, he could see she had been crying and he asked her, 'Is everything all right Miss?' She stammered, 'Y . . . yes . . . it's OK, I'm fine thank you.'

She sat there lost in her own thoughts, unaware of anything or anyone around her, when she picked her glass up she was surprised to find it empty. Still feeling thirsty she decided to have another drink. At the bar the same airman offered to buy her a drink, but she refused and again paid for it herself. He tried to talk to her, but she quietly told him she just wanted to be left alone.

Sitting at the table pensively and wistfully thinking of her future, she soon lost count of the number of drinks she had consumed. When she rose to leave, everything appeared quite normal until she reached the coldness of the night air, and although she felt unsteady she thought she would be all right, but she started to fall and stumble around. It was moonlight and a male voice called out, 'Are you all right miss?' She could see through her blurred eyes, that it was the same airman approaching her, who earlier had offered to buy her a drink and who had obtained the drinks for her.

Her legs felt weak and wobbly and knowing she needed help and because she felt slightly unwell, she started to cry again, then turning to the airman in a slurring voice said, 'Would you mind . . . (hic) . . . if you could let me lean on your arm? . . . (hic) . . . you see . . . I don't feel very well and I want . . . (hic) . . . to get to the cottage near the Hospital . . . (hic) . . . (hic) . . . where I live.' the tears were now streaming down her face as she said, 'I'm awfully . . . (hic) . . . sorry . . . But I've just been told . . . my husband is missing . . . (hic) . . . (hic) . . . from a bombing raid and I felt I needed a drink . . . Do you . . . (hic) . . . blame me?'

After hearing that news and seeing the state she was in, the airman's whole attitude and manner changed towards her, and he said very gently and sincerely, 'No Miss. I don't blame you. I think you are just fine and you did the right thing, because I think everyone else would have done exactly the same thing as you.'

He held her close to him as he gently helped her along the road, then passing the hospital she said, 'I work there.' At the cottage gates he held her head in his hands and very tenderly placed a kiss on her forehead as he said, 'Goodnight. God bless you and good luck.'

In a drunken fashion she staggered towards the front door, on entering the cottage and going to her room she removed her coat, letting it fall on the floor and with tears flowing freely down her face, she threw herself on to the bed and whilst her body was being racked by the torment of her sobbing, she was crying out loud, 'Oh why? Oh why?' repeating it time and time again until, exhausted, she fell into a deep sleep.

As time went by, with Kevin being missing she did not want to live in the cottage on her own, and she obtained a room in the hospital. Two months later she received a letter from the War Department informing her that Kevin was missing, presumed killed. Receiving this letter upset her and the weeks rolled into months. She carried on working in the hospital, but she became remote, impervious to idle discussion and not willing to mix with anyone.

It was just before the D-Day invasion of Europe, that two fellow staff nurses, Nurse Drayton and Nurse Mackenzie, entered her room and asked Margery to help them because they had a problem that evening. They and Nurse Rednow had arranged to meet three American airmen, who were going to take them to a dance at their aerodrome, but now Nurse Rednow had been confined to her quarters with a severe cold, and that meant one American being left on his own. As Margery was the only person available with time off, did she think she could make the party complete by joining them and taking Nurse Rednow's place?

Margery was shaking her head while saying in a mournful tone, 'I'm sorry I can't. As you know, my husband was reported missing presumed

75

killed a few months ago, and I haven't quite recovered from the shock of it. Anyway I don't think it right that I should go out gallivanting.' Both Nurse Drayton and Nurse Mackenzie looked at each in amazement, then Nurse Mackenzie said in her lovely Scottish accent, 'Ach away with yer, yer won't be being unfaithful to him, or to his memory, by living your life, but yer will be if yer carry on going the way yer are. Why yer so melancholy and have that sad woeful nature about yer and yer act as a remote person with all the worries of world on yer shoulders. Wake up and live yer life.'

Margery retaliated by saying, 'I think what you have said is horrible and very unfair. I don't think you realise I feel very lonely and I am still overcoming my sorrow and grief of losing my loved one.'

With an overt stark look, Nurse Mackenzie harshly replied in her Scottish manner, 'Ach away with yer. Yer no different from hundreds of other widows, who, I am sure, are making a better job of their lives and grief than yer are.' And then she unkindly added, 'from the way yer have carried on in this hospital over the past few months, I think yer have three choices to make, One – wake up and live yer life. Two – remain as yer are being morbid and becoming a cabbage, or three – commit suicide.'

Margery stood motionless, looking at them in amazement and bewilderment, and then as they went to leave the room, suddenly, vigorously she exclaimed. 'Right you buggers, I'll show you, I will come with you!' Startled by Margery's retort, the two nurses suddenly whooped with joy and said, 'Great! Be ready by 5 p.m. and don't put on anything too dressy.'

Margery dressed herself in a colourful flowered dress and went to meet the other two nurses at the main gate of the hospital, where they found the Americans were already in the jeep waiting for them and shouting to them to hurry up. The Americans helped them get into the jeep, but they found they were rather squashed, but the Americans who were still laughing and joking with them said, 'Come on girls, there's plenty of room.'

Margery found herself sitting on the lap of one of the Americans, who had put his arms around her waist and began speaking to her. During the journey, she asked the American, 'Where is this dance being held?' He replied in a drawling southern American accent, 'Why Honey, it's at our base at Little Gainsford, and when you get there, remember that me and my two buddies are meeting up at the dance with our buddies from Betsy Lou.'

She was embarrassed and very surprised when the American all burst out laughing after she asked, 'What part of America is Betsy Lou in?'

When they had all finished laughing they told her, Betsy Lou is a B.24 Liberator Bomber and their buddies were the crew that flew in it.

Arriving at the base after passing through the main gate check point, the girls were surprised when they saw the dance was being held in a large aircraft hangar. Inside they were also amazed to see how huge and spacious it was. They could see at the far end of the hangar an aircraft and just in front of it was the bandstand, and on one side of the hanger near to the bandstand were tables loaded with food, and then a little farther back towards them, on the same side, there were other tables where servicemen was serving beer and spirits. Above all the noise the band was playing, people talking and laughing, there were others who were dancing, and Margery could see and hear a girl singing to the music of the American Air Force band. When the band played 'South Rampart Street Parade' everyone cheered and jumped and danced.

Margery had quite a task making herself heard above all the noise, however two of the Americans they were with managed to make their way to the bar to obtain drinks, while the other American managed to find a table with some vacant chairs. Soon afterwards, she found out the Americans were officers, two of them pilots and the one she was with their navigator. Because the Americans were so happy and lively, she soon began to relax and enjoy herself and their company.

When she was on her own with the navigator, she said to him, 'I like the way you speak with that soft American drawl.' He stood to attention and said in a rather quizzical way, 'Honey, my name is Homer D. Standen. I am 22 years of age and I come from Fresno in California. I am engaged to a lovely girl called Donna, who is waiting for me back home. But tonight baby doll, I'm going to have a great time dancing with you.' Before she could say anything, as the band started to play 'In the Mood', 'Quick,' said Homer, 'let's dance.' After a short while, knowing she loved dancing and because he was good company and a good dancer and did not attempt to be flirtatious with her, she very quickly began to enjoy every dance with him and in between the dances she would have a quick drink and a sandwich, then go back to the dance floor and carry on dancing.

Just after they had finished dancing the band stopped playing, and as they were going back to their table for a drink, the drummer gave a drum-roll and the band leader announced, 'Ladies and Gentlemen, the American boys of the famous 259th Bomber Group . . .' as he said that, a terrific roar rose up from all the American airmen, '. . . invite every one of you to take to the dance floor and dance to the "Turkey Trot". This dance has been arranged by some of the boys of the band and is danced to the tune called "The Mississippi Mud". To you young English ladies I should inform those of you who do not know it, this dance is in the form of a military two step, coupled with the Palais Glide – Have a great time folks.'

Margery said to Homer, 'What do we do?' He immediately put his right hand in her right hand, then put their hands in front of his body and then held her left hand in his left hand and held that in front of her body. With every couple holding each other exactly the same way, the band began to play. Every now and then, everyone would stop dancing and they would bow down very low with their faces towards the dance floor and the men would raise their heads high in the air and make a sound like a turkey gobbling, then the band would start to play again and off they would go into another two step-dance.

With the men making those funny gobbling sounds, everyone was soon laughing and hooting, with tears of laughter running down their faces. Soon after that dance, the band began to play 'At the Woodchopper's Ball'. Homer grabbed Margery, saying, 'Quick Honey, let's dance, it's a jitterbug. Just let yourself go Babe.'

Looking at Margery being thrown up in the air and pushed through his legs and then thrown over his hips, Nurse Mackenzie cheerfully remarked, 'My goodness, she is human after all! She has certainly let herself go tonight and she appears to be enjoying herself dancing with Homer. And isn't she a good dancer!' After that dance the Band Leader announced, 'It's Night Night time, folks, take your partners for the last dance,' and the band began to play, 'My dreams are getting better all the time'. Margery and Homer danced cheek to cheek singing the words out loud with the rest of the dancers.

It was 11.00 p.m. and everyone started to make their out of the hangar, as they sat off towards the jeep to take them home, Margery knew that she and Homer, in between dancing, had consumed a fair amount of alcohol, and being very relaxed, she thought how it had been a lovely evening dancing with Homer, and felt a glowing feeling of relief and relaxation within herself.

In the jeep on the way back to the hospital, Margery was sitting on Homer's lap and everyone was singing the tune of 'My dreams are getting better all the time', when the jeep, which was going very fast, swayed causing Margery and Homer's faces to come very close together and he began to kiss her. At first she stiffened with fright, but because of the amount of alcohol she had consumed, and the warm glowing feeling within her, she found herself responding to his kisses. When the jeep was about a mile from the hospital, it stopped near some playing fields and they all went for a walk. Being in the warm night air, she soon began to feel the effects of the alcohol and began wobbling as she walked and she held Homer's hand.

The moon was shining very brightly as they both staggered along the footpath at the river's edge, and they could see their shadows quite clearly. Looking around for the other nurses, Margery realised she and Homer were all alone and Homer was still holding her hand, suddenly he flopped down on to the grass, causing her to fall down beside him.

Looking at him sitting there with his Officer's cap askew on his head, she started to laugh, which made him ask, 'Now what are you laughing at?'

She replied, 'It's your cap. You look rather comical with it all askew on your head.' As she reached over to put his cap straight, he put his arms around her, drew her towards him and began to kiss her. Within seconds she was lying on the ground with Homer kissing her, at the same time was caressing her breasts from the outside of her clothing. She could feel his fingers undoing the buttons on her dress then he eased her small firm breasts from her brassiere. With the warm night air wafting across her naked breasts, she laid there enjoying the ecstasy of the moment, as he kissed each nipple very gently she could feel his hot breath upon them and her body began to tingle and quiver. She could feel his other hand slowly going up her legs to caress her private parts. Very soon her body was yearning and throbbing for him to go further, Very, very slowly he lowered himself down and entered her.

Her whole body was responding in unison to his movements, but just as he was reaching his climax she was about to join with him, a low flying aircraft flew overhead it was the noise of its engines that reminded her of Kevin. The thought stopped her thinking of the ecstasy of the moment, causing her to momentarily to stiffen her body and cry out, but because of the movements of Homer upon and within her, she was unable to stop herself reaching a climax. Homer lay beside her panting and sexually exhausted, but knowing that something had happened to make her stiffen and cry out as they were about to climax together, he looked at her, and seeing she was crying he wiped her eyes and asked, 'Was that the first time for you?'

She shook her head because she was afraid that if she spoke she would start to cry again. Homer asked again, 'If that wasn't the first time, then did I hurt you in any way?' Again she wouldn't speak, just shaking her head from side to side.

With Homer sitting beside her, she moved her position to adjust her clothing, but as she did so he grabbed her by her shoulders and, looking straight into her eyes, could see the tears going down her face. He said to her with a great deal of concern, 'Look honey. For Christ's sake tell me what's wrong. Don't you think I have enough to worry about, than to worrying over whether I have hurt you?'

Before she could say anything he carried on. 'Tomorrow I could again be on operations with the other two and if it's going to the same place we went to the day before yesterday. It's going to be one hell of a trip.' Looking at him as he finished speaking, she could see that he was shaking, and though she was still upset and crying, she felt a great compassion for him.

'Was it a bad flight?' she asked quietly.

His voice was trembling, 'Yes, I know I can trust you. We lost 24 aircraft from our group, that's two hundred and forty men, and that is why we had today off. Tomorrow we could be going to the same place again and that is why we let our hair down tonight, because tomorrow's trip could be another bad one.'

Realising that she had another busy day in the hospital tomorrow she began looking at her wristwatch and noticed it was nearly midnight. She looked around for the others, but could neither see or hear them. She turned quickly to Homer and said, 'Homer, before we meet up with the other nurses, I feel I must tell you what made me stiffen up just now. It wasn't you. It was because when I heard that aeroplane fly over, it reminded me of my husband Kevin.'

On hearing her say the word husband, a look of horror came upon Homer's face. Seeing it, she wiped the tears from her own eyes, leaned towards him and taking his hand in hers said, 'It is my fault. I should have told you when we first met that I may be a widow, because a few months ago my husband was shot down over Europe on a bombing trip and is now reported missing, believed killed. Since then I have kept myself to myself because I have felt so lonely and miserable, and to help me forget, the other nurses asked me to accompany them to the dance tonight.'

She paused for a moment. 'Homer I really want you to believe me when I say that I've had a wonderful time dancing with you, and I have really let myself go and I have enjoyed your company very much. What happened between us just now, happened, and there must be no regrets. As far as I am concerned it was great for both of us.'

Homer thought for a second then said, 'Thank you for telling about your husband. I do feel for you.' She could tell by the crestfallen look on his face that he was not worried over her loss, he looked very worried about something else, so she asked him, 'Homer, is something else worrying you?' He replied with tears in his eyes and in a very worried tone, 'Yes. When you said your husband had been shot down and was missing, it reminded me of my great fear.'

Then with a very, very, scared look and with panic in his voice he said, 'Please please don't say anything to the pilots. I am their navigator, and every time we go on a bombing trip I am more nervous than ever. I'm very frightened that something is going to happen. I have never mentioned this to anyone else, but somehow you make me feel that I can confide in you, so I am going to tell you why I am scared. I am frightened of dying, and on some trips there have been times I have felt like a baby. I have been so scared that if an emergency arises I might show this fear and let the others down.

She put her arms around him and whispered in his ear, 'Don't be afraid. Just remember that you are a man in every sense of the word, you proved tonight to yourself and to me that you are.' With tears running down his face, she continued, 'Before you go to sleep tonight, why don't you say a few prayers to your God, not only for yourself, but for your Mum and Dad and for your girlfriend in California, and I am sure that when you wake up tomorrow you will not be afraid to tackle any task you are called upon to do.'

He was holding her tight with his arms around her and she could feel his wet tears against her face as he gently put his lips to hers. Then as they broke from their embrace he very tenderly whispered to her, 'Honey, no wonder you are a nurse, because you sure are some woman. You have made me feel much better and I would like to keep in contact with you and would take it as a great compliment if we could meet again.' Then rather anxiously he added, 'You will let me meet you again won't you?'

This took her by surprise and for a brief moment, not sure what to say but realising that she did not want to upset him, she replied, 'Yes, I think that would be lovely.' Homer's face began to break into a smile. They could heard voices calling them and when they had reached the jeep, it was from the way the others were brushing and adjusting their clothes, Margery knew what they had been doing.

Everyone was quiet and not talking on the short journey back and just before they arrived at the hospital, Homer whispered in Margery's ear, 'Thanks, Honey, for a truly wonderful evening. I will never forget you and I will be in touch.' After the Americans had kissed the girls goodnight, they drove away with the girls waving goodbye to them. Soon they were saying 'Goodnight' to each other, and they each made their way to their rooms, with their thoughts of a lovely evening still mingling in their minds.

Ever since the day that Kevin had been posted missing, Margery had always felt his presence and thought he was close to her, but tonight when she got into bed and said her prayers, she felt he was not around.

This made her feel very sad, lonely and guilty, and in an audible whisper she said, 'Kevin, I did have a lovely evening dancing and I am so sorry if I have let you down tonight.' Then, exhausted from dancing, she fell into a deep sleep.

When she awoke in the morning she lay there thinking of the events of last night and thought of Homer and his confession, and she remembered how her body had responded to his caresses. She knew she felt better physically, but psychologically she felt in a worse frame of mind, because she realised she had enjoyed every minute of the lovemaking, knowing that it made her feel wanted, desired and her body felt alive.

It also made her feel as though her body was still tingling for desire. She knew Homer had awakened a strong sexual feeling within her, and she let her thoughts dwell on this whilst she lay there. As she lay there breathing very heavily, she said out loud, 'Margery Hopkins, you are becoming one hell of a sex pot, and this has got to stop.'

While she was dressing she made a decision not to see Homer again, then she began to vacillate and said, 'What if he does comes here and asks me to go out with him, will I have the courage to say no?' She knew she would not be sure of the answer to that question, until the time came when he was standing before her.

On an American airfield some miles away, Homer and crew were being briefed for another daylight raid on Schweinfurt. They knew it was going to be a rough trip because they had been informed it was their turn to be in the low squadron, and this meant that they would be the first to get the wrath of German defences and also of the fighter planes.

Homer and the two pilots had always managed to keep together, ever since they became friends at the air base in Utah prior to leaving for England. Looking at the red tapes stretched across the map marker board, showing them the routes to the target and back to base, the three of them looked at each other and the map and it made them and everyone else shiver at thought of another long and dangerous flight.

After a quick early lunch they all made for their plane, and while they were discussing the briefing, Homer was looking at the name on the nose of their aircraft 'Bootiful Lady', and he sighed and remarked, 'Yes indeed . . . she is a beautiful lady.' Hearing Homer's remark both pilots stopped talking, looked at each other, then one of them said to Homer, 'Are you alluding to this lady,' pointing towards the aircraft, 'or to the lady you met last night?'

Homer's face reddened as he looked wistfully at them, and the pilots, seeing his blushing red face, said, 'Why you son of a bitch, you made it last night, didn't you?' Homer didn't answer but his eyes, which were laughing at them, giving them the answer. They were all nervously laughing and joking with each other when the order came to board the aircraft.

Crossing the coast over Cromer, they formatted their plane with the rest of their group and positioned themselves into their slot, right behind the leader of the last box of four, in the low squadron. It was when they reached the enemy coast Homer had to log the time and noted it was 2.15 p.m, then for a fleeting second he wondered what Margery was doing and remembering her encouraging words of wisdom he began to feel calmer and was concentrating on his navigation.

All hell was let loose 50 minutes later and it was soon chaos inside the plane with the noise being deafening. The enemy fighter planes began coming at them from all angles, and the gunners were firing their guns, with empty shell cases clattering noisily on the floor of the plane, then suddenly everyone in the plane was shouting to each other, 'Where are the enemy fighters?' Then the ground guns started firing and the shells were exploding all around them, suddenly there was an almighty explosion within the plane, and it disintegrated and fell to earth.

Margery was having a short break in the hospital canteen sitting drinking a cup of tea, when she happened to look at the clock on the wall and noted it was 3.05 p.m. At that moment a cold shiver went through her body which she knew she had experienced before and she somehow knew immediately that she would never know the answer to the question of whether she would have gone out with Homer again.

After slowly drinking her tea she thought for a few moments and went back to her work in the ward in a very lugubrious mood.

When she had said her prayers that evening, she sensed the presence of Kevin around her, and as she lay there she said out loud, 'Kevin I am sorry for breaking the trust you had in me. Please forgive me.' Then she thought she heard him say, 'It is all right, sweetheart. You did the right thing, you made someone happy. By the way, you are very clever because you can hear me. I wish I could have your psychic powers.'

Lying in bed thinking what she thought she had heard, she said to herself, 'I must be going insane, fancy thinking I can hear things like that. It must be all in my imagination.' Next moment she was in a deep sleep. When she awoke in the morning, she began thinking of last night and of the shivering incident in the canteen, and decided to bury herself in her work. A short while later she heard that Nurse Drayton and Nurse Mackenzie had left the hospital and she read in the newspaper that the Allied forces had invaded France.

One day she was listening to the wireless and the Andrews Sisters were singing 'Don't sit under the apple tree'. It made her feel very sad and it brought tears to her eyes, because the song reminded her of Kevin. It was because of her loneliness that she hadn't made any close friends or had close relationships with any of the nursing staff, however she never stopped working and devoted herself to her work and it was because of that attitude she was known to everyone as the, 'lonely workaholic sister'.

She began to feel that there was no one she could turn to, when suddenly she remembered Mrs Swinton. At first she thought she would write her a letter, but then she said to herself, 'Better still, I will go and visit her.' She managed to get a day off, and travelled to Hemelsham.

Waiting for the bus in Kirkbridge bus station brought back to her many memories of Kevin, and when the bus was nearing Hemelsham village, she could see the aerodrome in the distance and she could feel the tears in her eyes when she remembered the happy times she had spent with him. She didn't recognise any familiar faces as she walked through the village and was feeling very sad and melancholy, but hoped that Mrs Swinton could soon give her back some happiness.

Entering the shop, the first thing she noticed was that the layout was different and she didn't recognise the lady behind the counter. On being asked what she wanted, Margery said, 'Could I see Mrs Swinton please?'

The lady replied, 'I am very sorry she doesn't live here any more.'

'Oh dear,' said Margery, 'could you tell me where she has moved to? You see I used to live here and some of my personal things were in the back bedroom.'

The lady looked very concerned and apologetic as she said, 'Oh dear, all I was told was that Mrs Swinton had been very ill and after a period in hospital she was taken to a nursing home. I am very sorry I don't know what nursing home she went into. Shortly afterwards the shop was put up for sale and we were informed it was to cover the cost of the nursing fees and that is how my husband and I were able to buy it. When we heard about Mrs Swinton being in a nursing home, we specifically asked the estate agent about the furniture and he said everything had been removed, and I know when we moved in, all the rooms were empty. I have no idea who removed the furniture and things, or where they are now.'

Margery was devastated hearing that news, but she managed to thank the lady for giving her the information about Mrs Swinton before making her way back to Kirkbridge.

On the journey back to the hospital she was feeling very sorry for herself, and as the days went by, to help her forget her loneliness she immersed herself more deeply into hospital work, hoping that it would help her.

One day a vacancy for a ward sister arose in the hospital and she applied for it, and much to her surprise the hospital management appointed her.

Of medium build and with an air of aloofness and independence about her, and being smartly dressed in her starched sister's uniform, she appeared to have an air of mystique about her which enhanced her reasonably good looks. Over a period of time, this appearance made her very attractive to the male staff and to the patients. On hearing she was a war widow, there were several times when some of the junior doctors, as well as some of the young male patients who were being discharged from the hospital, would invite her out for a drink, but she always declined their offer. To everyone she remained aloof, austere and with an air of mysterious beauty about her which made her more attractive.

The war in Europe having ended, the government declared the 8th of May VE Day, and everyone was in a joyous mood to celebrate the ending of the hostilities in Europe. However she remained on duty to allow the other staff to join in the daytime celebrations, and when the night staff came on duty to relieve her, she went to her room intending to stay there. But the noise outside made it impossible for her to sleep.

Looking out of the window in her room, she could see the houses and buildings with all the blackout curtains removed from the windows and the houses lit up. The beams of the searchlights from the nearby army unit were weaving across the night sky backwards and forwards, making everything look bright, in contrast to the years of the blackout. She could hear joyous shouting and could see people dancing and singing in the streets.

She decided to change her clothes and go outside and have a closer look. As she walked along the streets she could see everyone being happy, and when she was near the 'Royal Jubilee' public house a line of people who were singing and dancing the 'Conga', coming out of the public house doors and went down the pathway of the house next door, through its side entrance and into the rear garden, then back through the side entrance of the house next to it and back into the street where the pub was. She was standing there watching the endless line of people dancing, when a very high pitched excitable voice called out, 'Come on Miss join in!' A young boy with a look of joy and excitement upon his face was holding out his left hand to her. She instinctively held her hand out, he grabbed it and she found herself in the line of dancers. Very soon she forgot her inhibitions and joined in the fun. Feeling his young hands around her waist it gave her a feeling of joy and hope. After a while, feeling thirsty, she stopped dancing and went into the pub for a drink.

Going outside again, she again felt the joyous feeling of the people around her and it began to permeate into her mind. She began to relax in their company, then someone seeing her without a drink offered her a glass of wine, then a little later a gin and tonic, soon she was singing and dancing with the people around her. Some of the hospital staff who were there were very surprised to see their austere ward sister dancing and enjoying herself with complete strangers. Among them was a young, extremely handsome, junior doctor called Nigel Cairnworth, who some of his colleagues thought had a lothario manner. Although he had a young lady nurse with him, he had noticed Margery's lithesome figure dancing and wriggling her hips in time to the music, in what he thought was a sensuous manner, and he was soon eyeing her with a long thoughtful sensual look.

During the evening he tried very hard to dance with her, but every time he was anywhere near he found someone else was dancing with her. It was just after midnight and the festivities were still going strong, when he at last managed to dance with her, and because she was enjoying herself, she was oblivious to the time and whom she was dancing with. But suddenly she became aware and felt uneasy about the way the person she was dancing with was holding her, also she felt very uncomfortable because of the lewd remarks he was saying. She could smell his breath and could tell he was slightly drunk. She thought she recognised him and she tried very hard to remember where she had seen him before. At that moment all she could think of was how quickly could she get away from his hands that were going all over her body. Luckily a couple bumped heavily into them, causing Nigel to lose his hold on her and fall to the ground. Whilst the other couples were laughing and helping him up, she managed to slip away through the crowds and hurry back to the hospital and the sanctuary of her room.

Sitting on her bed she reflected on the evening events and shivered at the thought as she remembered the last person she had danced with and the way his hands had been going over her body and what it might have led to. Thinking and hoping that Kevin might be alive, she pleaded out loud, 'Kevin, I'm glad I ran away tonight. I do love you very much and please hurry home to me.' In bed she prayed fervently for Kevin to be alive and although she knew he was missing, she could still feel his presence around her and somehow felt he was not dead.

A week later she was waiting in the corridor for the house doctor to inspect the patients in her ward, when she saw a male figure in a white coat approaching. It was not her usual house doctor, because this person was shorter in height, but as he approached she thought she recognised him. It was the way he walked by, smiling at her and moving his tongue slowly over his lips then letting his hands slide sensuously slowly down the sides of his body that she tried to recall where she had seen him before, and cold shivers went through her when she remembered he was the person dancing with her on VE night. The next hour was sheer agony and embarrassment for her during his walk around her ward, because she knew he had recognised her, and in between his visits to the patients, she was warding off his attempts to fraternise with her. During the next few months she kept herself very busy and avoided all occasions where she could be alone with any doctor, and she always made sure a nurse was in attendance with her when the house doctor visited her ward.

American's destruction of Hiroshima and Nagasaki by atom bombs brought World War II to an end. Shortly afterwards she wrote a letter to the adjutant of Kevin's squadron, asking him if he could give her any more information on Kevin. She received a letter from another officer who wrote informing her that he didn't have any new information, but suggested she write to the Air Ministry, and enclosed a stamped addressed envelope to the department he thought most likely would be able to help her. Because of the nice way he had phrased the letter, she immediately sat down and wrote a letter, and for a few days it raised her hopes. While she waited for news she kept herself busy and semi-isolated from the doctors and the male hospital staff.

She had still not heard from the Air Ministry when one day the nurses on her ward told her there was going to be an off-duty nurses' party and asked her to go with them. At first she declined, but as they kept imploring her, she eventually relented saying, 'I will only spend a couple of hours with you then I must leave.' On the day of the party she said to the nurses, 'I will not be staying late.' She went to her room and changed into a lovely pale blue dress which complemented her figure and made her look very attractive. When the nurses met her, they all said how lovely she looked and congratulated her on the way she had styled her hair.

When she and the nurses arrived the party was in full swing, and very soon everyone was speaking to her and saying how pretty she looked. As the party progressed she began to relax and felt more at ease, until she saw four doctors arrive. She recognised one of them as the doctor who had made those lewd remarks to her in her ward and who had danced with her on VE night. She started to stiffen with fright and felt the gaiety recede from her body. Pointing to the doctors who were on the opposite side of the room and were now surrounded by nurses, Margery asked one of the nurses standing by her, 'Is Dr Cairnworth with those other doctors over there?'

The nurse excitedly replied, 'Yes, and isn't he handsome?' Margery decided to leave the party, and saying, 'Goodnight nurses. Do behave yourselves!', she began to make her way through the crowd of people. But when trying to get past a dense crowd she suddenly found herself facing Dr Cairnworth, who was carrying two glasses, one in each hand. When he saw her he exclaimed, 'Why hello . . . you are like Cinderella, always disappearing when I am near you.' His breath smelt badly of drink and as he leant forward, as if to let someone go past behind him, he spilt the drink from the glasses all over the top part of her dress.

Hurriedly putting the glasses down, he took a handkerchief from his pocket and started to dab the top part of her dress that covered her breasts. She had just eaten some peanuts and the shock of him pouring the drink over her dress and dabbing at her breasts made some of the nuts become stuck in her throat, causing her to cough very badly. All the time he was dabbing at her breasts he was saying, with a big grin on his face, 'I do apologise for this, but I do assure you . . . I like this part of dabbing it up.'

The people all around were still talking, laughing and drinking and they appeared not to have noticed the incident. She was trying to move away from Nigel's hands, which were still touching her breasts, and she tried to speak to tell him to stop, but the nuts in her throat were making her cough even more. One the men standing close by, gave her a large glass of what she thought was water and she took a big drink from it. Unbeknown to her, it was one of Nigel's friends who had filled the glass with neat gin. This caused her to splutter and made her feel sick and cough even more severely.

Nigel suggested she went outside into the corridor for a few moments. There a number of people who were walking to and from the party avoided her because they could see that she was coughing very badly. Nigel opened the door of a consulting room opposite the party room and holding her firmly by the arm he led her inside and sat her in a chair, at the same time saying to her, 'I will soon get you something to stop that coughing.' Going behind the chair he unlocked a cupboard on the wall and took a small bottle from it and a piece of lint.

She was still coughing very badly as he put the lint in her hand and said, 'Hold the lint to your nose and sniff very hard.' She did so and he put one of his hands behind her head and with his other hand he held her hand with the lint and pressed it firmly against her face.

Because of the pressure of his hand on her head and the pressure of his hand against her face, she was unable to breathe properly and she started to panic, taking deep breaths and in doing so, she smelt a sweet aroma and the coughing partially stopped, but she became giddy and lost consciousness. When she regained consciousness she found herself lying naked on an examination couch, with Nigel standing nearby adjusting his trousers. At that moment the door opened and in walked Matron. She stood there disdainfully looking at her nude figure and declared in a rather loud, abrupt and indignant manner, 'I demand to know what has been going on here?'

Before Margery could regain her thoughts, or her speech, Nigel said, 'Well Matron, the Sister here became ill at the party.' At this point he made a gesture as if to infer Margery had been drinking, then carried on speaking, 'and I brought her in here to recover. Well, one thing led to another and I am afraid I did let temptation get the better of me . . .' and with a slight smile on his face he suavely said, 'I do apologise for the embarrassment I have caused you Matron.' In her befuddled state, Margery could not believe what she was hearing, and suddenly she remembered the sweet smell on the lint and realised she must have been drugged. But as she tried to sit up and speak she slurred, saying, 'Itch's on the lint . . . Itsh's on the lint . . . whersh that piece of lint . . .' As she tried to explain to Matron what had happened she was waving her hands around when she fell off the examination couch on to the floor. Looking at Margery spread-eagled on the floor in the nude, Matron gave her one more disdainful look and said in a very stern parting remark, 'Sister Hopkins, you will report to me in my office, at 9.00 a.m. tomorrow morning.'

When Matron departed, Nigel picked up his jacket and without saying anything, or even looking at Margery, he left the room closing the door behind him. For a few moments she remained on the floor in her nude state, to allow her befuddled senses to return to normality. When her mind began function she began thinking more clearly and she could remember Nigel spilling the drink over her dress and of him pinching and squeezing her breasts as he dabbed at her dress. Then she remembered someone giving her a glass which she thought contained water and drinking from it. As her mind began to clear she could see one of the other doctors handing her the glass, then she realised it was Dr Chalfont, one of Nigel's best friends, and she remembered seeing his face smiling at her as she took the glass from him and drank from it. She remembered herself choking and coughing and being taken into the room and put in a chair and she remembered feeling Nigel's hands on her head and pressing the lint into her face then passing out.

Looking at herself in the nude, it made her realise she had to find the lint and to know what Nigel had put on it, because without the lint she would be unable to prove what had happened. This spurred her to get up off the floor to look for the lint, but seeing her clothes all over the place she started to clothe herself and as she picked up each article of clothing she was still looking for the lint. When she was fully dressed, she went to the cupboard on the wall and tried to open its doors, but found them locked shut. She began looking for the keys but could not find them anywhere and after searching the rest of the room, she couldn't find any trace of the keys, or evidence of the lint.

Remembering Matron's stern warning of wanting to see her at 9 in the morning, panic began to set in and from the way her body felt and the feeling inside the top of her legs, she knew that intercourse had taken place and she had been raped. It was then she realised the hopeless situation she was in, because how could she prove she had been raped without the evidence of the lint, or any witnesses. Making her way back to her room, she threw herself on to her bed crying, feeling as though her whole world had collapsed around her. After a while she stopped crying and decided to have a bath, to rid her on what she termed was, 'a sexual act of ghoulishness'.

The following morning she entered Matron's office very apprehensively and stood before her desk. Matron was writing and a few moments later she stopped, looked up and in a very stern voice said, 'Sister Hopkins, before I submit my report to the hospital governing body, I want a full account of your version of that disgraceful incident yesterday. I would also like you to know that I have received a report from Dr Cairnworth giving his version of what transpired and I must warn you, if what he has written is true, your conduct was disgraceful and you are a disgrace to our profession.'

Tears came to Margery's eyes as she began to relate the events that had occurred and how the drink was spilt over her dress. Soon tears were streaming down her face when she related what she could remember had happened in the consulting room. In between the crying she said, 'Matron, all I can tell you is that he held a lint, which had a peculiar smell, tight to my face. I have no recollection how I became undressed, or what actually took place.' Pausing for moment, taking a deep breath, she sobbed, 'But I am absolutely certain sexual intercourse took place and it was without my knowledge, or consent.'

Matron looked momentarily startled, hearing Margery say that, and said, 'Are you actually accusing Dr Cairnworth of raping you?' Then before Margery could answer, Matron quickly looked through some papers on her desk and said, 'Yes that's it, I thought I was right, Dr Cairnworth said you were drunk. Can you remember how many glasses of drink you had?'

Margery replied, 'Yes – I only had one and I do assure you he spilt his drink over my dress and as I was trying to get away from him he had a handkerchief in his hand and was dabbing at my dress, and I could feel him tweaking my breasts. I panicked and started coughing because I had just eaten some peanuts and they had stuck in my throat. I remember seeing Dr Chalfont standing close by, and I'm sure and believe, it was him who gave me a glass, and thinking it was water I took a big drink of it, but I now realise it was neat gin and it made me choke and cough even more.'

Stopping to gain her breath she said, 'Dr Cairnworth took me outside into the corridor and because I was choking and coughing very badly, I do remember he took me into the consulting room, where he sat me in a chair. Then a little while later he told me to hold some lint to my face. I can still feel the force of his hands on my head and the strength of his hand holding the lint against my face, but I must have passed out. I am sorry Matron, that is all I can remember, except that when I came to, I was lying naked on the examination couch and you were standing just inside the room.'

Earlier that morning, Matron had been reading the various hospital reports on Margery's work in the hospitals where she had previously worked, and had noted that the reports were of a very high standard, and together with letters of commendations from the senior doctors and consultants, that gave a very good impression of her character and conduct. Matron had also made a few enquiries from the staff in the hospital and had heard the 'gossip' concerning Dr Cairnworth being a lustful, licentious 'ladies' man'.

Looking into Margery's eyes, Matron could see a look of fear and anxiety and felt quite sure that Margery was telling the truth. With those thoughts in her mind Matron said, 'For obvious reasons Sister Hopkins you will not go to your ward, or report for work today, but I would like you to come back here at 5 p.m. and I will give you my decision.'

When Margery entered Matron's office that evening, Matron was not in her uniform and after inviting Margery to sit down, she began to explain to her the position of a Matron. After having explained the duties attached to that office, she looked at Margery and said in a very stern voice, 'I believe you are already aware that the incident in which you were involved has become the talking point of the hospital staff, and because of that, it has left me no option but to report it to the Hospital Board of Governors.'

Seeing the look of horror on Margery's face, Matron voice softened as she hastened to say, 'However, having read your previous hospitals' conduct reports and having listened to many of the hospital staff here as to your usual behaviour, and that of Dr Cairnworth, as well as having heard and read both versions of this unfortunate incident, I will be submitting a recommendation to the Board, that your version should be believed.'

Margery was surprised and very pleased to hear the Matron say that, and replied, 'Thank you Matron for those kind words of support. It is at least comforting to know that someone believes in me.' The following day she was delighted when the Matron told her that Dr Cairnworth was going on holiday and she could resume her duties.

Ten days later she was ordered to report to the Hospital Board of Governors. When she arrived at the hospital boardroom she was told to wait outside while Dr Cairnworth gave his version of the incident. After giving his evidence he jauntily came out of the Boardroom and as he passed her he gave her a derisory smile and sensuously passed his tongue over his lips. Seeing him do that she shuddered at the thought of him touching her.

Then she was summoned in to the boardroom, and she was grateful to see Matron there, because after a while she felt that from the questions being put to her everything was going her way and the Board of Governors believed her version of the incident. Then one member said to her in a superior manner, 'Dr Cairnworth is a highly respected doctor, are you actually accusing him of serious sexual misconduct and rape?' Fear, doubt and dark thoughts began to enter her mind, as she momentarily thought of the answer she should give, and she looked hesitantly at the members of the Board, but all she could see through her tear clouded eyes was their blurred faces as she replied, 'I have told the truth', and her voice quavered as she said, 'Yes I am.' Hearing her reply, some of the members gasped and looked at each other in a rather bewildered way, then after a long pregnant pause she was asked to wait outside while they considered their verdict.

Outside the boardroom she saw no sign of Dr Cairnworth, nor was he inside the boardroom when she was called back to hear the decision of the Committee. Before the Chairman began speaking to her, he appeared embarrassed and to be having trouble adjusting his glasses. He kept putting them on and then taking them off again and then said in a very hesitant, quivering voice, 'Ahem . . . Sister Hopkins . . . um . . . um . . . from all your reports it appears that you are a very good nurse, and I feel I must also tell you that . . . um . . . um . . . Matron has spoken very highly of you. Now . . . um . . . this committee has heard from Dr Cairnworth of what . . . um . . . he says occurred and we have before us . . . um . . . your allegation and the Committee . . . um . . . have taken into consideration both versions of the incident . . . um . . . However . . . um . . . you have made a very serious accusation against a highly respected doctor . . . um . . . who is the son of a very eminent surgeon, and therefore this Committee . . . um . . . has no alternative but to direct this matter to the GMC at Hallam Street in London, from whom . . . um . . . no doubt you will be hearing. But because of the seriousness of the charge you . . . um . . . have made and the embarrassment which . . . um . . . could occur if you were to carry on working here, the Committee . . . um . . . have temporarily suspended you from all your duties, pending . . . um . . . the result of the GMC hearing.'

The verdict shook Margery and she left the room very dejected and in low spirits, however during the next few weeks, the Matron became a great friend and comforter to her in trying to help her overcome her anger of not being believed and the feeling of the grave injustice of being an innocent victim. She kept saying and repeating to herself, surely the Board of Governors must know he is lying.

A few weeks later she received a terse letter from the GMC informing her to report for a hearing on Tuesday of the following week, at 10.00 a.m. In order that she would have enough time to compose herself and not worry, she arrived early at the GMC building in Hallam Street. She was called into the room where the hearing was being held, and saw it was a very large room, with a pair of large gold plated chandeliers hanging from a decorative ornate ceiling, and she noticed that the investigating committee sat at a horseshoe shaped table.

Standing alone in the middle of the room, looking at the surroundings, which appeared rather forbidding to her, she was startled when she heard a voice telling her to sit down at the table on her right. Sitting at the table looking around, she noticed that to her left sitting at a separate table were two people, one was Dr Nigel Cairnworth and the other person was someone she did not know. Turning her head to look at the members seated at the horseshoe table, she noticed an elderly man, seated on a chair against the wall, behind the committee members.

The Chairman opened the proceedings by introducing the committee members to everyone present, then turning looking at the table where Dr Cairnworth was sitting, the Chairman introduced the other person, as a barrister called Mr Trevor Ainsley KC. She was instantly shocked, and very concerned hearing that that was who the stranger was.

However she soon felt fairly confident answering the questions of the Chairman and knowing that the letters of her character references from the Charing Cross Hospital, as well as those from the Matron of her current hospital, had been submitted to the GMC beforehand. Also remembered the verse her father had told her about the wise old owl who, the less he spoke, the more he heard, she decided only to speak briefly and to keep to the truth.

After answering a number of questions, she looked at the faces of the committee seated at the table, and noticed they were mostly elderly people, whose questions to her, and those of the Chairman, all appeared to be sympathetic towards her.

Then chairman invited Trevor Ainsley KC, who was dressed in a black coat and pin-striped trousers to open Dr Cairnworth's defence of the allegations made by her.

Mr Ainsley rose from his chair and standing in front of the horseshoe table addressed the committee members saying, 'I am appearing on behalf of my client Dr Nigel Cairnworth, and, members of the committee, I will prove to you beyond any shadow of doubt, that the allegations made against my client are false. I am going to suggest, in fact prove, that Mrs Hopkins' version of the incident is a complete fabrication of her imagination, because I am given to understand on good authority, that she is not a habitual drinker and therefore I suggest she is unable to consume strong alcohol.'

He proceeded to put Nigel's version forward as evidence. Hearing this, Margery's mind was in turmoil, and when he said, 'I now call Mrs Hopkins to the witness stand', she was very nervous answering his opening questions, which were all about her family and upbringing, and whether her parents had money to pay for her nursing training. Then his questions began to be of a more intimate nature concerning her relationship with men and with other people and his questions on sex embarrassed her and made her answers appear very inadequate, in fact when answering some questions she was incoherent and close to tears on many occasions.

When his cross examination of her had finished, she noticed that when Nigel was called to give evidence and cross examined by Mr Ainsley, none of the questions he put to him about the alleged rape were embarrassing, nor were there any awkward questions for him to answer. She also noticed when some members of the committee did ask Nigel questions, the questions were mainly about his family and of his ambitions to become a surgeon and not about the incident, or of her allegations of sexual assault or rape. The last question Mr Ainsley asked Nigel to answer was, 'Mrs Hopkins has sworn on oath that you raped her without her knowledge, or consent. What is your answer to that?'

Nigel slightly bowed his head, clasped his hands together and kept looking at them as he replied, 'I met her at the staff party where we had both been drinking quite heavily. We got into conversation, shortly afterwards she said she was feeling a little under the influence of drink and suggested we go outside. In the corridor she suddenly threw her arms about me and began kissing me. It was because I didn't want any one openly seeing a ward sister kissing a doctor that I opened the door of an adjacent consulting room and we went inside. I do admit that I was aroused because she was, and is, extremely attractive and then the situation began to get more amorous and I admit I did have intercourse with her and it was definitely with her consent.'

She was absolutely astounded when she heard him say that and was about to stand up and speak, but having finished his cross examination of Nigel, Mr Ainsley immediately addressed the committee saying, 'Mr Chairman and members of the committee, I now wish to call my next witness, Professor Cairnworth.'

This caused a gasp from some of the committee members, whilst others looked at each other in amazement, turning in their seats to look at the person seated behind them. Margery was surprised to see the person who had been sitting behind the committee, stand up and approached Mr Ainsley. When he was seated, Mr Ainsley said to him, 'Would you please tell the committee your name and your profession and what your connection is to the defendant.' Smiles appeared on the faces of some of the committee members, especially when he replied in a haughty, ostentatious manner, 'My name is Professor Cairnworth. I am a member of the medical profession, I am a neuro-surgeon and your client is my son.' Margery's heart sank. Mr Ainsley KC cross-examined Nigel's father for approximately 15 minutes, during which time the questions and answers were all about Nigel being a very trustworthy person who had been educated at a very well known public school, before going to Cambridge University, where he obtained a degree in medical studies, and he finished his testimony by saying that Nigel was now studying hard to qualify as a surgeon.

When Nigel's father went behind the committee at the horseshoe shaped table and resumed his seat against the wall, Mr Ainsley KC addressed the committee saying, 'Gentlemen, you have heard of the good character of the defendant, especially from his father who is, as you are all well aware, a very well known and respected person in the medical profession. You have also heard the evidence from this woman, who comes from a working class family of humble stock. The inarticulate answers she gave to the questions I put to her, concerning the intimate points of this unfortunate incident, make her, in my opinion, an unreliable witness. She has sworn on oath, that she cannot remember anything that happened to her on that eventful day, and even though she has not produced any evidence, or witnesses, to support her allegations, she still maintains that the defendant drugged and raped her. I submit to you, that on the day in question, this lady was inebriated and knowing the defendant's affluent position, was hoping to benefit from it, by what means I know not. I also submit to you, she encouraged and allowed the defendant to have sexual intercourse with her, and I feel I should remind you, the defendant has admitted that sexual intercourse did take place. It is only her word that it was not with her consent. Then having been caught in the act by the Matron of the hospital, Mrs Hopkins is now trying to discredit the defendant.'

Mr Ainsley began walking in front of the horseshoe table. Looking at the faces of the committee he said, 'You have heard the evidence from Professor Cairnworth, who has stated that he is very proud to be the father of the defendant, who is a normal, happy, fun loving son, studying hard to become an excellent member of the medical profession. Having heard all the evidence, I do earnestly call upon you to dismiss this allegation and exonerate Dr Nigel Cairnworth of this awful charge of rape.'

After hearing the summing up by Mr Ainsley KC, Margery could see by the smiles on the faces of the committee, that he had made a good impression upon them.

Her mind was in a state of turmoil when the Chairman asked her to submit her submissions. Not knowing the correct procedure or what to say, and being very nervous, all she could say with her voice quivering with emotion, 'I have told you the truth of what happened and I can honestly say I was not inebriated and I do remember what happened before he drugged and raped me. I did not encourage, kiss, or cuddle him, or ever want to have sexual intercourse with him. I did not like him then as a individual, nor as a doctor, and I like him even less now after what he did to me.'

She broke into tears and was crying profusely, not was unable say anything more. The Chairman said to her, 'Mrs Hopkins, would you please retire from this room whilst the committee considers its verdict.'

She stood in the corridor quietly crying outside the room waiting to be recalled. She couldn't bear to be near Nigel, but found it very hard to avoid him, because his counsel was standing nearby him taking up a lot of room. Nigel was smoking a cigarette leaning against the wall and he kept looking at her in a lascivious manner. It was because he was looking at her in that way, that she suddenly shouted at him, 'I never knew you were such a mendacious person.' Mr Ainsley immediately rebuked her for speaking, so she turned her back on Nigel, so that she did not have face him or to see that look in his eyes. After a short wait, they were called back into the committee room.

On entering the room, Margery went be seated, but the Chairman asked her to remain standing in front of him, until everyone else was seated. Standing before him and the committee, he said to her in a very solemn voice, 'Without any substantive evidence to support your allegations, the committee have found the charges and allegations you have made against Dr Nigel Cairnworth to be groundless, and therefore the charge of rape will be quashed. They also feel that in trying to tarnish a respectable doctor's reputation and your drunken behaviour, a severe reprimand will be entered in your documents and a letter will be sent to the Governors of the hospital where you work, containing the decision of this committee, together with its recommendations. This concludes the hearing. You are free to retire.'

Margery could not believe her ears and for a moment stood there stunned, then as she turned to leave the room, she saw the committee members talking to Nigel's father, while others members were congratulating Nigel and shaking his hands. Someone with a loud voice said, 'Well done Nigel. Mind you it was your father that won it for you.' Margery quickly turned to see who had spoken, but she couldn't connect the voice to anyone.

It was a lovely warm sunny day when she came out of the building, but she didn't notice the sunshine, all she did was wander around the streets dreamily out of touch with everything around her.

She didn't hear, or see anything and nothing registered in her mind, except whilst she walking around she kept repeating to herself with tears in her eyes, 'Why! Oh why didn't they believe me?' It was later, when she looked up and saw the busy traffic and noticed the large shops and stores that she suddenly realised she didn't know where she was. Turning into a side street, she found herself outside a cafe and going inside she ordered a cup of tea and asking the waitress, she was told she was near Oxford Street. Leaving the cafe she made her way back to Kings Cross railway station and on the train, she thought of the extreme difficult position she was in and decided to visit Matron for advice.

It was late when she arrived back at the hospital. The following morning she went to the Matron's office and informed her of the decision of the GMC.

Hearing of the GMC verdict Matron was astounded, saying with much astonishment in her voice, 'Do you mean to tell me that they have not believed you and dismissed your allegations? Why that is preposterous. How they came to their decision is beyond my comprehension.' then a worried frown came upon Matron's brow, as she said, 'Oh dear! I suppose we shall have to wait for the letter from the GMC, and then we will see what the Board of Governors of this hospital will do.'

Margery came away from the Matron's office with mixed feelings. She was pleased to know of Matron's support, but fearful of that last remark of, 'Oh! Dear', and this made her very worried over her future position within the hospital.

Five days later she was summoned before the hospital Board of Governors and stood before the Chairman, who again appeared very nervous as he fiddled and rustled with his papers. Then adjusting his glasses he glanced at the paper in his hand and said, 'Sister Hopkins we have received a letter from the GMC ... ahem and they have stated that your allegation against Dr Cairnworth was not proven and the recommendation from them is, ahem ... that as you are a disgrace to the nursing profession you are to be dismissed from this hospital and ... um ... from the nursing profession, this means you cannot work in this hospital or any other hospital for some time to come.'

At this point he couldn't look at her as he carried on speaking. 'Ahem ... Umm ... this Board cannot go against the recommendation of the GMC, who are, as no doubt you are well aware, our governing body, therefore we have no option but to terminate your contract with immediate effect and this means you must leave the hospital immediately.'

Hearing the Chairman telling that, she was devastated and burst into tears. She could hear the Chairman still talking, but she could not mentally grasp what was being said to her. When the Chairman had finished talking she asked him if she could appeal against the GMC decision and was told to enquire at some future date.

When she came out of the room, Matron was waiting for her, and took her arm and led her straight into her office. Once inside, Matron locked the door and sat Margery in a chair and proceeded to make her a cup of tea, at the same time commiserating with her. While Margery was drinking her tea, Matron said to her, 'Sister Hopkins, having heard and read your version of the incident and knowing the general behaviour of Dr Cairnworth, I do not know how the GMC could have arrived at their verdict. All I can say is, there are a number of us here, who believe in you.' Handing Margery a cup of tea she continued, 'I am sure that one day the truth will come out. In the meantime however, there is nothing that I can do to go against the decision of the GMC or of this hospital's Board of Governors who have cancelled your contract. But I am going exercise my right as Matron to give you permission to stay in your accommodation for the next seven days, to enable you to find somewhere else suitable to live. Now drink your tea and remember, if I can be of any further help, please do not hesitate to come and see me.'

Margery tearfully thanked Matron for all her assistance and guidance and solemnly promised to leave the hospital within the seven days.

Knowing that Nigel was still employed and living within the hospital and being fearful of meeting or coming into contact with him again, she knew she couldn't look for a place to live nearby. The very next morning she was up early and caught a fast train to London, and because she had limited time to search for work, she knew her first priority was to get a room somewhere, she concentrated her search within the vicinity of the railway station, deciding to look in the Islington area.

Walking up Caledonian Road she went into a newsagent's shop and took note of the advertisements of rooms to let, and after writing down four addresses, she went to view them. With the first two she was not impressed, however at the next one she decided to look inside the house and although it was sparsely furnished, it had the basic things she required and after agreeing terms with the owner, she agreed to move in within the next five days.

On the way back to the railway station she bought a newspaper and read the headlines: 'Nazi Leaders Hanged'. Reading further on, she read that Hermann Goering had committed suicide. As she was reading this, she began to say to herself, 'At least there is some justice in this world, because if Kevin is dead, at least his death with his crew, and all those others who died fighting for peace, was not in vain.'

She then began think about the difficult situation she was in, and mentally said, 'I don't know what have I done wrong to deserve the punishment and the treatment I have received . . .' Tears began to fill her eyes and suddenly looking around and seeing that no-one was nearby, she spoke out loud saying, 'Now I must remember that Kevin always said I must stop feeling sorry for myself and to think positively, then my luck will begin to change for the good. So I must start smiling, because at least I have found somewhere to live, and I must fight because I do have something to live for.' Her spirits began to rise and she started to think about her next priority, of where she was going to get a job.

6

LONDON AGAIN

On the journey back, Margery was sitting in the train and reading the situations vacant columns in the paper, thinking to herself, 'If I can't apply for a hospital position until the turmoil has settled down, I must do something else.' It was then she saw an advertisement for waitresses in J. Lyons corner house in the Strand. She felt that was a lucky omen, because she was remembering it was the same place that Kevin had taken her to celebrate their engagement.

On the day she left the hospital she was feeling fairly optimistic for her future, and then as she was walking past the Matron's office, Matron called her in and to her surprise put her arms around her, saying, 'Keep cheerful – every cloud has a silver lining and I am sure yours will soon be shining through the dark clouds. Goodbye and good luck.'

Sitting in the train taking her London and remembering Matron's parting words, she was feeling very sad at the prospect of leaving the profession she loved, but told herself, 'I must cheer myself up. Spring time is here.' But looking at the rain beating against the windows of the train, she remarked, 'Oh! dear just my luck, another miserable wet day.' Picking up her newspaper she read that Great Britain had experienced the worst floods ever recorded. She cheered herself up by thinking about the personal items she had managed to bring with her, which as well as her ration book and identity book were the letters she cherished that she had received from Kevin, and the little porcelain clock decorated with hand painted yellow porcelain flowers, that her grandmother had given her when she was a little girl.

Arriving in London she went into the house where she had agreed to live and after arranging and leaving her personal items in her room, she went immediately to J. Lyons in the Strand to apply for the job, which to her surprise was still vacant. Having obtained the position she knew it was shift work, and she kept repeating to herself, 'I'm very lucky, because I've got a place to sleep and I have a job with money coming in, so I must now stop worrying and concentrate on saving money and making myself look presentable and trying to get my old job back in a hospital.'

She soon began to feel that her lifestyle was improving, because by not going out and only buying the cheaper foods, she was able to save a little money each week. This made her feel better and happy.

It was raining again on Thursday 20th November, as she stood near Westminster Abbey to watch Princess Elizabeth go by to marry Lt Phillip Mountbatten, and watching the happy couple return to Buckingham Palace, she remembered her own wedding day and thought how lucky she had been, because her day had been a lovely sunny day, which was quite a contrast to the wind and rain of today. She was standing with crowds of people, in the rain, and began thinking of the type of reception the Royal couple were going to have and how much it would cost, and comparing it with the cost of her own wedding. She remembered how Kevin had saved his flying money to pay for their wedding and how his friends had managed to make the wedding cake and provided such a lovely banquet for her.

Thinking of her wedding, she began laughing to herself about how she had saved her clothing coupons and how Mr Rabonovitch had manipulated the number of clothing coupons she had to give, to enable her to have that lovely peach two-piece wedding suit. As those thoughts went through her head, she unintentionally said out loud, 'I wonder how many clothing coupons Princess Elizabeth had to give up for her wedding dress?' Her face began to blush with embarrassment when the people all around her started laughing, especially when one elderly Cockney lady quipped, 'I don't care how many coopons she hat ta give up for 'er wedding dress luv. It's made my day just seeing 'er, but it's a bloody shame that the sun isn't shining on 'er, cos she really looked bootiful.'

The days rolled by, and when Christmas came she was feeling lonely, remembering how during the war she had walked round the wards with Helen and the other nurses singing carols to the patients, and she remembered the other happy Christmases she had spent as child and compared them with the one she was now spending, all alone, and she felt the loneliness and became very depressed.

The next day she awoke and began vomiting. It was later that day that she began to analyse her condition, and she realised that she had missed the last two of her periods. Could she be pregnant from that rape? She began to cry, saying out loud to herself, 'Oh why did that dirty rotten doctor have to pick on me and make me pregnant? What can I do? Where can I go?' She began thinking that at work she had made friends with a nice young girl called Sadie, who was about 25 years old. When she went to work the next day she told Sadie of her condition and how she had been raped and asked if Sadie knew where she could go to have the baby, without costing her too much. Sadie looked at her and said to her in a serious way, 'Do you really want to have the baby? And can really you afford to bring it up?'

Margery burst in to tears, saying, 'No, I don't want to have his child, and No, I can't afford to bring it up because I haven't much money, let alone feed another mouth.' Sadie looked around to see if anyone was standing nearby before she quietly said, 'Well that settles it, because it only leaves one thing for you to do and that is to have an abortion.'

The thought of an abortion shook Margery and she began crying very hard, because she was thinking of the serious implications involved, and remembering all the Acts of Parliament and laws she had been taught during her nurse's training. 'Oh what a mess I'm in. I've hardly any money left to pay for an operation and I'm sure that the hospitals will not abort my pregnancy. And I know that by the Offences Against the Persons Act of 1861, it is an offence to have an abortion. Oh my God, what can I do?' Sadie was looking at Margery crying profusely, and leaning forward she held Margery around her shoulders and whispered to her, 'Don't worry about all that because I believe I can help you, if you want me to?'

Margery looked incredulously at Sadie, saying, 'What do you mean you can help me?' Sadie again looked around before whispering to Margery, 'Well, I know of someone who might be able to help you stop having the baby. Mind you, you might have to pay for her time, and before you start saying you can't afford it, let me tell you I was in the same condition as you last year, and that person helped me, and I managed to find the small amount of money that she asked of me.' Hearing Sadie telling her of how she had overcome her problems and what it had cost her, Margery stopped crying and within a short moment of time she was anxiously asking Sadie to help her.

Sadie told her that she knew of a lady who lived not far away, who would have to see Margery first before committing herself to helping her. After she had finished work and was on her way home she began to feel much more at ease knowing that Sadie was trying to help. When she was at work a few days later Sadie came up to her and whispered, 'Mrs Mossad is an old lady who has lived in the area for many years and I know, because my mum told me, that before the war Mrs Mossad used to help the local women have their babies and laid out the dead people ready for the undertaker. I have told her all about your rape and the condition you are in, and she has agreed to meet you on your day off to discuss things with you. Is that alright?'

The following week, she and Sadie met Mrs Mossad in a small café, and after listening to Margery telling her of her plight and how she had been raped, Mrs Mossad leaned across the table, holding Margery's hand as she gently said, 'I always feel very sorry for young girls like you who have been abused and used by those disgusting men, so I will agree to do the abortion, but you mustn't tell anyone about me doing this for you.'

Having agreed to get the abortion done, Mrs Mossad began asking questions, and having been given the facts she knew she would have to do it very soon, otherwise it would be too late, so she arranged for Margery to have the abortion within the next two days. Sadie, who had been listening, hurriedly said to Margery, 'Don't worry about work because you will have to have a few days off to get well again, and I will tell them in work that you have a nasty cold and will back again in within seven days.'

Two days later Margery went to a house where Mrs Mossad was waiting, and it was in that house that she had her pregnancy terminated. Mrs Mossad made Margery stay with her the house until the following day, when Sadie came and helped her back to her lodgings. When they arrived there Sadie put her to bed, telling her not to worry because every would be alright now.

Margery felt very ill for a few days afterwards and Sadie came each day and helped her and told her that she had informed the management at J. Lyons that Margery had caught a very bad cold and would not be able to work for a few days. A week later, still feeling pretty sore and weak, she went back to work, and while she was there she thanked Sadie for helping her. It was then that Sadie told her she was leaving. The news upset Margery because she had become fond of Sadie and she knew she would feel very lonely when Sadie left. After she left work that day Margery bought a bunch of flowers for Mrs Mossad and gave them to her as a thank you present. Mrs Mossad was very grateful for the kind thought and told her that she was glad that everything had gone well with the abortion.

A few months later as she was reading the newspaper she saw that J. Lyons was going to be closing some of its restaurants, and the staff at those would all lose their jobs. But when summer came the staff at the restaurant had not heard of any closure and Margery started to relax and think of her future. She was also reinforced by the knowledge that due to the wartime bomb damage to buildings, there was plenty of rebuilding work taking place and there appeared to be plenty of other opportunities for work, especially in the nursing profession. There was also talk of a Festival of Britain, which would create more work.

Knowing there were nursing vacancies in the hospitals and thinking of her current situation, she thought enough time had elapsed for her to write letters to various hospitals, and decided to apply for a nursing position. A few days later she received replies inviting her to attend for interviews at hospitals, and at the penultimate interview she thought everything appeared to be normal and was going very smoothly in her favour, with the interviewer being very impressed with her records. All until they read a letter which was in their file.

It was after reading that letter that the interviewer said, 'Mrs Hopkins, we are interviewing a number of other people, we will let you know in due course whether your application has been successful' After the interview was over she realised that the contents in the letter must be the reason why the result of all the interviews was the same.

When at the next and final interview the interviewer adopted a similar attitude, she was ready and said to the interviewer, 'Would you please tell me what is in that letter you have just read, and who it is from?' Seeing the look of astonishment on the interviewer's face, Margery continued. 'The reason why I have asked you that question, is because at every interview I have recently attended, everything appears to be going in my favour until that letter is read, then I am told I will be hearing in due course, which in effect means that I am unsuitable for the nursing position.'

Being a very kindly considerate person, the interviewer looked at Margery's worried face and realising of her concern, opened the file, picked up the letter she had just read and said, 'I should not be telling you this, but this letter is addressed to all hospitals and is from the GMC.' And she proceeded to show Margery the letter. 'It states,' she said, 'that under no circumstances are you to be employed in the nursing profession in the foreseeable future.' The interviewer put the letter back in the file and said, 'It does not state why you cannot be employed, and all it says is "in the foreseeable future", but from the excellent reports from your two previous matrons and seeing the length of time since this letter was written, I can see no reason why you should not know of its contents and if I may add my own observations, may I suggest that you must not give up hope, but apply again within the next six to twelve months.'

Leaving the hospital and remembering the kind comments made by the interviewer, she walked away feeling happy and reasonably confident, especially knowing the contents of that letter and the favourable reports of the two matrons. She said to herself, 'I must keep myself neatly dressed, but to be able to do that I must acquire some more clothing coupons and I must also sort out my financial position.' She began thinking of her money problems, because after paying her fares to and from work, buying food and paying the rent, she knew there was not much money left to save.

The following year, because the rent of her room had been increased, her financial problem had not improved, in fact it was decidedly worse, so she had decided to move a mile away from her present home, into cheaper accommodation. The room in the new house was small with a single bed hidden behind a curtain and she tried to make it as cosy as possible. There was a small earthenware deep sink, with only one tap for cold water. Next to the sink, was a small gas oven and nearby an open fireplace, with a single bar electric fire standing in its hearth.

She had to share an outside lavatory with the other residents, but considered herself lucky, because she was able to walk down the passageway to a side door leading to the garden where the lavatory was. Surveying all this she said to herself, 'Right, my girl, the time has come for you to step off with your right foot and get on with your life and have no more feelings of being sorry for yourself.' Due to the overloading of the main electrical grid systems, there were many electrical breakdowns occurring to the domestic and factory users, so she ensured that she had plenty of candles to provide herself with light when there was a power failure.

A few months later, on a lovely spring Sunday morning, she decided to go for a walk, and although there had been an early morning frost, the sun was shining down from a beautiful clear blue, cloudless sky. She had dressed herself in her best clothes and was looking reasonably smart. She felt pleased to be out, because for some unknown reason, she had the urge to retrace the steps she and Kevin had taken on the day he had proposed to her.

It was early in the morning when she arrived on London Bridge, and looking down the Pool of London towards the Tower of London, she could see in the distance the paddle steamer *Golden Eagle* tied up at Irongate Wharf waiting to take passengers to Southend and Margate. Then she saw at New Fresh Wharf a large ship laden with cargo was just leaving and sailing down towards Tower Bridge. Its passengers were waving up to the bridge and the people standing close by her and were shouting to them, 'Have a lovely time in the Canary Islands!' As she was watching, Tower Bridge raise its arches to allow the ship to sail down the river Thames towards the sea, she was whispering, 'Oh how I wish I was going with them . . .'

Soon she was walking along the riverside towards the Tower of London, when suddenly she heard the clock in the Tower strike eleven times. As she walked along she thought she could feel the presence of

Kevin very strongly around her, it was so strong that she looked around just in case someone was creeping up begin her, but all she could see were other people some distance away.

The sun was shining brightly and there was no wind, however because of the strong feeling of someone being around her, she shivered and began feeling very cold. That cold feeling momentarily frightened her and because of that strange cold feeling she knew Kevin was dead and was never coming back to her, yet somehow she felt she could still feel his presence strongly around her.

In a small village in France in the Haute Marne region, it was 12 a.m. and a small party of French army cadets, together with the minister of the local church and a group of people from the village, were standing near to a small monument and laying a wreath beneath a plaque which read:

> 'En memoire de L'Equipage
> Du Lancaster OW 492 RAF
> Tombé sur notre commune
> Le 11ieme Mars 1994' ?
>
> Flt/Lt. M.K. Ospring RAAF DFC. F/O J. Etheridge RAAF DFC
> P/O. P.H. Pautaune RAAF DFM. Flt/Sgt. K. Hopkins RAAF DFM
> Sgt. D. Chiltern RAF. P/O. N.M. Nicholson RAAF
> Flt. Sgt. E.K. Redway RAF DFM

Back in England Margery knew the cold feeling she was experiencing was unreal and inexplicable, she felt strange because she felt very cold, but the sun was shining and it was a very warm day. With no one around or near her she remained quite still, near the spot where Kevin had proposed to her. She stood there just letting the rays of the sun warm her body trying to reason with herself on what was happening. Within a few moments she began to feel much warmer and as she was about to walk away she thought she heard Kevin's voice saying, 'Don't worry, I will always be close and watching over you.'

With her head held high and tears in her eyes, she straightened her back and with stronger strides, she walked along the path she and Kevin had walked together, and for the first time in quite a long time, she felt at peace with everything, and felt that living now had a purpose. The trials and problems she had endured over the past few years seemed to roll away and the day became sheer bliss for her. She walked around not caring where she was walking, just thinking to herself, 'He is near me'. Later in the afternoon when she sat on a riverside seat trying to analyse the strange feeling she had experienced, she eventually came to the conclusion she must be suffering from sunstroke. But lying in bed that evening, as she reminisced over her day, and with her knowledge of medicine and her own common sense, she knew she had not had sunstroke, though she could find no logical answer why she had experienced that cold feeling, or why she thought she had heard Kevin's voice. After saying her prayers she closed her eyes and in an audible whisper said, 'Thank you Kevin for a lovely day. God bless, I do love you.'

Since leaving the hospital, due to her movements from one address to another and not leaving any forwarding addresses, Margery's whereabouts had been largely unknown, and for the past two years the Air Ministry had been trying to trace and inform her that not only was she was entitled to a serviceman's war widow's pension, but there was a plaque with Kevin's name upon it on a memorial monument near a small village in the Haute Marne area of France.

Later that year, being a very warm sunny Saturday morning with a smattering of clouds wafting through a lovely blue sky, she decided to go for a short walk. Wearing a floral dress that had buttons down the front, eventually she found herself in Exmouth market where, because of her shortage of money, she could only purchase a small amount of shopping which included a packet of egg powder to have some scrambled egg on toast.

As she was making her way home and was walking along Farringdon Road she thought she would look at the second hand book stalls and found a book she liked in an excellent condition, by Daphne du Maurier. As she picked it up, she saw a large bible beneath it, and being very curious, she put the book down and opened the bible. On the inside cover she saw the family tree of the person who once owned it – Elijah Forrester, who had married Emily Middleton at Dirksworth in 1893, who had given birth to two children, Felicity Jane in 1893 and Martha Phyllis in 1897.

Knowing that Dirksworth was a village near Kirkbridge, she began to imagine the type of country house in which that family could have lived and began to compare it with the little cottage in the village of Hemelsham where she lived. She was thinking about the descendants of that family and where they might be today, when suddenly she was awakened from her slumbering thoughts by the sound of a cough from the stallholder. Looking up she could feel his eyes upon her and to cover her embarrassment, she asked him how much the bible was. 'It's a good bargain for two pounds ten shillings,' he replied.

She began to fiddle with the electric flex that was attached to an old wireless set, as she replied, 'I'm awfully sorry, I can't afford that.' The stallholder, who hadn't had many customers, saw her fiddling with the flex, and as she went to walk away said, 'Look lady, that's a lovely wireless set you have been touching. It's made by one of the best wireless companies, called Bush, and it is in very good condition and has a lovely sound. It's a good bargain at ten shillings, and for that price I'll even throw in two new spare valves.'

Knowing she had only twelve shillings in her purse and therefore she really couldn't afford it, and hoping to put the stallholder off, she said, 'I'm very sorry, all I have is five shillings.' Much to her surprise he replied, 'All right luv, you've made yourself a bargain. I'll accept your five shillings,' and proceeded to put the wireless set in a paper carrier bag. Margery was surprised, but accepted it. She found carrying it along with her shopping rather heavy and when she arrived home her arms were aching. But after a short rest she managed to connect the wireless to the single electric socket in her room and was able to listen to music from the 'Light' programme.

After her experience at the Tower of London and the cold feeling that embraced her, and still feeling mentally troubled by the thought of Kevin being close to her, she began to find solace in going to church on Sunday morning and meeting other people there. One Sunday morning as she came out of church she spoke to a couple who had been sitting near her inside. A conversation about life and death followed, and she told them about her experience at the Tower of London and the cold feeling she experienced, together with the feeling she often has of Kevin's closeness about her.

The man looked at his wife as she said, 'How strange! my husband and I experienced a similar incident when we lost our son in a motor-cycle accident. We were recommended to see Mrs Gaffney, who is well known locally as a spiritualist. I forget who recommended her to us, but having been to see her we think she is very good, because she helped my husband and me overcome our troubles. Now I know she attends the spiritualist church in Aldridge Street, and I believe she could help you and explain to you what happened.' Her husband nodded his head in agreement.

As the couple departed Margery said, 'Thank you very much indeed. I was beginning to think I was going mad, thinking I could hear voices. I have been so worried and I'm most grateful to both of you for telling me how you overcame your problems and recommending Mrs Gaffney. I will do my best to see her as soon as possible.'

A few days later, after work as it was getting dark she was walking along Aldridge Street towards the spiritualist church. Two women had come out of the church gate, and as they passed her, she asked one of them, 'Excuse me, was that the spiritualist church I saw you coming out of just now? The woman replied, 'Yes it was. Why, did you want some healing?'

At first she did not know what to say, but heard herself saying, 'Yes, I understand there is someone in the church who might be able to help me and possibly give me some healing and advice.' The other lady said, 'Oh, so you want to see Mrs Gaffney do you, well the church is locked at the moment, but if you would like to come with us, we only live in the next road,' pointing to a side road, 'we might be able to help you. Come on. Would you like us to help you get some healing?'

Margery walked with them, and when they stopped as they were about to turn into the side road, one of the women said, 'That's our home over there. Do come in.' Margery could see it was a small terraced house and though she was feeling uneasy, she found it difficult to refuse their offer. On entering the house she went into a darkened passageway with a door on the right and another door at the far end. Halfway along the passage there was a flight of stairs leading to the floor above. After being shown into the room through the door on the right, she began to regret going into the house, somehow she had a premonition that all was not right. It was the way one of the women spoke when she said she was going to get something that made Margery feel very uneasy, and unsavoury thoughts went through her mind.

Looking around the room she saw there was a small single electric light bulb that was suspended from the ceiling by a lamp holder with no shade. There was a three-seater leather settee whose fabric had seen better times, and then there was an unusual smell, a smell she had smelt before but couldn't remember where. Now she was in the light, Margery saw the woman standing near her in the room had a short cropped hair and looked very masculine. Suddenly a very nasty thought came into her mind, which began to work very fast, and she hastily made an excuse and a very hurried exit from the house. She was shaking with anger and frustration as she hurried away, saying out loud to herself, 'You were very lucky. First of all there was Dr Cairnworth, and now those two women, who I feel were lesbians.'

Safely in her own room again she made herself a pot of tea, sat holding the porcelain clock her grandmother had given her and switched on the wireless. She was listening to Nat King Cole singing 'Unforgettable', and began reminiscing. Picking up the bible, something within her seemed to urge her to remember what her father had told her many years ago about being lonely and being able to find help from the bible, and she opened it.

Edmundo Ros and his band were playing a samba, and she was drinking her tea, feeling safe and warm. She said to herself, 'Oh! this is lovely, this music is making me feel so relaxed.' Suddenly she felt as though she wasn't alone and as she sat in a chair listening to the band playing another samba, she closed her eyes and thought of a tropical island, and imagined she and Kevin were lying on the sands in the warm sunshine. While those thoughts were going through her mind that she fell into a peaceful sleep and dreamt again.

Very soon another Christmas was upon her and she was cooking her Christmas dinner and listening to Jean Metcalfe broadcasting Two-Way Family Favourites from England to Cliff Michelmore, who was with Armed Forces network abroad visiting a military hospital. He was speaking to a patient who said he was looking forward to going home to England, because his 3-year-old daughter had just learnt to sing the nursery rhyme 'Oranges and Lemons'. The thought of that young child singing that nursery rhyme to her parents made her think of the happy times she had singing that rhyme to her own parents when she was a little girl, and made her feel sad and brought tears to her eyes.

However a few moments later her mood changed again when a record was played of Louis Armstrong's band playing 'I can't give you anything but love'. The tune brought back happy memories to her and she remembered when she and Kevin went dancing at the Covent Garden Opera House and Kevin was singing those words in her ear. She started remembering how he held her and it made her want to dance, whereby she threw off her slippers and started to dance merrily round her small room wriggling hips in time to the music, at the same time letting her hands slide sensuously down the sides of her body, all the time she was thinking of Kevin holding and dancing with her and how he sang that song to her. This raised her spirits, and the thought that she still had retained her petite figure made her enjoy the rest of her Christmas. And so not long after Christmas, when she read in the newspaper that because of the shortage of staff in the hospitals, some Italian ships were bringing in foreign people to fill those positions, remembering the comments of the last interviewer, she was feeling very confident as she wrote another letter applying to work in a hospital.

When she went to work on New Year's Eve, she was having a tea break with some of the other waitresses when the manager walked in and, quite casually, said to them, 'This is the last New Year's Eve party we will be having here because we are closing down in the next two months.' She became very worried because she had had a letter of refusal from the hospital, and now the news of the restaurant closing made her realise that she had to walk around again looking for work.

It was a cold February day and the job situation looked very bleak, and although there was an abundance of work, the weekly trade union strikes made companies very wary of employing more staff. Having walked around for some time looking at the shop windows she was in a side street just off of Oxford Street and was on the point of giving up hope of finding work, when she saw a notice in a shop window of a Ladies' and Menswear store, advertising for a shop assistant. She went inside and applied for the position, and was delighted to be told that the job was hers. On the way home she began to feel more contented with life.

Not long after she began working there, due to the increase in factory production and the increase in demand for electrical appliances in the consumer sector, plus the lack of expansion in the power generating stations, the electrical supply to homes, shops and factories began to fail on a fairly regular basis. It was causing mayhem, because it stopped machinery in work places and caused the street lighting to fail and plunged everywhere into darkness. The staff in the shop were getting used to the electrical breakdowns and knew what to do in an emergency. However one afternoon, just as it began to get dark and all the shops, factories and homes had switched on their lights, she was in the small stock room checking the stock with one of the senior male staff, when all the lights went out and the shop and stock room were plunged into sheer darkness.

Having previously been told not to worry and to stand still if the shop lighting failed until the emergency lighting came on, she could hear the man with her moving around in the stock room and as she began to speak to him, suddenly she felt a hand on her shoulder then she felt his other hand groping her legs under her dress and his fingers sliding under her panties. She tried to move, but the hand on her shoulder kept her pinned against the wall, at the same time he was whispering to her to be quiet and to stand still. She about to shout out when the emergency lighting came on and someone was calling out if everybody was all right. The man immediately withdrew his hand from beneath her dress and whispered to her, 'If you dare say anything about this to anyone, I will see you are dismissed.' Looking towards the door she saw that a large box had been wedged against it to hold it shut and prevent anyone entering.

On the way home that evening, she thought very hard about the incident, saying to herself that she didn't want another Dr Cairnworth affair. She realised that if she remained in the store, she would have to inform the manager, and she feared nobody would believe her, and if the lights failed again, the same man would try the same thing. So she felt she had no alternative but to leave. The very next day she made a feeble excuse to the manager for wanting to leave and she ceased her employment at the end of the week.

Having been unable to find any work in the shops and knowing that the Festival of Britain was going to open, with many stalls around St Paul's Cathedral, and the 'Dome of Discovery' had been built together with a very big fairground with water fountains near the new Festival Hall at the south end of Hungerford Bridge, she thought she stood a very good chance of obtaining work there, if only for a short period.

Knowing the gates were being opened at 12.30 p.m. and hoping to avoid the crowds, she walked fast across Hungerford Bridge towards the Fairground and the 'Dome of Discovery'.

Arriving at the end of the bridge and seeing from Big Ben that it was only 8.30 a.m, she saw that big queues had already formed, with many more people arriving all the time. Seeing all those people she went up to a policeman standing nearby and asked if there was any chance of being allowed inside to apply for a job. The policeman, smiling, replied, 'Not a chance, young lady.' When she eventually arrived inside the fairground she made numerous requests for work, but all were refused. After many thankless hours, and feeling very low, she heard a man being very irate with a catering manager, because he had been charged five shillings for the cost of an afternoon tea and sandwiches. She looked at the menu chart and saw cheese and tomato sandwiches were one shilling each, and even though she was very hungry she knew that she would never be able to buy a sandwich at those prices. Because of the huge crowds, especially round the 300 ft 'Skylon', she was finding it hard to move around looking for work, and decided to leave. As she was passing one catering place she overheard the manager saying to one of his staff, 'The place is crowded with people but we haven't had hardly any customers! Business has been very bad today, tomorrow we will have to reduce the prices of the afternoon cakes and teas from five shillings to three shillings and the price of a cup of coffee to nine pence in the hope that will entice more customers.'

Walking away she said to herself, 'Oh those poor souls. How would they like to be in my position where I don't know where the next week's rent is coming from.' During the next few days she looked everywhere for a job, all to no avail, and knowing she had to find some money from somewhere to pay the rent, she looked at the engagement ring on her finger and with tears in her eyes, pulled it off and walked slowly towards a pawnbrokers shop nearby.

Inside, the man looked at the ring through a large magnifying glass and offered her ten pounds. She knew the ring was worth more than that, and knowing Kevin had paid thirty pounds for it, she tried asking for more, but he shook his head and offered her the ring back. Knowing he wasn't going to offer her more, she was so desperate for money that, close to tears, she sadly nodded her head. Walking away, her sorrow at parting with the ring was lightened by the thought that she had enough money for three weeks rent, with some money left over for food.

At the end of three weeks, still unable to obtain work, and having been very frugal with the remaining money by not buying enough food, she made a very serious decision. She knew she had only enough money to pay the rent, but she also knew from the stomach pains she was experiencing that she had to choose either to pay the rent with the remaining money, or eat. She chose to eat.

7

HOMELESS

Two weeks went by, and knowing the owner of the house would soon be knocking at her door for the backlog of rent, she began wrapping the porcelain clock in plenty of paper, together with the bible, and putting them with Kevin's letters and hiding them in one of her shopping bags waited for the dreaded moment of his knock.

When he eventually did knock on the door and he found she had no money he said in a surly manner, 'I fawt so!' Looking at her body he went on, 'Nah yer can eiver pay me in kind, or I'll ave ta confiskit some of yer belongings.' Seeing she was shaking her head he said, 'Right,' and proceeded to take her wireless and her good top coat, together with other things which he thought were of value, leaving her with just a few pieces of clothing which she had managed to hide in the carrier bags. Then pointing towards the door he said, 'Yer can git out of 'ere right away.' Quickly grabbing hold of her things and clutching the bags containing the remainder of her things, she came out of the house. Wandering around the streets knowing, and worrying, that she had to find somewhere to sleep that night, she eventually made her way to Kings Cross Station where she hoped to find shelter. Then an idea came to her, she would ask someone for a few coppers.

With her bags at her feet she stood alone on the pavement asking people for money as they walked by, and after a short while she was surprised to see that she had collected eleven shillings and sixpence. She immediately went to a tea stall that was round the corner and bought two cheese rolls and a cup of tea, saving the rest of the money for another meal. She managed to find herself a suitable shop doorway, where she was able to have a short sleep. She woke up very early in the morning and her body was aching and feeling stiff.

After hiding her bags, she went to the nearest labour exchange where she was seen by a very kindly elderly clerk, who, after hearing of her job record and of her ordeal in the hospital, took pity on her and told her he didn't have any hospital positions, but offered her a job in a restaurant near Covent Garden, that was offering a reasonable wage. He then suggested she go to Carrington House in Farringdon Road that would provide her with shelter and a little stability. Whilst she was thanking him for his kindness, he looked around to see that no-one was watching and he took from his wallet a pound note and pressed it into her hand, at the same time wishing her good luck.

On her way to Carrington House she thought that if only she had met that kind man a few weeks ago, things might have turned out different for her. At Carrington House after being told there was a room available, she paid twelve shillings and sixpence for five nights stay and was given the key to room No. 312 on the third floor, and was also told that everyone had to be in their rooms by 10 p.m. every night.

When she opened the door of her room the first thing she saw was the bed with two blankets and an uncovered pillow. There were no sheets or pillowcases. Looking at the walls she thought they had been painted a dull yellow, but on closer examination she found the walls were discoloured and had many stains upon it. The room also smelt of disinfectant. As she closed the door she said, 'My God! What a place to be in.' then she remembered where she slept last night and said, 'At least I have a roof over my head, and if it rains tonight I will not get wet.'

Leaving her bags in a secure place after locking the door of the room, she went to Covent Garden to enquire about the job at the restaurant. She had to walk through Covent Garden Market to the restaurant and was interviewed by a man with Latin American features, who informed her the position was for a kitchen assistant and the wages were £1.17s.6d a week and the hours were from midday until 9.30 p.m. with a short break from 4.30 to 5.15. He added there was a possibility of overtime if she wanted it. After hearing about the work she was expected to do, he asked her if she still wanted the job, and being desperate for money, she agreed to start work the following day.

Within a few weeks of starting work, she found that, being on her own in the kitchen, the work was hard. Some days the pressure would slacken off at 4.30 then build up again during the evening to such an extent that there would were occasions when, because of the heat in the kitchen and the pressure of work, she would work non stop without a break until the end of her shift at 9.30. On those occasions she would leave the kitchen soaked in perspiration and sweat and would hurry to get home before the 10 p.m. curfew.

Most evenings when she arrived at Carrington House she would notice a peculiar smell inside the building. At first she wondered what it was, until one evening, when she saw the drunken people staggering around the corridors, she realised the smell was a combination of turpentine, stale beer, urine and disinfectant. Aware of the type of people living there, she withdrew into herself and resolved never speak to any of them, and in doing so she became a lonely hermit, which soon made her lose her enthusiasm to return to the nursing profession and mix with people.

One Sunday morning she was having her usual walk she went towards St Paul's Cathedral. Although it was slightly damaged from the wartime bombing, to her it still looked very regal in the bright sunshine. Looking at the remains of the bombsites and the rebuilding work going on around the Cathedral, her thoughts went back to those wartime days when she and Helen had attended to people who had been trapped in the bombed buildings adjacent to the Cathedral. Later, sitting on the Cathedral steps, she thought of those wartime days, which seemed a lifetime away. She began to think of Helen and wondered whether she was still married, or if she was a widow too, and thought of the baby, and wondered to herself where Helen was now and whether she ever thought, or even remembered, her.

At that precise moment, in a comfortable house in Exeter, Helen, Ian and their two children were about to leave home to meet Ian's parents at the railway station. Just as Helen was about to leave, for some unknown reason, hearing the laughter of her son Mark, she suddenly thought of her old friend Margery Hopkins. She felt very grateful to her for her advice about her affair with the pilot, Mark, who Helen definitely now knew was the father of the boy playing with her husband Ian.

Often when Helen was alone, she would think of her nursing days and the joy and fun she had with her room-mate and friend Margery, and would wonder if Margery was still in nursing, and whether she and Kevin were still together and had any children of their own. Then she would think about Mark, and wondered whether he and Kevin had survived the war and if they had, whether Mark had ever tried to contact her through Margery, and whether after the war he had gone back to Australia. She was remembering it was on advice of Margery that she had named her baby Mark, but said nothing to her husband, Ian, about Mark the pilot. Then when her daughter was born she named her Margery, telling Ian that because of her great friendship with Margery, she wanted the children to have the same initial for their Christian name.

Back in London, Margery was walking along Farringdon Road towards Spitalfields Market also thinking of Helen and how close they had been, and of all the crazy antics they did together. She remembered how they had enjoyed life, and the time when they had met the two Australian airmen, and especially that lovely sunny day when she and

Kevin were married. Then she remembered Helen telling her of how she and Mark had behaved at her wedding and had slept together, and how Helen had cried when she realised she was pregnant and that Mark was the father.

While she was thinking of all those things, knowing that no one was around to hear, she said out loud, 'I wonder if Helen ever told Ian that Mark was the father of her child, and I bet she doesn't even know that Mark and Kevin are dead.' She was still reminiscing about Helen when she said, 'Oh! I do wish I knew where she lived and could see her again. But if I was to meet her, I certainly wouldn't like her to see me in this scruffy condition.' At that moment she passed a shop window displaying a brightly coloured advert on how to invest and make more money, and all thoughts of Helen disappeared, because the advert reminded her of her own precarious financial position and made her realise that the luxury of having a bath at the local baths every week would have to be curtailed to once every two weeks.

When she eventually arrived at Carrington House, she saw some of the residents outside the front entrance staggering around in a drunken state. Very despondently she looked at them and said very quietly to herself, 'Oh how I wish I could earn enough money to get away from here and live in a decent place with nice surroundings.' But she realised the more she thought about saving money, the more she knew that unless she obtained a better paid job, there was no hope of her saving anything.

The next Sunday she was sitting on a seat on the Embankment opposite Zion College, watching the river Thames flowing by and trying to relax and think of how to save money. She knew she was now working harder and longer hours for the same amount of money and she knew she wasn't getting much sleep because of the noise of the drunken residents in Carrington House, and she also knew it was making her more irritable with people. With the cold breeze coming off of the river, she pulled the collar of her coat up around her neck and was sitting there thinking of how hard she had studied to qualify to become a nurse and how all her training in hospitals was not being utilised. Believing what had happened to her to be an injustice, she vehemently cried out, 'I'm not able to work as a nurse because of those lies told by that doctor, and I'm having to suffer for it.'

The more she thought about Nigel and how he and the GMC had ruined her life, the more despondent she became, and she began to think about Kevin and his death, and suddenly she shouted out loud, 'Oh God! Why did you have to take my Kevin from me? What have I done to deserve all this suffering and misery? Please, God, please believe me, I did tell the truth at those hearings.' As the people walked past they looked at her, but she was quite unaware of them until she became noticed a small girl about eight years old standing in front her smiling and saying in her childish way, 'Is anything the matter Miss? Have you lost something?' Margery face went very red with embarrassment and she replied, 'No! No! It's alright my dear, I haven't lost anything. Thank you very much for worrying over me.' When the child had gone Margery quickly jumped up from the seat and began to walk towards Waterloo Bridge. At the same time she was quietly admonishing herself for her stupidity and telling herself to more careful over her behaviour.

When the Festival of Britain finally ended and all the exhibitions and sideshows had closed, she knew that all the people who had been to the Festival would have happy and lasting memories, but all she would able to remember of it would be the hard work of washing up those dirty soiled food dishes. The autumn months passed by and soon the harsh winter began to set in. She went to work a little earlier on Christmas Eve because she had been told that the restaurant was closing early. She was pleased it closed at 7 o'clock, and as she wandered through the deserted streets going towards Carrington House, she began thinking how lonely Christmas was going to be again, when suddenly she said, 'Oh, I'm going to miss my meals at the restaurant! My goodness where am I going to get anything to eat if everything is closed?' These thoughts were worrying her as she was about to go into Carrington House when she overheard one of the residents saying, 'Tom don't fogit ab-bout the soup kitchin at twelve o'clock near Trafalgar Square, an' the Silver Lady van, which ab-bee on the Ombankment sumwhere near the Temple underground station ab-bout ten er-clock on Boxing night. Don't be late will yer, uverwise yer won't git nuffing to eat or drink.'

She gained great comfort from this, because now she knew that besides the two ham sandwiches the staff at the restaurant had given her, she would at least be able to get some soup and perhaps bread that would nourish her over the next few days. On Christmas morning she rose early and dressed herself in what she considered were her best clothes, but as she put them on she could see that the blouse was grubby and badly creased. Going through the rest of her clothes she found them all in equally poor condition, and holding them up and looking at them she said out loud, 'I don't know what I'm going to do. These should be washed and ironed, but I can't do that here.' Looking at them made her feel despondent and before she went out into the coldness of the day to walk to Trafalgar Square she began moaning to herself as she put on her flimsy topcoat and wrapped a tattered scarf around her neck.

It was nearly 12.15 p.m. when she arrived at Trafalgar Square, and seeing a small queue she joined it. Within a very short time she could see other people joining the queue and could hear the shuffling and the talking going on behind her. The doors of the hall opened and she was amazed at the quickness of those people who were serving the soup, because within minutes she was sitting at a table with a bowl of soup, bread and two chicken sandwiches. Whilst she was having her soup she noticed that nobody was paying for the food and what surprised her most of all, as they went out of the hall there was a person at the door handing to everyone who left two mince pies wrapped in clean paper. Having finished her meal she was walking along the Strand feeling much better and looking in the shop windows, when she picked up from the pavement an old newspaper. In her room she sat down and was eating her mince pies, when she read from that newspaper that the King was recovering from an operation and it was hoped he would be well enough to give his Christmas day message to the people. Then she read that the BBC hoped to televise the broadcast to people with television sets. Pausing for a moment she said to herself, 'I wonder what it is like to watch television, Um! I suppose it must be like watching a film.'

With Christmas being over she went back to the restaurant and began working very hard again, especially on New Year's Eve. The days simply flew by and she was trying to save some money, and was pleased when the springtime came, because she was beginning to hope for better things and was looking forward to starting work again in a hospital.

It was early in April when she arrived at the restaurant that she was surprised to find it closed. She thought it was strange because there were usually two or three people there when she arrived. She waited about an hour when two strange men came and began to unlock the main doors but she did not recognise them. She went up to them and asked them who they were. One of them replied in an educated voice, 'We are from the Bank and we have come her to look over the premises to take a value of the stock.'

She was bewildered and said, 'Why? What for?' and she was very shocked when he replied, 'The owners have vanished, owing my Bank a lot of money.' She stood there devastated and was dumbfounded for a moment before saying, 'I was looking forward to getting some wages today. Will there be any chance of me getting my pay?'

Both man laughed derisively at her, as they looked at what they considered a pathetic figure of a woman. Then the other younger man turned towards her and said in a rather sardonic and cynical harsh voice, 'No! We are not giving anyone any money, we are taking the goods away. Now clear off and let us do our work.'

She left the restaurant and slowly walked miserably back to Carrington House where she spoke to the clerks at the desk informing them of her problem. They listened very sympathetically before saying to her, 'Now don't you dare say anything to any of the other residents, but because you have been a good resident and have not caused us any trouble, we are going to let you stay in your room until the end of the week, by which time you may have found other work. If you cannot pay for your room by then, we are sorry but you will have to vacate it.' She thanked them and immediately went out and walked to the Labour Exchange, where she hoped to find that nice man again who had helped her the last time she had been there.

Going inside the Labour Exchange she noticed the interior had been redecorated. Looking for that nice man she couldn't see him and decided to queue with the other people standing there. After an hour she arrived at the counter where a haughty obese man was looking impassively at her grubby appearance. When she asked him if there was any work for a nurse in a hospital he sarcastically replied, 'No there are no work vacancies anywhere! And we've no vacancies for nurses and if there were, they wouldn't be for the likes of you.'

She came out of the building with a heavy heart and slowly walked along the road, realising that things were going to be harder for her now. She knew she would have to call on all her resources and willpower to overcome her problem of finding somewhere to live. Leaving Carrington House she had packed her things tightly into bags and trundled along Farringdon Road towards Ludgate Circus, where she knew of some bomb ruins by the railway arches that would give her shelter for the night.

When she arrived there, she found other people already there, and after a short while and being rather naive to this type of living, she began to realise that whenever she found a comfortable spot, someone would come up to her and tell her to move. Having made a number of moves, when she found another comfortable place she said to herself, 'Right; I don't care who comes along now and asks me to move, I am definitely not moving.'

Soon as she had settled and made herself comfortable, a man appeared who smelt heavily of beer. 'Come on, move on, that's my place yer 'ave . . .' She stood up and in a rather irascible manner said, 'Buzz off, you silly old sod!' The drunken man, shaken by Margery's stern voice, just turned and mumbling to himself staggered away.

Awaking early in the morning, Margery still felt tired and her joints were stiff from the uncomfortable position she had slept in. Looking around her, she saw the others were still asleep. She knew she couldn't trust anyone, which meant that wherever she went, she must always take her belongings with her. Panicking a little she rummaged in her bags to make sure the porcelain clock was still there, and taking her frayed handbag from the bag, she looked inside and found the remains of her money safe and Kevin's letters, her wedding ring and the small bible were still there.

Sitting there looking into space and enjoying the early warm sunshine, she visualised Kevin's face and imagined him saying to her, 'Don't you worry, sweetheart. You are all right because I am watching over you. Don't forget there is always someone worse off than you.' Just as those words were going through her mind and she could feel her head nodding in agreement, suddenly she could feel nature calling and wondered where she could go to the lavatory.

Seeing no one was awake she went behind a big piece of bomb damaged stone and as she was coming away from it, she remembered that on the Embankment was a horse trough where she knew she could have a wash. She went there, and having washed herself, she was walking up one of the side streets leading to Fleet Street, when she found on the pavement an early edition of the *Daily Tribune* whose headlines read 'King George VI Dead'. Looking at those headlines she was reminded of the time during the war when the King and Queen had come to the bombed sites where she and Helen were helping with the rescue teams, close to where she had slept last night.

Deep in those thoughts, she was suddenly surprised when a man suddenly appeared from around the corner, grabbed her arm and put a sixpence into her hand, saying, 'Good morning Mary, have a cup of tea on me.' And with a smile and a wave of his hand went on his way. Visibly shaken, watching the figure of the man disappearing into the distance, she kept opening and shutting her hand to see if she had imagined it happening. On opening her hand once more she saw that it was a real coin, and being near the 'Press Cafe', she decided to go in and ask for cup of sweet tea and a cheese roll.

The counter-hand who had been very busy during the night serving the print workers, was feeling tired and when he turned round to see who was speaking, he nearly exploded when he saw a bedraggled haggard woman standing in front of the counter. He was on the point of ordering out when on looking into her face and seeing the sixpence she was offering, he took great pity upon her and said, 'All right then, you can have a small carton of tea and a cheese roll, but I must ask you to eat it outside.'

Margery felt her temper rising and was on the point saying something, when her sanity and common sense appeared to take over, because she heard herself saying, 'Thank you very much young man, I appreciate you serving me.' Without saying anything else to her, the counter-hand wrapped the cheese roll in clean white paper and gave her a steamy carton of hot tea and took the sixpence.

Having quickly eaten the roll, she was drinking her tea and feeling it warming her stomach. Thinking the counter-hand had made a mistake, she went to the door and looked inside at the price board, where she read that a cheese roll cost fourpence and the tea twopence. Feeling much better now she had eaten she began to think about money and how easy it had been to accept money from that man. She thought it was a good idea to hold out her hand to people for money and see how much she could collect.

Later on in the afternoon, after standing on the pavement near Covent Garden Market for nearly two hours, she was just counting the money she had been given, when a rather corpulent policeman appeared before her and taking the money from her hand said in a very deep voice, 'I have been watching you for the last twenty minutes and you have been begging from the public. I am therefore charging you under section 3 of the Vagrancy Act of 1824. Now come along.' And he escorted her to Bow Street Police station where she was formally charged and put in the cells for the night. She felt quite dumbfounded by what had happened to her and in the morning she had to wait until all the prostitutes and drunks had been dealt with by the magistrate.

When it was her turn to appear and stand in the dock, she thought the magistrate seemed a nice person, because after the charge against her had been read out, he said, 'Is it true you were standing on the pavement with your hand held out, inviting the people passing by to put money into it?' Looking at him with her head held high she said very politely, 'Yes, Your honour, that is right.'

Hearing her answer in a very polite manner, the magistrate asked if she had anything to say in her defence. In a very punctilious way she looked at the magistrate saying, 'Sir, I do not understand what I have done wrong, because I was not begging. Please could you tell me what the Vagrancy Act is and what does the section I have been charged under means? Thank you.' The magistrate who was surprised and very impressed by her candid and very polite manner, leaned forward and said to the person sitting at a desk, below his bench, 'Mr Stacey would you please hand me the Green Book? Thank you.'

The magistrate opened the Green Book and finding the page he required said, 'Mrs Hopkins, I will read to you what Section 3 of the Vagrancy Act says: Every person wandering abroad, or placing himself, or herself in any public place, street, or highway, court, or passage, to beg, gather alms, or causing, or procuring, or encouraging any child or children to do so . . .' at that point the magistrate paused for a moment before saying, 'I believe that part explains what you want to know and as you have admitted that you were attempting to obtain money, it means, Mrs Hopkins, that you are guilty under that section of the Act of the offence, as charged. However as you have been very polite, and this being your first offence, I am going to let you go free, but if you ever appear before this Court again, I shall have no option but to send you to prison. You are discharged.'

Leaving the Court, having been charged then set free and knowing the money she had been given had been taken away from her, and having therefore no money at all, she was in bewilderment as she wandered around, not realising it was getting dark until the bright lights of a passing car shone in her eyes and momentarily blinded her, making her understand it was evening time. On reaching Fleet Street she went down a side road, and walking past a building, she felt cold air being emitted from extract fan outlets, which were at pavement level. Feeling that air coming out, suddenly she realised that if cold air was coming out of those ducting outlets now, hot air would be coming out of them when winter arrived.

Later in the year she was sheltering and trying to sleep in a doorway, when the sound of bursts of thunder, together with the flashing streaks of lightning woke her up and torrential rain came down when a thunderstorm broke. The flashing of the lightning and noise of the thunder frightened and reminded her of the bombing during the war and she became very scared. The heavy rain was splashing into the doorway, wetting her clothes and making her huddle closer in the doorway. She was very scared of lightning, and tried very hard to get further inside the doorway. When the rain eased off, she stood up and, remembering the warm air ducting outlets, she walked to the building down the road and was standing in front of them, and could feel the warm air from them blowing on to her damp clothes, when along came the man who had given her the sixpence. This time he stopped and said, 'Good morning Mary. I can see you got wet last night. You must try and keep dry. Here's an early morning paper for you. See you tomorrow morning outside the Music pub ok?' and as he was talking to her he was again pressing another sixpence into her hand. 'By the way,' he added, 'the Music pub is the Harp of Erin round the corner near to Shornfield House. Be there tomorrow morning, about this time . . . Bye.'

Feeling very grateful to that man for giving her another sixpence, she was standing there watching the steam coming off of her clothes, when her eyes caught sight of the headlines on the paper which read: 'Severe Storms and Flooding in the Lynton and Lynmouth Area. Many Deaths.' Reading those headlines she felt very sorry for the people who had lost someone and who had suffered through the storm, and was grateful that all she had wrong were damp clothes, and felt happy now she had money to go to the Press Cafe to buy something to eat.

When winter came she saw a placard that read: 'Government to Abolish Identity Cards'.

This made her temper rise and she shouted out loud to the people walking by, 'Government to abolish Identity Cards – that makes me laugh. I had my identity taken away from me and now I haven't an identity or a card. Nobody wants to know me because I've been arrested, and in prison, all because I accepted money from strangers. I get so mad when I think of that doctor who raped me and got away with it. Then I lose my job, my home and my respectability and also my identity, and you strangers are not even allowed to help me. No wonder people like me get annoyed.'

Standing watching the people walking by and not saying a word to her she thought, 'I wonder what my Mum and Dad, or even Kevin would think of me if they were to see me now?' she started to cry and as the tears ran down her face, she thought back how very hard she had tried to overcome the adversities that had befallen her.

As people walked past not taking any notice of her standing there, openly crying, she thought back how the main stumbling block to her problems had been that letter from the GMC, and she asked herself why they had been so vindictive. Not knowing the answer to that question made her very despondent. She began crying again, remembering how hard she had worked to obtain her nursing grades, and she thought of the money Mrs Swinton had spent on her to achieve those results, and now all she was, was a homeless vagrant. These thoughts made her rant and rave even louder and she gave vent to her frustration by shouting towards the people as they walked past.

Two policemen, one of whom was a sergeant, appeared, warning her to stop annoying the public. One rather brusquely asked her her name, out of sheer cussedness she insolently replied, 'I'm known as Mary.' The other, a sergeant, seeing what he thought were tearstains down her grubby face and sensing that she had been upset by something, said to her in a kind way, 'All right Mary, just behave yourself and no one will bother you, but if I see you shouting, or harassing the people walking by, I will charge you. Now be on your way.' With that sharp rebuke ringing in her ears, she trundled along Fleet Street carrying her four bags.

However because of her appearance and the heavy bags she was carrying, people were still trying to avoid coming into contact with her as they passed by. This made her feel terrible, and she said out loud enough for them to hear, 'Everyone is treating me as though I'm a flaming outcast, so why don't you treat me as a leper, because that's the way you all see me. I know all of you don't think that I'm a human being anymore.' Some of the people passing by hearing her outburst looked at her and just smiled and nodded their heads in agreement with her.

A few days later she was standing against a wall, again talking out loud to herself, saying, 'It's my birthday today and I am going to wish myself a happy birthday.' While she was speaking, a very smartly dressed lady stopped, opened her purse and took a pound note from it saying, 'Here you are my dear, happy birthday and buy yourself something to eat and drink.' As she put the pound note into Margery's hand she said, 'and I do wish you a happy birthday my dear.' This took Margery by surprise and she was amazed at the consideration shown to her. It took a few moments for the kindness to sink in, then as the lady walked away, Margery shouted out to her, 'Thank you very much indeed.' Unbeknown to Margery, standing a short distance away was PC Atkinson, who had noticed the lady giving something to her, and hearing Margery calling out thank you, he approached Margery and rather sternly said, 'What have you got in your hand?' Seeing the pound note he said, 'Right. I'm arresting you for begging and harassing the public.' All her protestations went unheeded and again she was taken to Bow Street Police Station and charged. She was still protesting in the police station and it was only when the police sergeant read the charge to her and she heard him saying, 'That you were observed by Police Constable Atkinson No.512E at 10.32 a.m. to be begging and receiving money from a member of the public', that she immediately interrupted him and said, 'It's my birthday today and that lady only gave me the money because I happened to be speaking out loud to anyone who wanted to listen that it was my birthday. Suddenly she stopped walking past and gave the money to me as a birthday present.'

Hearing her say that, the sergeant sneeringly laughed at her saying, 'Nobody gives money to people like you, unless they were begging, so I'm going to charge you.'

When she appeared before the magistrate she was very apprehensive because it was the same magistrate who had seen her before, and told her that if she appeared before him again she would go to prison. The magistrate was writing while her charge was being read out, but when he heard of her denial, he stopped writing, looked up and said to her, 'First of all my dear lady, I am given to understand that today is your birthday and to show you, and to others, that this court sometimes have feelings, a kind heart, and consideration for others, I am going to believe your story, that a kind lady did give you money as a birthday present, and therefore in the hope that you will not appear before me again, I am going to dismiss this charge and release you, so that you may enjoy the rest of your birthday with freedom, and I extend to you my best wishes for a happy birthday.' When the magistrate had finished speaking, many people in court began laughing and clapping their hands, which he quickly brought to a halt by looking sternly at the court usher, who immediately stood up and called out 'Silence in court.'

Still amazed by being released from the court, when she was outside in the cold sunshine air, she was spoken to by a number of people who wished her a happy birthday and were also congratulating her on being released by the court because it was her birthday. This caused her mind to be in a muddle and she wasn't really listening to them, because she was thinking of another occasion when she appeared before the GMC and they had found her guilty of a crime she had never committed, and yet today she had been found not guilty just because it was her birthday. Walking away from the court, she was shaking her head in disbelief, but rejoicing that she was not going to prison.

Then winter came and being homeless on Christmas Day she went to Trafalgar Square, where she knew she was able to obtain some hot food. After she had queued with the other vagrants and had eaten the only decent meal she had had for a long time, she came away and wandered around Trafalgar Square, then stopping to look at the Christmas tree and began to read the notice on the large placard that read:

> The tree has been given by the Norwegian Government to the British Nation, to commemorate all those people who had died during the war in assisting those loyal Norwegians overcome their struggles against the Norwegian Quislings and the Nazi aggressors occupying their homeland.

After reading the notice she began to feel cold and as it was getting dark she huddled into her heavy topcoat and was standing in a doorway near Canada House, looking at the Christmas tree with its white lights swaying backwards and forwards in the wind, that appeared to be twinkling because they were slightly hidden by its branches. As she stood there looking across the square at the tree, the effects of the twinkling lights made her remember the Christmas tree given to her mother by Mrs Swinton, and how proud she had been having a small tree. Then she remembered how the flames from the fire had made flickering shadows on the wall in her parents' cottage, making the silver decorations on the Christmas tree twinkle.

Suddenly she began to see herself, dirty, scruffy and bedraggled, and cried out loud, 'This is how people see me – scruffy, dirty and bedraggled. Oh how can I help myself, I know it's very hard, because every time I try to improve myself something always seems to be pushing me further backwards.'

It was while she standing there feeling cold and alone saying those things, that Dr Nigel Cairnworth was in a large six-bedroomed house at Broxbourne, where only a few moments earlier, he had enjoyed eating a lovely Christmas dinner with his parents and Phillippa, his fiancée, together with her parents and a coterie of friends.

It was after dinner and they were all sitting in a large L-shaped drawing room in a corner of which stood a large Christmas tree with twinkling lights upon it, with many beautifully decorated Christmas presents beneath it waiting to be handed out. Everyone sitting there in the room had a feeling of contentment as they looked at this very lovely Christmas scene, especially with the hidden subdued electric lighting shining, allowing the flickering shadows coming from the burning logs in the large ornate fireplace to shine on the walls.

As the evening darkness began to fall, someone said to Nigel's father, 'John it's so lovely sitting here looking out at the Thames flowing by at the bottom of your garden. It must be beautiful here in the summer time with all the flowers in bloom!' Another man, smoking a large cigar, looked over to Nigel and said, 'Nigel, you and Phillippa could, and probably will, inherit all this one day, you lucky young things!' Nigel looked at the speaker first then at his parents, giving them a wry smile, then he looked at everyone else sitting comfortably drinking their coffee and port and nodded, at the same time putting his arm round Phillippa's shoulders and giving her a big hug and kissing the side of her face.

Nigel's parents were close friends of the Parkinsons and so they had been delighted when Nigel became very friendly, and then engaged, to Phillippa Parkinson. They were pleased his carefree days appeared to be over, and he was now beginning to settle down, and they were also very pleased that he was marrying into the Parkinsons' influential stock-broking family.

Ever since the day of the GMC hearing, when he had been told very sternly by his father that he must behave himself and not to become involved in any more affairs with the opposite sex, especially with the nurses, Nigel had tried very hard to be on his best behaviour, not only in the presence of his parents but also at work, because he knew if he did not behave, his family would disown him. And knowing that Phillippa's father and his father were very close friends, having been to the same public school and university together, he was well aware that to upset them would bring catastrophic consequences for him.

Early one morning, just after Christmas, Margery, having washed and cleaned herself from the horse trough on the Embankment, was standing outside the building of Shornfield House with some other vagrants, who were also waiting for the man to appear to give them sixpence each. When he appeared and was giving her the sixpence he said to her, 'My my Mary, you do look nice and clean this morning. Keep up the good work!' Then with his cheery smile and a wave of his hand he called out to her and to the other vagrants, 'See you all tomorrow.'

Watching him walk away and hearing him saying she looked clean bolstered her self-esteem and confidence and she felt very pleased with herself. Later on that morning it began to rain very heavily and not being able to find shelter to get out of the rain, her clothes soon became very wet, until she eventually found shelter in the driveway of Shornfield House.

Standing in the driveway in her very wet clothes she said to herself, 'I am so fed up – no sooner do I try to smarten myself up, then this happens and I'm soaking wet. I've nowhere to go to get dry and all my other clothes are in my bags hidden away on the old bombsite. Oh Lord! Why do I have to suffer like this? What have I done to hurt you so?' Suddenly she could hear metal rattling and looking around she saw it was the grill on the covering of an air vent that was moving with the pressure of the air being emitted from the air duct. Going up to it and putting her hand against the vibrating grill, she could feel hot air coming from it. 'Great!' she shouted. 'Now I might be able to dry these clothes that I'm wearing.'

Standing in front of the grill she could feel the warm air hitting her clothes and shortly afterwards she could see the steam coming from them. Every now then she would turn round to allow the hot air blow on the other part of her clothes.

It was while she was turning round that she noticed a billposter that read 'Sweet Rationing Ends Today!' 'Wouldn't be nice to have some money to buy some sweets,' she cynically said.

The following day she went the bomb damaged site and retrieved her clothing, and after she had changed some of her damp undergarments, she found a partially torn newspaper lying on the floor. Picking it up she saw that it was the current day news and she read that over 280 people had died in the storms on the east coast, and Canvey Island was swamped by a sudden flood of water. Twelve US servicemen had drowned near Hunstanton, with a number of others missing. She read that the villages of Cley and Salthouse had almost been devastated where the sea had rushed inland for five miles, causing widespread flooding. Then she read that parts of Lincolnshire had flooding up to 20 feet deep, and this made her think of her village of Hemelsham, which she knew was not far from that flooded area.

Tears began running down her face as she read another headline 'US Airman Wins George Medal'. Eagerly she read that the US Airman was called Reis Leeming, and was only 22 years of age and stationed with the 67th Air Rescue Squadron in Norfolk and had rescued 27 people from the floods in Hunstanton.

Margery was crying because she began remembering the time in Trafalgar Square when she met Kevin before they were married and Kevin was wearing the small ribbon on his uniform jacket and when she asked him what it meant and had shown her a piece of paper saying that he had been awarded the DFM. Afterwards she remembered how very proud she was of him and how she had told him to be very careful.

Thinking of Kevin, the tears were still on her face as she looked up at the grey sky and said, 'Thank you, Kevin, for not letting me get too wet yesterday. By the way I am still hoping my luck will change.'

Thinking of the American hero and how very brave he must have been, she started to look inside her bags for some of Kevin's letters to read. Rummaging through the bags, she found his letters in her old tattered handbag and taking one of the letters out, she settled herself down on a piece of masonry. Looking at the post date on the envelope she noticed that it was one of the last ones she had received from him just before he was killed, and she thought this was strange because at the time of his death they were living together in that cottage near the aerodrome.

At first she was reluctant to reopen it, because she felt by reading that letter again it would remind her of his death and would upset her again, but somehow she felt that Kevin was around her and something within her made her open it. When she looked at it she realised it was not his last letter, and began to read it.

My dearest Marge,

I'm sorry that I haven't written to you lately, but I have been very busy training and learning new techniques. I can tell you the one good thing that has emerged from this training, is that we are all staying together as one crew, with Mark being our Skipper.

He has been promoted to Flt Lt but he is still the same Mark we like. By the way I haven't said anything to you about this before, or when I have been home on leave, but there is something strange happening here, because whenever Mark and me are alone, he keeps talking to me about Helen and about our wedding and saying how he and Helen got on well together.

Then recently he confided in me and said that shortly after our wedding, he received a letter from her saying she was pregnant, but as there was no forwarding address he couldn't answer her letter. He now appears a little worried and keeps on asking me if I know how she is and could I obtain her address from you.

Sweetheart, I know Mark is very keen on her and wants to contact her. Can you help him in any way? Is there something going on between those two that I should know? If there is, please let me know when I next come home, so that when I get back I don't say the wrong thing and cause an upset. I still don't know when I am able to get leave again, hopefully it will not be too long, because I miss you terribly and want to feel your arms around me again.

In the sergeants' mess the other day we were talking about the end of the war and our demob and it has set me thinking that when this war is over, would you like to settle down in this country of England, or would you prefer to live in Australia, because we have been told that is where we are going to be demobbed, and if we have married an English girl, we can take her back to 'Aussie' with us.

Let me know how you feel about this when I am next home on leave. It will give us something to think about and look forward to. This is all the news I have for now sweetheart, and remember whenever you are feeling lonely and think the world is against you, and I know you do that very often, just try to remember that I am around and think of those positive vibes and try to remember you are all I have in this world and I love you very much and I need you to keep me sane and cheerful. With all my love, until we meet again

Your ever loving husband,

Kevin

Putting the letter back in her handbag, she was feeling very melancholy thinking what Kevin had written and decided to think positively and hope things would start to improve. A few days later she was asleep in a doorway in Fleet Street when she was awakened very early in the morning by a very young policeman, who told her he was arresting her and escorted her to the police station. After the young policeman had written out the charge sheet, the sergeant began to read the charge to her. She was standing there completely bewildered but it was when the police sergeant read that the charge was 'Sleeping out' that she interrupted him in a rather questioning manner with her voice quivering with disbelief as she said to him 'Sleeping out? What the dickens does that mean? Are you telling me that I am being charged for being asleep? Haven't you got enough work to do without picking on the likes of me for being asleep?'

The police sergeant opened the drawer of his desk and taking a book from it. Looking at her, telling her to be quiet and then looking rather sternly at the young police man, the sergeant said, 'This constable has charged you under section 4 of the 1824 Vagrancy Act, which states "Every person wandering abroad and lodging in any barn, or out-house, or in any deserted or unoccupied building, or in the open air, or in a tent, or cart, or wagon and not giving a good account of himself or herself . . ."' then turning very quickly towards to the young policeman the sergeant said to him in a querulous way, 'And as he has arrested you I am going to see that the cell you occupy today is properly cleaned out by him. Do you get that constable?'

Two weeks later when she was released from the police cell, she was walking up Fleet Street when she saw a placard which read: 'Elizabeth to be Crowned Queen.' Soon she found a dirty copy of a newspaper lying on the ground containing the news of the ceremony to be held in Westminster Abbey and the ceremonial route the Queen would be taking. After reading that news, she said to herself, 'I think I'll go and watch it. It will be lovely to see history being made.'

On the eve of the Coronation she knew she wouldn't able to see the procession because of all the people coming to London, so she settled herself down in a very secluded spot, which was partially hidden from view but she could hear what seemed like hundreds of people walking past, all heading towards Westminster Abbey and the processional route, which had been gaily decorated and was soon to be lined with servicemen. Even though it was summertime, it was a very cold night and she was pleased she was able to have her heavy topcoat covering over her, but it was the noise of the people walking past that kept her awake most of the night. When she did manage to get to sleep, she awoke very early to the sound of more people passing. While she watched them, she was mentally saying to herself, 'I know those people won't let me stand near them and therefore I wouldn't be able to see the procession, so blow them.'

Then she thought, 'I am luckier than they are because I have seen the decorations being erected, and they are lovely.' After clearing and packing her things away, hiding the bags from view, she made her way to Shornfield House as she felt it coming on to rain.

It was still drizzling when the man appeared from Shornfield House to give her, and the other vagrants who were waiting with her, their usual sixpence. When he came to give her the sixpence he said, 'Are you going to watch the procession today Mary?' Looking up to the damp sky, she said, 'No I think it is going to rain all day today.'

'Then why don't you go to that large electrical shop in Holborn, near Seven Sisters Road?' he replied. 'I am given to understand the shop is going to have a television set in its front window, showing the whole procession, and it's there for anyone to watch.'

Later that morning she was walking up Chancery Lane towards Holborn, when it began raining very heavily. Luckily she found shelter in a doorway until it eased to a drizzle, then she made her way to the electrical shop. On her arrival, she was surprised to find that she was the only person there. She was able to sit on the floor in the doorway and still manage to see the picture from the television set. Although only in black and white, she was thrilled by the clarity of the picture of the procession leaving Buckingham Palace and she felt as though she was actually there.

Later that day she was enthralled at the ceremony from Westminster Abbey, she tried to imagine the colours, then later she was so engrossed in watching the new Queen and her consort standing on the balcony of Buckingham Palace waving to the crowds below, that the sudden roar of low flying aircraft frightened her and watching the Queen pointing towards the sky she knew that the planes were flying on their way to salute their Queen. During the closing moments of the television broadcast, she felt she had a marvellous day watching history being made, and she felt so happy she said, 'How lucky can I be? I've seen everything and I'm dry, not like all those people who have stood outside in the rain getting soaking wet.'

A few weeks later she began to worry again, when she read in a newspaper that John Christie had been sentenced to death for killing seven lonely women. The danger of being alone and homeless made her think of the precarious position she was in of not knowing how to stand up and defend herself, especially when it came to a confrontation with the other homeless people and from those who drank methylated spirits.

One morning at the end of September, with everyone was experiencing the cold nights and damp days, she was standing against the wall opposite Australia House, when a very well dressed man came up to her and in a well educated voice said to her, 'How are you today? I do hope you will go and buy yourself something to eat with this,' and he placed a ten shilling note in her hand. His action frightened her, because it had taken her completely by surprise, and remembering the last occasion this had happened, she quickly looked round to see no policemen were watching before she turned back to thank the man, but he was walking smartly away.

She had moved her head so quickly that her hat fell from her head and was now lying on the ground. People walking by could see her looking at the money in her hand and with her hat on the floor some of them began to put money into her hat. It was about an hour later that she looked towards the Strand and saw a policeman coming slowly towards her. She panicked and quickly picking up the hat with the money in it, and gathering her bags together she made a hurried departure in the direction of Kingsway, dodging between the trams as they came out of the subway tunnel, then made her way to Covent Garden market. She soon found a secluded spot where she was unobserved, and began counting the money she had been given, and was amazed that it amounted to £2.16s.5d.

Putting the money into her handbag she made her way to a fruit stall and bought some fresh fruit. By buying the fruit, it made her feel like a normal person once more and her spirits rose knowing she had more money left in her handbag.

A few days later it came as surprise to her that Christmas Day was drawing near, because the days had been very sunny, and the nights very warm. After Christmas she was reading a day old newspaper where it stated that it had been the mildest Christmas for over 200 years, but as she put the paper down she read that an aeroplane called the 'Comet' had crashed into the sea off the island of Elba, with the loss of 35 lives. She felt sorry for the families of those who died, but said to herself, 'At least they know where their loved ones died, I don't know where my Kevin died.'

At the end of January the weather changed for the worse and it became intensely cold, with a biting wind. One night whilst lying in front of the extractor grills she found it difficult to sleep, because the hot air being emitted only warmed one side of her body, whilst the other side of her became extremely cold. This made her keep turning round to warm the cold side, which caused her to become very irritable. A little while later, tired of twisting and turning, she made her way to a little niche she knew near St Paul's Cathedral, which she hoped would give her a little more comfort. During the night a small sandy coloured dog snuggled into her clothing and fell fast asleep. In the morning when she awoke she felt nice and warm and was startled to see the dog lying against her. It didn't move but opened its eyes and immediately she took pity on it and began stroking its fur. This pleased the dog, who turned on its back and let her rub its tummy. Doing that to the dog, Margery thought at last I have found a friend, and decided to call it Sandy. Later that morning she went to the horse trough on the Embankment to wash, but found the water frozen. Picking up a large stone she managed to break the ice, and she started shivering as she washed her face with the cold water while the dog had a drink.

A short while later she standing opposite Shornfield House waiting for the man to appear from the *Daily Tribune* to give her and the other vagrants sixpence each. When he appeared and gave her the money and he saw her face was clean and red and hands were clean, he said, 'That's a good girl, you look much better today, keep up the cleanliness.' It was as he departed she suddenly remembered that when her parents had been alive and they had been discussing their own poor financial position in her presence, they had said to her, 'Whatever difficult situation you find yourself in, never lose your self respect, or lower your standard of morals, because if you do you will lose all faith in yourself.'

Thinking of her parents' words and knowing her own homelessness and her financial situation was putting her morals to a strict test, she resolved that if she didn't keep to her parents' beliefs she would become like a number of the other vagrants, who were just sitting around drinking a concoction of methylated spirits and cider. It whilst she was thinking those thoughts that she felt a tap on her shoulder. On looking around she couldn't see anyone, suddenly she thought she could feel the presence of Kevin very strongly around her, and it gave her great comfort feeling that he was close to her.

As the months went by she decided that when it was raining, she would get into a routine of sleeping unobserved in a niche near to St Paul's Cathedral, and when it was warm and dry, she would sleep by the buildings where the newspapers were being printed. It was during this period that she read a placard saying 'All Food Rationing Ends Today', and a derisory smirk came upon her face as she said to herself, 'I wish rationing would end for me.'

The next day she was standing by a wall when a smartly dressed lady came along and stopped, opened her handbag and gave her five shillings, saying to her, 'You look hungry, here you are my dear, buy yourself a cup of tea and a bite to eat.' Margery was so surprised that she could only mumble, 'Thank you'. The lady quickly walked away, but a few moments later two policemen were standing in front of her, with one of them pointing to the money in her hand and aggressively saying, 'Where did you get that money?' When she replied, 'That lady gave it to me,' and she tried to explain to them what actually happened, one policeman said, 'We don't believe you. We saw you begging to that woman, so I am going to charge you with begging from the public and' (pointing to the other policeman) 'he is my witness.'

'Honestly I am telling the truth, said Margery. 'That lady stopped and said that I looked hungry and then opened her purse and gave me the money.' But all her pleadings went unheeded, and the more she protested the more the policemen wouldn't listen until eventually one of them kept saying to her, 'Shut up, you old hag. You vagrants never tell the truth, and you are going to be charged, and that's that.'

On the way to Bow Street Police Station, the policemen were talking to each other when one of them said, 'You know Bert. I don't know about you, but I am finding it hard to manage on our police pay. What with the increase in the police rent for our house and the food prices going up, and the increase of the TV licence from £2 to £3, the wife and I are going to have to make cut backs on the way we are living.'

Hearing those policemen's remarks, made Margery grimace and a wry smile came on her face, as she thought, 'I wonder what he would do if he was in my position, being homeless and penniless.' It was while those thoughts were going through her mind that one of the policemen looking at her face, said to her rather brusquely, 'What are you smirking at, you old hag? All you lot do is scrounge off the public and you don't have any of the worries we have. All of you ought to be locked up and put away for ever and save us a lot of trouble.'

She was livid with anger hearing him say that to her, but inside Bow Street Police Station, she recognised the police sergeant at the desk who rather cheerfully said to her, 'Hello Mary it's you again. Well what have you been up to this time?' Before she could answer, the policeman who arrested her said, 'I arrested her because I observed her begging from the public, sergeant.' At that point she shouted to him, 'You lying sod. I've told you time and time again, but you won't listen me, because if you had been observing me as you said you were, you would have seen and heard that lady, who was dressed in a blue coat, come up and say that I looked hungry. When I nodded my head, she opened her handbag and put the money in my hand telling me to buy myself a cup of tea and a bite to eat.'

The police sergeant hearing her reply he said, 'Now come on Mary, that's a likely story. Nobody gives money, especially to the likes of you.' Margery interrupted him saying, 'Sarge, they do and they did, honestly.' The sergeant replied, 'Now stop making up stories Mary, it's no use. You are only making things more awkward for yourself.'

The policeman who arrested her said, 'Sergeant, she has been making one story up after another, just telling a pack of lies.' Hearing him say that, and remembering what he had said to her on the way to the police station, she lost her temper and shouted at him, 'Does it really matter if I am telling the truth?' Then pointing at the two policemen, she vehemently said to the sergeant, 'You only want to believe those two lying sods, so carry on and bloody well charge me then.'

'Right, Mary,' said the sergeant, 'you are being charged with begging and using abusive language whilst being charged.'

This time magistrate was a woman, someone she had not seen before, and after the policeman had given his evidence, the magistrate began speaking to her in a haughty manner. Margery wasn't listening, because she was looking at the hairstyle of the magistrate, and she knew it was called a chignon and this brought a smile to her face. But when she heard the supercilious voice of the lady magistrate speaking: '. . . as you seem to disregard the law. I cannot allow people like you to go about begging and I certainly will not allow anyone to use abusive language to the police. I am therefore fining you £10 for begging and £10 for using abusive language, or 21 days in jail.' Margery was dumbfounded, knowing she could not pay the fine, and it wasn't until she was put in a cell that due to her frustration at not being believed she burst into tears again.

When she had served her sentence, she went straight to the bombed site near St Paul's, where she had hidden her bags containing her possessions, and looking around to see that no-one was watching, she delved into the hiding place. She was relieved to find they were still there, but as she retrieved them and put her hand inside one of the bags to take out one of her woollen jumpers, a mouse jumped out. Screaming with fright, she picked up a piece of wood lying nearby and holding the bag in one hand and with the piece of wood in the other, she began to withdraw her clothing from the bag, and in doing so she could hear squealing of other mice. Tilting the bag upside down, she shook it until all her clothes were on the floor. As the mice ran around, she tried hitting them with the piece of wood and screamed when a mouse ran over her foot. Within seconds she was jumping up and down smashing the wood up and down, as though she was at a Red Indian war dance, at the same time she shouting out loud hoping her friend Sandy the dog would come along and help her, because the mice were running everywhere. For a few moments bedlam reigned all around her. She was hitting out at anything and everything including her clothes which lay on the ground, as she tried to hit the fleeing mice that were scampering all around her. Eventually there were no mice to be seen, or heard.

Standing there puffing and blowing with exhaustion, she waited a few moments to compose herself, before she looked closer at her clothing to make sure that all the mice had gone, then began checking to see what damage they had caused. Although the clothing was grubby and dirty, she was grateful that the mice had not touched the bag containing her peach two-piece wedding suit and her diary.

Looking at all of her clothing on the floor, she saw it was covered in mice droppings, and picking up a woollen jumper she saw it had many holes in it where the mice had been gnawing at it, and felt pleased that the mice had only been in the bag containing her woollen clothing. She was nearly in tears when she finally finished picking all the mice droppings off of her clothing, it had taken her a long time and her eyes were very sore, and just as the tears began running down her face, she suddenly felt a strong presence of Kevin around her. It was the thought of him being close to her that gave her great comfort, so gathering up her tattered clothing and putting them into the bags, she decided to settle herself down for the night.

It was her usual custom before going to sleep to say her prayers, and it was on this particular night, with Christmas approaching, she decided to say an extra prayer, for someone to give her a small present of clothing. What a delightful Christmas present that would be.

One evening on her way to get her usual nightly drink from the 'Silver lady' van on the Embankment, she suddenly felt very strange, because somehow as she walked along she viewed herself from an astral-plane and was able to look down upon herself. It made her realise that from the way she was living, and particularly after the mice had gnawed at her clothing, no matter how she tried she looked a dreadful sight in her tattered clothing. As she despondently and wearily approached the 'Silver lady' van, one of the two ladies who were serving the tea, looking at Margery's face, which she thought was nice in spite of everything, and at her tattered clothing, leaned forward and whispered to her, 'In the mornings I work for the WVS, and tomorrow morning we are giving away some nice clean clothes. Would you be interested if I brought some for you tomorrow night?'

Hearing that strange lady offering to help her made Margery very suspicious, but then she remembered the astral-plane feeling she experienced earlier that evening, and that she had been praying very hard for someone to help her with clothing. She looked very intently into that lady's face and thought she could only see kindness in her eyes, and she found herself saying, 'Yes please, and thank you very much for thinking of me.'

The following evening when she arrived at the 'Silver Lady' van, there were only two drunken male vagrants leaning against the river wall, and this enabled one of the ladies to come out of the van and give Margery two bags of clothing and a heavy top coat, which came down to her ankles. Handing her the coat the lady said, 'I am sorry the coat is a little too long, but at least it will keep you warm during the cold winter.'

Margery was so shaken by the kindness shown to her that all she could say was, 'I don't know how to thank you. You see most of my clothing was ruined by mice, and only recently I have been praying every night for someone to give me a present of clothing for Christmas, and now my Christmas present has come a little early, because this is my Christmas present from you. Thank you very much indeed.'

Carrying the bags back to her little niche near St Paul's Cathedral, she found that they contained blouses, skirts and a few items of underwear, all nicely cleaned and ironed. She now felt she could face another winter out in the open and felt so happy, knowing that she had decent clothing and a heavy top coat to keep her warm.

A few days later she was thinking of the clothes she had been given and was rummaging in her bags when she came across her small bible. As she held it in her hand, suddenly she could see herself as a little girl in the small garden in Hemelsham with her father talking to her, and remembered how he told her about being lonely and in the need of help, and that she could always find comfort from the bible. She could hear him saying, 'Ask and it will be given you; seek and you will find.' Then she remembered him reading that passage from the bible to her and looking in her diary she saw she had written 'Luke'.

She was trying very hard to remember what page he had read it from, when something prompted her to look at the top of every page in the book.

With the light beginning to fade her eyes became very sore from straining, looking at each page, and she was on the point of giving up, when suddenly she saw the name 'Luke', and cried out, 'That's it! I'm sure that's it'. Very slowly she looked at each page that had 'Luke' on it and her heart missed a beat when, in her excitement, she found the passage of scripture she was searching for. As she read it, she could still hear her father's voice as he read it to her all those years ago saying

> So I say to you; Ask and it will be given to you
> Seek and you will find;
> Knock and the door will be opened to you;
> For the one who asks, always receives;
> The one who seekss, always finds:
> The one who knocks, will always have the door opened to him . . .

Feeling the tears running down her weatherbeaten face, she stopped reading and felt very tired. She cried out loud, 'Lord! I have knocked at your door. What did I do wrong? Have I been that bad that you cannot open your door and help me, must you punish me this way and make me suffer all this anguish and hardship?' She stopped for moment before speaking again. 'You know I have tried to do good by tending to the sick, yet you took my Kevin from me, and then you allowed that horrible Dr Cairnworth to rape me and get away with it, and then you allowed them to stop me from working in the hospitals. I have asked you many times for help, all to no avail. I have even lost the dog I had as a friend. So what must I do? You seem as though you want to ignore me and not help me. Is it because I had that abortion? If it is not that Lord, why do you make me suffer like this?'

Sitting there, she stopped speaking, just letting the tears run down her face, and could feel the frustration growing inside her. Feeling there was not going to be any answer to her questions or improvements in her current circumstances, she threw the bible rather hard into one of her bags, shouting out vehemently, 'I don't believe what my father said, or what is written in that bible.' Sobbing with frustration at her sudden disclosures and of her disbelief in the Deity, she threw herself down on the floor and putting her head on her bags she closed her eyes, trying not to cry. Suddenly the tears stopped and she felt herself becoming sleepy and her body quivered as she thought she felt a warm hand upon her head, then it was gently brushing over her body, which made her feel quite calm and contented. Quickly opening her eyes, she looked around but she couldn't see anyone who could have touched her. She brushed her face with the back of her hand to wipe away the tears and anything that might have crawled onto her face. She didn't feel afraid, but for a long time she laid on her side with her eyes open, then as she closed her eyes she remembered the evening prayer her mother used to say to her when she was a young child, and she began saying it out loud:

'Lord God keep me safe this night secure from all my fears.
May angels guard me while I sleep, until morning light appears,
Amen'

Somehow saying that prayer had made her feel different, and she said, 'Lord if you are listening, I am sorry for my outburst, but I am finding it very hard to understand why I am having to live this way, please do forgive me because if my belief in you is correct, then please keep me safe and free from harm.'

A few weeks later, it being a nice sunny day, she decided to sit on a seat near St Paul's where she found that someone had left behind a newspaper. She began reading that Grace Kelly the film actress was going to wed Prince Rainier who ruled Monaco, and that the film actress Marilyn Monroe had married Arthur Miller the playwright. Looking at the date, she suddenly realised it would soon be the anniversary of the date of her own wedding and she began remembering how she and Kevin came out of the church and how Kevin's friends had formed an arch with broom handles for them to walk beneath.

Thinking of all the fun they had at the wedding, she smiled and began to sing out loud *'Only tonight, I will hold you tight, while the moon beams shine. My dreams are getting better all the time'*. Her reverie was halted by the voice of a man who was saying to her, 'You have a nice voice and such a lovely smile on your face while you're singing, and I would love to give you a penny for your thoughts.' Then, laughing, he went on his way. Hearing his remark made her feel quite contented and she remained sitting there in the warm sunshine reminiscing over her lovely wedding day, with all the fun and games everyone played afterwards in the Red Lion Hotel in Kirkbridge, and she again began thinking of Helen telling her how she and Mark had slept together. That evening, she walked back to her little niche, feeling very satisfied and contented with herself, with the happy memories of her day still very prominent in her mind, and again wrote in her diary.

When she awoke in the morning she had the euphoric memories of her wedding still in her mind, but looking around and seeing thick mist, her mood changed to depression. Looking at the mist and the dampness it was bringing, made her shiver and shrug her shoulders and think of the cold, damp foggy nights she was going to have to endure, and this made her feel very miserable.

One evening when it was getting dark, as she made her way to her little niche near the Cathedral, the fog had become so thick, damp and choking, that it made her snuggle more closely into her top coat to keep warm. With the fog being so thick it was also causing people to bump into each other, but when they bumped into her and saw what she was like, they pushed her roughly out of the way. She was trying not to be pushed into the road, because she could hear the noise of the engines but could only see the shadowy glare of the headlights as the vehicles went slowly by, and this was making her very nervous. Because the fog was so thick she could only see a few feet in front of her and it made everything look eerie and frightening.

The following morning when she walked along Fleet Street, the fog was still very thick and she was surprised when she arrived at the *Daily Tribune* building that she couldn't hear the voices of the vagrants, and she wondered where they were. Standing there all alone, she was surprised and for a moment and was frightened when out of the fog appeared a ghostly figure of a man, but as he came closer, she could see it was the man from the *Daily Tribune*. As he gave her sixpence and a copy of the morning paper he said, 'Where are all the others – couldn't they make it this morning?' Before she could reply he said, 'Keep yourself well wrapped up this morning, Mary, this fog is very cold and damp. I hope to see you tomorrow morning. Bye for now.'

She was thanking him as he disappeared into the fog, then looking at the headlines of the paper she was shocked when she read: '92 die in rail crash at Lewisham. Two trains collide in thick fog with a 500-ton fly-over bridge collapsing onto the wreckage.' She shivered reading that news, but she didn't know whether it was from the cold, or from what she had just read. She crossed the road and stood against the wall of the building next to where the extract fan was emitting hot air. Standing there feeling the warm air blowing on to her clothing made her feel nice and contented and she said a silent prayer: 'Lord thank you for keeping me safe last night. Please help those unfortunate ones still trapped in that train crash.' It was while she was saying this that she thought she could feel Kevin's presence around her and was sure that a soft warm hand went over her head and body.

She always tried to look dignified even in her bedraggled clothes and she knew by her own silent behaviour that she was becoming more and more introverted, because she rarely spoke to any of the other vagrants, and this annoyed them, and there were many occasions when they tried taunting her by calling her names, one of them being 'Saint Mary'. One morning whilst waiting for the man from Shornfield House, one drunken vagrant, seeing Margery standing well away from them all alone, called out to the other vagrants, 'Looks at Shaint Mary standing there all 'lone bee 'erself, all lie-dey like.' And at that some of the other drunken vagrants standing nearby started to look and point to her, and began to drunkenly sing out loud:

'Shaint Mary, Shaint Mary she aint got a care
She stands there alone wish ah dishnified air'

Standing there listening to them, she was inwardly laughing at them, and while they tried dancing and staggering about the pavement, repeatedly singing that ditty and derisively laughing at her, she was saying to her herself, 'They will be sorry because they will all have bad headaches later on.' Having received her sixpence, she decided to walk her 'circuit'. She began walking from Ludgate Circus along Fleet Street, into the Strand and along Drury Lane into Covent Garden.

In Covent Garden she avoided the porters as they pushed their trolleys, loaded with baskets of fruit, over the cobblestones when occasionally she would stop and pick up some fruit from the fruit baskets that had fallen to the floor. Walking along Long Acre and going into Great Queen Street, she made it a long devious route avoiding Lincoln's Inn Fields, because she knew the violent drunken vagrants would be around that area, then she made her way back to Fleet Street. She felt exhausted after that long walk and made her way back to her little hiding place near St Paul's Churchyard to have a rest and then eat the fruit she had collected.

It was after she had rested and eaten the fruit, she began thinking she must try and improve her living conditions and make herself more presentable, and if possible try and find a proper place to live. 'But,' she thought, 'to have somewhere to live like that requires money, but how can I get money when no-one wants to employ a vagrant like me? I just don't understand it. I am not a drunkard, nor am I a dipsomaniac. I am a qualified ward sister with a good medical history record, yet no one wants to employ me and if it wasn't for that letter from the GMC I could be working in a hospital today. Oh I do wish I knew how to overcome this problem.' Just as she was thinking of money, she heard the loud voices of two workmen who were standing close by. One of them, in a very deep voice said, 'Wha'cher fink of the July budget Joe? Did yer see 'ow the Chancellor has increased the price of fags, from 4s.2d to 4s.6d for twenty. An wha-ba-out the cost of petrol going up from 4s.7d to 4s.10d a gallon?' Then other voice said, 'Yer I know it's bow-ned to affect us, cos they'll put up the price of fares, an' wot wiv fags going up, our wages won't be wurf nuffing, so we'll 'ave ter put in for a rise.'

Sitting there listening to their conversation she was smiling to herself saying, 'There are those two lucky devils with a home go to, earning money, and all they can moan about is the price of cigarettes and petrol going up. Yet here I am with no home, cold and hungry, wondering where the next meal is coming from, and I'm not moaning.' She sighed. 'Ah well I'll have manage somehow.'

A short while later, she was looking through the window of an electrical shop and she could hear music coming from inside the shop. She overheard two people standing near her say it was Perry Como singing 'Hoop-dee-doo'. Listening to the music it made her tap her feet on the ground in time to the beat of the music and she felt she wanted to dance and she began humming the tune. Slipping her feet from out of the boots she was wearing and even though her toes poked through the holes in her tattered stockings, she twisted and danced on the pavement in time to the music. Seeing her dancing and twisting around, the couple nearby started to laugh but she didn't care because she loved dancing. Then she heard the same singer singing a song called 'Maybe' and she felt as though she wanted to dance again, but because people again began laughing at her, she stopped dancing and hurried away thinking to herself, that even though she was getting older, she was still a good dancer. She was still humming and thinking about the title of that song and hoping that maybe her lifestyle would alter after all.

Later on in the year, it being a lovely sunny Sunday afternoon, she was seated on a parapet wall looking at the vapour trails of the aeroplanes in the sky thinking of Kevin, and suddenly decided to go for a short walk. On reaching the Royal Courts of Justice she noticed a number of people all hurrying towards Trafalgar Square.

Not thinking or worrying about them, she quietly ambled along the Strand looking in the shop windows at the ladies' dresses, and had just reached Bedford Street when she saw in the distance that Trafalgar Square was full of people. It was then she noticed a number of policemen with police vans parked nearby, and suddenly everything became bedlam. People started shouting and running around and the police who were working in pairs were chasing, catching and arresting them, and bundling them into the waiting coaches and vans waiting nearby.

She was standing in a shop doorway watching this mayhem taking place, when two policemen came running past. One of them looked round and recognising her shouted, 'Mary, for Christ sake sod off, or you'll be arrested again.' She didn't need a second warning. Hurrying very quickly she arrived in Covent Garden market, hot, sweating, and gasping for breath, and very quickly made her way back to her little niche near St. Paul's churchyard.

In the morning she met the man from the *Daily Tribune* and asked if she could have a copy of the morning newspaper. He smiled at her as he gave her one, also giving her sixpence. She was soon reading of the trouble in Trafalgar Square, where 15,000 people had been attending a 'Ban the Bomb' demonstration and Canon Collins, John Osborne and Shelagh Delaney the playwrights, Vanessa Redgrave the actress, Mr. Fenner Brockway a Labour MP and George Melly the jazz singer, were among 1,314 people arrested. Reading of the large number of people arrested she was grateful to that policeman who had recognised her and told her to move.

As the months went by, and because the horse troughs had been emptied of water and filled with earth and flowers, she was unable to wash herself, or her small clothing, and she was beginning to look dishevelled and dirty. It was on one of those days when she was feeling at a very low ebb that she overheard two men talking about the suicide of Marilyn Monroe. Thinking of her she began talking to herself, saying, 'What made a beautiful woman like her commit suicide?' then she remembered the time when just after she had heard the news of Kevin being missing when she had thought of committing suicide, and she remembered Sister Drayton saying and telling her to:

1. Wake up and live your life
2. Remain as you are and become a cabbage, or
3. Commit suicide.

It was a warm day as she reflected on the merits of those points and ambled along the road, trying not to bump into people who were making their way to their offices and said to herself, 'How often have I tried to get up and live my life, but every time I do, something comes along and stops me from doing so. Well I can assure you Margery Hopkins, I don't care what fate has in store for me, or how cold and hungry I am, there is no way I am going to commit suicide because I intend to fight this problem out until the last.' With that great determination within her, she ambled along, blissfully unaware of all things around her.

During the summer she was wandering around and came across an old newspaper and she began to read about the resignation of John Profumo, the Secretary of State for War who, it was reported, had lied to Parliament over an alleged scandal. That news did not impress her because it reminded her of Dr Cairnworth who had lied about her, and she was saying to herself, 'What's new about that? All those people in those high places lie, it's their trade mark.'

Then she began to read about his trial taking place, where it was alleged that two women called Miss Christine Keeler and Miss Mandy Rice-Davies had been having sex at Lord Astor's home in Buckinghamshire, with Douglas Fairbanks Jnr (the film actor); John Profumo (Minister of War); Dr Stephen Ward and Capt. Eugene Ivanov (Soviet attaché).

She stopped reading the newspaper, because reading of Buckinghamshire reminded her of the times she passed through that county on her way home to her village in the Midlands and she began to think and remember the village of Hemelsham with those quaint little cottages and those lovely open spaces and green fields.

She began to remember when after the night rain, she would go into the field at the bottom of their garden and she could always smell the freshness of the early morning air as she picked the wild mushrooms, which her mother would cook for them at breakfast. Suddenly she could see her bedroom with that lovely view overlooking the small rear garden of their cottage, where across the fields she able to see RAF Hemelsham Manor airfield.

Then she thought I wonder if the village has expanded and wouldn't it be nice if I could visit it again. Just then her reminiscences were rudely awaked by a loud crash.

Looking up she saw that two cars had collided with each other and the hooter of one car was sounding out its sorrowful tone. With the arrival of the police and a breakdown lorry to tow one of the cars away, the noise began to subside again, enabling her to resume her reading, and she read that Dr Stephen Ward was a well known and highly respected osteopath, as well as being a very accomplished painting artist. From the reports given, she read that he would have to fight very hard to prove his innocence and whatever happened, he still might lose his social and professional standing. The next paragraph took her by surprise when she read he had taken a huge overdose of sleeping pills and was now very ill.

She began worrying over this and was thinking of his qualifications and how long and hard he must have studied to obtain them. She began talking to herself saying, 'I wonder if he is innocent, because if he is, I know from my own experiences how hard it is to prove to people that you are telling the truth, especially when all the other parties want you to be guilty and then they all tell a pack of lies to make it harder for you to prove your innocence.'

Those thoughts were going through her mind, when she realised that through Dr Cairnworth she had lost her profession in nursing, her home and felt very unhappy at the thought that she had lost everything, except the respect she had in herself. She also knew her present plight was due to his lies and the incompetence of the GMC committee, whose members had only been concerned and worried over retaining their own positions on the committee because his father was Chairman, and they had preferred to believe Dr Cairnworth's story rather than a mere nurse from a poor family. She started to lose her temper, but she suddenly quietened down, saying to herself, 'But my girl, through all this trial and tribulation you have not lost your pride and dignity.'

This made her think of Dr Ward, and she thought perhaps he would rather commit suicide than face his accusers. When her feelings had calmed down, she began to think about the two women in that trial and momentarily thought as she said to herself, 'They must be women of low morals, fancy giving your body to any man. I couldn't do a thing like that.'

Then suddenly she remembered the evening when with two other nurses, she met the three young American airmen and they were taken to the party at the American base, and after a lovely time dancing with one of them, she remembered that she gave her body to him.

She asked herself, 'Now Margery Hopkins, what makes me any different from those two young ladies? Don't you dare forget I broke the law when I had that abortion, it's only my standard of morality against theirs, and what criterion does one have to use to measure other people's morals? I do believe that just because I'm homeless, dishevelled and wearing tattered clothing, many people think I don't have any morals. Well they're wrong. I do have morals and I am proud of it.'

It was at that moment some people were walking past and with her thoughts making her anger rise, she shouted out to them, 'Let me tell you I have a higher standard of morals than many of you have.'

A few of the people laughed a little derisively at her, which made her shout even harder, and it was fortunate that there were no policemen around to arrest her.

The winter came and she was finding it very hard to keep warm, especially when the dampness seemed to penetrate her body and make every bone ache, and she was hoping that the ginger dog would come along again to keep her warm. It was a cold, damp miserable afternoon and she was feeling tired and cold as she walked along Fleet Street. Suddenly she heard a great commotion as the people rushed up to buy a newspaper, then she saw someone come running out of one of the newspaper offices and put a notice in the placard, then looking up at the buildings she noticed that some of the offices were flying their flags at half mast. She rushed along to see what the big news could be, being inquisitive, but because of the crowds of people she had to wait a few moments she could get to see the placard which read: 'The President of the United States Assassinated!'

The people walking by tried to avoid her, but they heard her say out loud, 'My God! What is this world coming to? Killing people like that!' Not one of them bothered to answer her, but she noticed that when she had spoken they all looked at her and they had a sickly smile on their faces and appeared to agree with her because they were speaking to each other and nodding their heads as they walked away.

Making her way slowly back to her little niche near St Paul's, she was thinking of the President and saying to herself, 'I know they are a very wealthy family, but they do have two young children who are going to find it very hard now that their father is not coming home again. But at least they have someone they can call upon to help them, which is more than I had.' When she had reached her little niche and settled herself down for the night, just before she fell asleep she wrote in her diary about the President's death, then offered a silent prayer to God to give help to the President's widow and her children.

A month later, she spent another miserable lonely Christmas, but when Spring came, and she was preparing her bed by laying newspaper on the ground, she read that a gang who had robbed a GPO train had been sentenced to a total of 307 years in jail. She also read that the stolen money had been in old banknotes and had been in sacks, and one sack had been left in a telephone kiosk in Southwark Bridge Road. 'Oh! my goodness,' she gleefully cried, 'I wish I had known that, because I could have walked over Blackfriars Bridge and helped myself to some of it. I'm sure a couple of handfuls of banknotes wouldn't have been missed!'

Sitting down on her makeshift bed, she was contemplating how she would have spent the money, and said, 'The first thing I would buy would be a home of my own.'

For a few moments she could see herself in some lovely clothes, smart shoes and was relishing the thoughts of ridding herself of the lifestyle she was now enduring, and said to herself, 'What a lovely feeling, to be free of this drudgery and misery, but do I honestly think I would, or could, have taken that money?'

While she was dwelling on that question, she closed her eyes and fell asleep.

The year passed and soon another cold miserable Christmas was upon her and just after Christmas she read of the death of Winston Churchill, and wrote that in her diary, because she remembered him coming to the ruins in Fleet Street when she and the other nurses were there tending to the injured. A few days later she watched hundreds of people walking towards Westminster and overheard some of them saying they were going to Westminster Hall where his body was 'lying-in – state', and he was to be buried on Saturday and it would be the first State funeral of a commoner since that of Gladstone in May 1898.

On Saturday morning she was waiting outside Shornfield House, when the man came out and gave her sixpence and said to her, 'Mary are you going to see the State funeral of Winston Churchill?' she answered, 'Yes I would like to, but . . .' before she could say anything else, he interrupted her saying, 'Well, his body is being transported by barge from Westminster down the river to Tower Hill, now I suggest you go to London Bridge where you will get a better view, but you must leave now to get a good place.'

Immediately the man had departed, she hurried towards London Bridge and was hot and sweating when she arrived, but she managed to get a good view downriver. When the funeral barge came under the bridge and entered the Pool of London, she saw the dockers lowering all the crane jibs in a salute to the statesman of the Battle of Britain.

While she was witnessing that spectacle, she began remembering the time when she and Helen were attending to the injured in the ruins around Fleet Street and St Paul's Cathedral and Winston Churchill arrived and was seen encouraging the rescue teams and telling the residents not to lose heart, and she remembered his deep resonant voice saying to everyone, 'Don't lose faith. We are going to win this war.'

After the funeral cortege had passed by, as she began to make her way back towards Fleet Street she began experiencing slight pains in her chest and arms, so she stopped walking and noticed she was breathing heavily. Waiting a few moments for the pains and the breathing to get better she said to herself, 'This can only be indigestion due to me not eating properly and also having too much walking around, so when I eat I must eat slowly and I must not walk around too much, and also walk at a slower pace.'

It was on a warm spring evening, and she had decided to settle herself down for the night in a doorway in Fleet Street when she again felt severe pains in her chest and arms. Although the pains were still troubling her, she drifted into a light sleep, and a short while later she was awakened by loud voices, 'Oh God!' she exclaimed, 'surely it's not Turpsy Ted again?' but as the noise got closer she realised it was northern voices she could hear singing. The noise of the singing brought some of the print workers out of the café and they also joined in the song

'One two buckle my shoe, Germany scored only two
Three four knock at our door, England scored two more,
Five, six, seven, eight, Geoff Hurst sealed Germany's fate,
Nine, ten, we've won the cup and we can win it again.'

The singers of the joyous English supporters were being discreetly escorted by police, and Margery who was in the doorway and was glad that England had beaten Germany, but all she wanted to do was to go sleep and was pleased when it all became quiet again.

A few months later it had been raining very heavily with thunder and lightening all night, which had frightened her and it kept her awake, because it reminded her of the wartime bombing. In the morning, when it began to get light, she found that she had damp clothes, and as it was still raining, she decided to find shelter in the van yard of Shornfield House.

In the van yard, looking around she found a newspaper whose headlines read: '83 Dead, 46 Entombed in Welsh Avalanche'. She continued to read that after torrential rain, a mountain of coal dust, which had turned into a black sludge, had tumbled down onto a Junior school full of young children. She started to cry as she continued to read how the mothers of the children had stood in the rain and waited in vain for their young ones to be rescued, and then she remembered how she had an abortion to kill the child she was expecting by the man who had raped her. Somehow she began to feel guilty about the abortion, but at the same time very sorry that she and Kevin had not had a baby. It was then that she felt she knew how those mothers must be feeling because she was remembering how she felt when she heard about Kevin being missing, and was thinking how she would have loved to have had a child by him and mothered his children, when suddenly she stopped thinking about herself, closed her eyes and offered up a silent prayer of sorrow and sympathy. Later that day while she was seated in the little dry hideaway, near St Paul's and was thinking of those children she was gently arguing with herself, that if Kevin had lived and they had had children, whether they would have looked liked him or her. And when she said out loud, 'I am sure they would have looked like me,' she was certain she heard Kevin's voice laughingly saying, 'No you twerp, they would have looked like me.' Quickly turning her head, because she was certain she had heard his voice, and looking around, again she couldn't see anybody.

Shortly before Christmas she was feeling very hungry and was reading in an old newspaper that the Wholesale and Multiple Bakeries paid their male workers £13.9s.6d and this was being increased to £16.2s.7d per week and the female workers who were receiving £9.6s.6d, were going to get £11.8s.4d. Then she read that the price of a single loaf of bread was 1s.7d, but due to the pay increases to the bakery workers, the standard price of a single loaf of bread would cost more. 'My goodness,' she cried out, 'how much more do those workers want? I wish I had that amount of money paid to me each week. I know I wouldn't be as hungry as I am now.'

It was in January near evening time and being a warm evening, she was in her little niche near St Paul's laying some cardboard down on the floor as underlining for her bed, when she heard a number of people walking past, all talking with Irish accents. Being very curious, she left her hiding place and crept a little nearer and looked out from her advantage point and could see many people standing outside the Cathedral, with many more going inside. She saw that some of the men were dressed like priests and wearing 'dog-collars', then she saw a car arrive and a very important looking person wearing a purple shirt and a 'dog-collar' with a large pectoral cross hanging from around his neck got out of the car, and about a hundred policemen standing by the entrance rushed forward to guard him, because the men in 'dog-collars' standing nearby began to jeer and boo him. She thought it was unusual to boo and jeer a person of that standing.

She was wondering what all the trouble was about and was thinking it was odd to hear men who were looking like priests wearing 'dog-collars', booing a very important priest. A short while later she heard more loud shouting and commotion, then a few moments later she saw policemen coming out of the Cathedral holding, in an arm-lock, a number of struggling men wearing 'dog-collars' and bundled them into the black police vans that were nearby. Very shortly afterwards she saw about thirty policemen surrounding another man, whose head, shoulders and suit had been splattered by burst tomatoes and he was shouting out, 'They are proving that Popery is a thuggery'. Seeing all the policemen around, Margery decided it was time to retire into her little niche and hide herself.

The following morning she managed to obtain a newspaper and read about the mayhem and how the newspaper described the demonstrators, as the 'Irish Paisleyites' who had demonstrated inside the Cathedral just as Cardinal Heenan, the Roman Catholic Archbishop of Westminster, had risen to speak on Christian unity and how Mr Paisley, the Northern Ireland Protestant Leader, had accused Dr Ramsey, the Archbishop of Canterbury, of 'Betraying the Protestant Church'. Looking around to see that no one was nearby, she said out loud, 'That commotion is above all my understanding, because I believe there is only one God, who is for all the people and for all the religions, and everyone prays to their God through their own particular faith and belief.' As she put the paper down she thoughtfully said, 'Ah! Well. I suppose some people will do anything for a little piece of publicity.'

8

SHIRLEY WITHERS

The months went by and the pains in her chest and arms were becoming more frequent, and she began to feel very despondent and to think that her life was not worth living.

It was due to her constantly going round the newspaper firms in Fleet Street, that many of the print workers of the *Peoples News*, the *Daily Echo* and the *Daily Tribune* watched her go from one print house to another to get hot water and also to get warmth and shelter, and they had heard stories of her descent into vagrancy, and it was because someone had called her 'Mary from the dairy' that she was always known to everyone as Mary.

Margery knew that if she didn't hinder the night workers and found a quiet spot near to a fan that was extracting the hot air from the machine rooms, it would also warm her frail tired body, and she would get a nice warm sleep on the thick paper that came of the newspaper reels.

Margery was diminutive and petite, but in her badly worn clothing she looked a sorry sight. Some days she could be heard talking to herself and holding a conversation with someone nobody could see. On the odd occasion she could be abrupt, but most of the time she would be quite rational and would talk in an eloquent manner, and always try to walk in a dignified way, which was hard because of the clothes she wore. Many print workers had formed a sympathetic feeling for her and had tried to find out why 'Mary', as she was known, was a vagrant, because they had heard that at some time earlier in her life, she had been a state registered nurse. It was because of that story that many approaches were made to the staff of the Features department of the *Daily Tribune* and the other newspapers to try and unravel the mystery of 'Mary' living the way she seemed to prefer. It was due to one of those approaches that Shirley Withers decided to speak to her.

Early one hot morning, looking out of the window of the Features office of The *Daily Tribune* in Shornfield House, Shirley saw 'Mary' standing with her back to the wall, which was near the pub called 'Harp of Erin' and thought it was a good opportunity to speak to her. So she went to the canteen and purchased two sandwiches.

Margery saw Shirley emerging from the main entrance of Shornfield House, crossing the road and walking slowly towards her. When Shirley got close to her Margery sourly said, 'What do you want?'

Shirley held out the sandwiches, at the same time with all the kindness and sweetness she could muster, said, 'I'm Shirley Withers. I've brought these for you.' Margery quite churlishly asked, 'Why? What for? Why me?'

This took Shirley by surprise but she quickly regained her composure, replying, 'Well, I thought you might like to have a fresh sandwich.'

Margery was looking at Shirley with great suspicion and was about to say 'No', but because of the great hunger she was experiencing and the sandwiches looking so nice she took them, at the same time saying, 'Thank you'. While Margery ate them, Shirley stood nearby.

After she had finished eating Margery said, 'I haven't tasted such nice fresh sandwiches for ages.'

Shirley very quickly asked, 'Why not?'

With a belligerent tone in her voice Margery replied, 'Well, when I can afford it and if the price is right and also if the café staff will let me go in to buy something, I usually end up with their stale bread that has been left over from the day before, and then even though the food is stale, the blighters will always charge me.'

'Oh that's not nice,' said Shirley and in order to carry on speaking to Margery, she asked, 'by the way don't you find it hot in that heavy top coat you are wearing?'

Margery sourly replied, 'It's all I've got to wear.' Suddenly Shirley had an idea. 'Look, I have some summer clothes that I am getting rid of and I wondered if you . . .' But before Shirley could continue Margery sourly said, 'Why? Why have you picked on me today and why do you want to get rid of those clothes and give them to me? Do you think I am need of your charity?'

Shirley very quickly replied, 'No! No of course not. It is because I have been told by my husband that I have too many clothes because the wardrobe is packed tight.' Shirley was hoping that her lies did not show in her voice or eyes and carried on speaking, 'I was not going to throw them away, I was going to give them to the local charity, but if you want them I could bring them to you. Of course I will make sure that they are all washed, cleaned and ironed for you.'

While Shirley had been talking Margery had been looking into Shirley's tender attractive face, and seeing nothing to mistrust, and thinking of those nice clothes, she quietly said, 'Oh alright, thank you. Mind you I don't know why you are doing this for me because most people think I'm too dirty to speak to and not worth bothering about.' And still being apprehensive and suspicious about Shirley's approach to her, Margery again began looking around to see if anyone else was nearby.

Shirley felt that by the tone of voice used by Margery that she was warming towards her. There was a moment's pause so Shirley quickly began asking, 'When I bring these clothes to you and if you are not here, where can I leave them for you and what name shall I put on the parcel so you can claim them?'

Margery was still being very suspicious and paused for moment, because for a fleeting second she saw herself clothed as she was in 1943 and she remembered the recent dream she had had and this brought back to her some of the events that had occurred in her life over the past few years, and even though it seemed a long time before she replied, all this happened in a fraction of a second.

While Margery was lingering with those thoughts, Shirley was looking into Margery's eyes and saw tears appear and wondered what traumas she had suffered, but the tears quickly disappeared, because Margery was saying, 'As long as you promise to keep it to yourself, my name is Margery Hopkins.'

Shirley felt a great surge of relief and elation go through her because she was sure she had gained Margery's confidence and trust. There were many questions Shirley wanted to ask Margery, but Shirley knew that to pry impertinently and too quickly into a person's mind was wrong, because everyone has pride and no one should never take away a person's pride by asking them impertinent questions. It was at that point that Shirley's eyes had strayed over to Margery's bags laying on the floor beside her and Shirley observed a skull cap and realised that is the first question she must ask.

Shirley rather tentatively and innocently asked, 'Why do you carry that skull cap with you?' the question had hardly left Shirley lips before Margery was blurting out, 'It's because of those rotten sods who drink methyl alcohol and get drunk, and they sneak up when I am asleep and try to steal my things, and.when I wake up and try to stop them stealing they hit me about my head and face.'

Shirley felt sure that from tone in Margery's voice and the manner in which she had pronounced some of her words she was sure that Margery had been educated to a high standard. Then Shirley remembered the way Margery had pronounced the word face and Shirley detected a Midlands dialect.

The sun was now beating down on Shirley and she was beginning to sweat a little, and she began to feel that it was not the sun that was making her sweat, but that lovely feeling a columnist gets when they are on to a very good story. Shirley's thoughts raced forward on how she was going to get that story without alarming and frightening Margery.

Shirley's instincts began to tell her that she was sure something dreadful had happened to Margery in her younger life to make her become a vagrant, and those instincts made Shirley more determined than ever to find the answer.

Standing there for a moment she thought, I will speak to Margery but use her proper Christian name, and said, 'Margery, I work for that newspaper called the *Daily Tribune'*, pointing across the road, 'and it is printed in that building. I have to go back to work, but would you allow me to meet you again tomorrow morning at about 10.30, and I can give you that parcel of clothes?'

'Oh! Yes please', replied Margery, 'and thank you very much.' Shirley noticed again that when Margery spoke it was with a slight accent, and her voice also appeared to be more refined.

As Shirley walked backed back to Shornfield House, her thoughts of Margery were mingled with the folklore story of Lord Shornfield that still persisted in Shornfield House. The story related that Lord Shornfield, the owner and founder the *Daily Tribune*, was a hard taskmaster who on his weekly visits to the various offices and departments, spoke gruffly to his staff but listened to their views and even supplied beer to the machine men because they were covered in a thin film of ink and he found the machine room very hot. The reason given for Lord Shornfield's odd behaviour was, that he believed in the old philosophy of demanding respect for himself and treating his workforce with the same respect, thereby preserving the dignity of his workforce but at the same time expecting them to do a fair day's work for a fair day's pay. When Shirley entered the main doors of Shornfield House, she stopped, looked at the photograph of Lord Shornfield hanging on the marble faced wall in the foyer, and silently whispered to herself, 'You were right mi-lord,' because she remembered how she had been taught the philosophy of respecting people and treating people from all walks of life with the same respect as she applied to herself.

On reaching her department she went into the Features Editor, John MacAndrew's office, without knocking on his door, and excitedly explained to him, 'John, I think I'm on to a good story. Can you recall that vagrant lady who we all know as Mary who we think was a nurse, and who sits around the nooks and crannies we have about this building – well today I've managed to have a conversation with her.' John looked up from his desk and seeing her flushed excited face, with her pale blue eyes glowing, he knew from his past close relationship with her that to rebuke her for her unusual entrance into his office or to stop her from proceeding would be futile, because he knew that when she sensed a story it would be a good one. That is why a few moments ago he had been writing to the directors to recommend her for promotion.

John was remembering their previous relationship before her recent marriage as he looked at her petite sensuous body, and also thinking that Shirley's husband was lucky having her as his wife, as he said, 'Well, want do you want from me?'

Shirley said, 'I have bought her a round of sandwiches today from our canteen and I have arranged to meet her tomorrow to give her some of my old clothes. I was thinking that tomorrow I could also buy her a decent meal in the Press Café and that way she might reveal if she was a nurse and how and why she became a vagrant.'

John was tapping his lips with a pencil, as he spoke. 'I don't think buying her meal would be a good idea, you have to remember that those people have a different digestion to us because they are not used to eating big meals.' He paused for a moment because of the look on Shirley's face, then said, 'Now don't get too upset, because you and I couldn't exist on the types of food they eat and we would be very ill, that is why when we try to bring them back to our standards of eating and living they must be gradually eased into it.'

John could see from the look on Shirley's face that she was not convinced, so he said, 'When it's Christmas time those vagrants go to the Church of St Martins in Trafalgar Square, and are given a Christmas meal that has been prepared by the hygienists and experts in the local health authorities who know the right amount calories and size of meat and vegetables that will sustain those people, so that there will not be an outbreak of diarrhoea amongst the vagrants.' When he had finished speaking he hoped that his explanation would be accepted, because he was not sure if what he had said was true, but he was happy when he saw the smile on Shirley's face as she said, 'Would it be all right if I bought her a couple of sandwiches and a cream cake, and if so, can I have some money please?

Taking his wallet from his pocket, John rose from his chair walked towards her and as he handed her a £10 note he put his arms around her shoulders and said, 'Please be careful! I don't want my best girl getting hurt. And remember, don't get too intimate with that lady by raising her hopes of friendship.' Listening to what she thought were words of wisdom from John, he gently kissed her on her forehead. His doing so it reminded her of their previous relationship, and she realised that his feelings for her had not lessened since her recent marriage to Robert.

That evening at home Shirley excitedly related to Robert the progress she had made with Margery, and when she explained that she was going to give Margery some of her old clothes, Robert asked, 'How do you know her size?'

Shirley replied, 'I am about 5ft 7ins and take a size 14, and Margery is slightly shorter and probably about the same size, therefore the clothes I'm going to throw away will fit her.'

She went into the bedroom and selected some blouses and a couple of skirts, together with a lightweight topcoat that had a small black tar stain on the back of it. Sorting through the rest of her clothes she came across a red dress she hadn't worn for ages and put it on. Robert walked into the bedroom and seeing her in that red dress he remembered the last time she had worn it and how sexy and sensuous she looked in it, and within a few moments he was making love to her. During all their ferocious lovemaking not a word was said between them and Shirley hoped that it might enable her to conceive the baby she longed for.

The following morning getting ready to go to work, for some inexplicable reason Shirley wondered where Margery had slept last night. The coffee shop in Fleet Street called 'Dampers' was open all night and was full of print workers. It was while Shirley and Robert had been making love the previous evening that Margery had been trundling along Fleet Street carrying her bags with her personal things in, which she treasured, and made for a doorway opposite the 'Dampers' café, where she intended to make her bed and sleep. After settling herself there making her bed, it was very late and she felt a somnolent mood come upon her and started to doze. But just as she was falling asleep she heard loud voices, which immediately awakened her. She shivered because she recognised the voices of those people she detested. One voice belonged to 'Turpsy Ted' who always drank methyl alcohol, and the other voice to his mate called 'Puffer Phil', and she remembered that earlier that day she had overheard 'Turpsy Ted' say to 'Puffer Phil' that he had no money for drink and she knew he would now be suffering from a bad attack of the 'bends'.

As 'Turpsy Ted' was crossing one the side roads he became very upset, because he was nearly run over by one of the *Daily Tribune* vans taking the early morning editions of newspapers to the mainline railway stations. Then as he crossed over another side road he was again nearly knocked over by another van returning from the stations. The van drivers knew him and had a good laugh at the abuse he shouted.

With their taunts still ringing in his ears, he was swearing as he staggered along Fleet Street in his 'bends' stupor, with 'Puffer Phil' puffing and staggering behind him. Hearing him shouting and swearing, Margery put on her helmet and pretended to be asleep. When 'Turpsy Ted' was near the doorway he saw her, and believing she was asleep he bent down and made a grab for one of her bags, which he thought contained money. However Margery was too quick for him and hit him with one of her heavier bags, causing him to fall over and hit his head against the wall, making him yell out in pain.

'Puffer Phil', seeing 'Turpsy Ted' fall and shout out in pain, and seeing Margery standing up with bags in her hands, panicked and hurriedly puffed away leaving 'Turpsy Ted' alone to fend off Mary's onslaught.

'Turpsy Ted' got up from the pavement and began shouting and cursing her, and to protect himself from her swinging bags, he managed to hit her on the face and again on the nose. These blows hurt Margery and incensed her so much that she swung her bags hard at him and was shouting, 'Get away from me you thieving buggers, and leave my things alone.'

It was because they were making so much noise that the workers in the 'Dampers' café opposite them came out to see what the commotion was about, and seeing what was happening and noticing 'Turpsy Ted' was being hit by 'Mary', they laughing and jeeringly egged her on, shouting across to her 'Goo on Mary, 'it 'im agin an' give 'im annuver one.'

In his befuddled state 'Turpsy Ted', on hearing the shouting coming across the road from the print workers and receiving many blows from Margery's bags realised he was not going to win, and only have a sore head, so he staggered away towards the Strand with Margery shouting obscenities at his retreating figure. When all seemed quiet, she went back into the doorway and settled herself down, but because of the painful battering she had received she had a bad headache and a bad night's sleep.

On the train next morning, after putting the bags containing the clothes for Margery up on the rack, Shirley settled herself into her seat and was feeling blissfully happy thinking of last night with Robert when her face reddened with the reminder of their passion for each other. As the countryside fields passed by, Shirley felt guilty because she realised that due to last night's passion with Robert, which she so hoped would result in her having a baby, she had forgotten to prepare herself on what she was going to ask Margery, and as those thoughts went through her mind she said to herself, 'Whatever happens in work today, I am going to endeavour to find the answers about Margery.'

When Shirley arrived at the Shornfield House everything appeared quiet – very unusual, as there was usually something happening somewhere. Taking advantage of the calmness around her Shirley began to concentrate on the strategy she was going to adopt to avoid upsetting Margery. Looking out of the window she saw Margery standing against the wall, and a few moments later, carrying the bags containing the clothes, Shirley walked out of the building and crossed the road, wondering what type of reception she was going to get from Margery.

When Margery began opening the bags and saw all those clothes her eyes shone bright and she had tears running down her face and kept saying over and over again, 'Thank you – oh thank you very much, they look great!'

While this was going on Shirley was determined to try and discover Margery's age, but when she looked at her, she saw her face looked swollen, and she was shocked to see two red marks and bruises beginning to show on Margery's nose and face.

While Margery was looking at the clothing, Shirley anxiously enquired, 'What on earth have you been doing to get those bruises and marks on your face?'

Margery looked apologetic, then forlornly replied, 'It was those rotten blighters 'Turpsy Ted' and 'Puffer Phil' who tried to steal some of my things last night, but they didn't succeed because I hit 'Turpsy Ted' with one of my bags and he fell over, but he got up and hit me back a few times and caught my face.'

Looking at Margery's sore bruised face, Shirley felt great sympathy and sadness at the thought of Margery's hard life. She felt that underneath Margery's features there seemed to be a compassionate nature, and she did not deserve to be treated like that. She felt this was a great opportunity to find out as much as she could about Margery's life without hurting her feelings.

Margery was taking the coat out of the bag and held it against herself when Shirley said, 'I'm not sure if you'll want that coat because I feel it was meant for an older woman, not for a youngster like you, but if you don't like it, don't worry I will give to the local charity shop.'

Margery was smiling when she looked at the light blue satin lined coat and said, 'Oh don't do that, I do like the coat very much. Mind you I like that piece you said about me being a youngster, I'm a lot older than you think I am because I was born well before the last war.' Shirley very quickly said, 'You do surprise me! If you are that old, what did you do during the war? Were you in the ATS or in London in a munitions factory?' As she finished asking those questions she noticed Margery was gazing into space, as if she was looking into a distance memory. It seemed to Shirley that for an instant Margery's eyes glowed and appeared to come alive with hope, but a few moments later Margery said, 'Yes it was something like that, and it was through the job I had that my friend and I met two Australian airmen, one of them that I married. We had only been married about 18 months and he didn't come back from a bombing raid.'

'He was in the RAF then?' asked Shirley.

Margery began to cry a little and her voice fell into a whisper as she replied, 'Yes, in Bomber Command. He was a wireless operator, air gunner. Look I don't want to talk about now.'

Shirley could see that Margery was upset and decided to leave her with her memories so she said, 'Margery, today is Friday and I can meet you again on Monday next week if that is all right with you, and hopefully you will be wearing some of the clothes I've brought you.'

She walked quickly back to Shornfield House feeling very pleased that she had been told something of Margery's past life, and she crossed the road she called out, 'Bye. Margery!'

John saw her coming in, and waved a greeting to her and beckoned her into his office. He pretended to be busy, so as not to reveal the feelings he still had for her, though he was wishing that they could renew their previous friendship as he looked up, saying, 'Are you winning with that vagrant?'

'I think so,' Shirley replied, 'because she is taking me more and more into her confidence, and I'm meeting her again on Monday. I was considering taking a tape recorder with me on that occasion.' She paused for moment on seeing the look of horror on John's face, and very quickly added, 'Don't look so aghast, John, I only said I was considering it.'

John was looking at Shirley while she was talking and was only half listening to her, because as she stood before him in her smart cream coloured two piece suit looking very sexy, he was reminiscing on their previous relationship and how close they been to becoming engaged to be married, and he was regretting the error he made that made her cancel their courtship. He was thinking what a lucky fellow her husband was having her as his wife, but it was when he heard the words 'tape recorder' that a frown appeared on his face. He recovered quickly, hoping the lies did not show in his eyes as he was saying, 'Sorry Shirley, I was not looking aghast, I was thinking of our legal position.'

Shirley said, 'John, I do believe that I am on to a very good readership story that I believe will interest our women readers. I feel I could get from Margery the events that have led her to degenerate from a normal human being into the bedraggled old woman that you and everyone else see. Now if you say I cannot have a recorder then let me remind you that

I cannot take a pen and notebook with me, because she will run away and all my hard work in gaining her confidence will have been ruined. I would like you to know that all the conversations I've had with her are in my head and in this office because of all the noise and talking taking place we do need notes.'

Understanding the force of her objections John compromised saying, 'There's a tape recorder on top of that cabinet and if I don't see you taking it, the onus is entirely on you.'

John turned his back so that he did not see her take the tape recorder and as Shirley was walked out of his office she was deliberately wriggling her bottom and he gave a wry smile to himself, thinking, 'Just you wait my dear, my time will come.'

On Saturday afternoon Margery was in her secluded sheltered spot amongst the bomb rubble near St Pauls and had changed into some of the clothes and one of the blouses Shirley had given her, and she felt so nice in a clean change of clothes.

As she put on the satin lined coat, she couldn't feel the fleas on her body because they were in her old clothing. She tightened the belt of the coat around her waist and she felt that she was living a normal life again. She wanted to dance as she remembered the time she danced in the village hall to the records of Henry Hall and the Jack Payne dance band. With sun shining upon her and being one of the hottest days in June for years, she sat quite still in those clean clothes, enjoying the moment of reminiscing, until she realised that it was getting late. For a long time she had felt a pain in her chest which sometimes made her cry, and sometimes went down her arms and made her fingers tingle, but today she realised that she had not felt it, and she said to herself, 'Margery Hopkins, that pain is only indigestion and is caused by bad eating times, so you must not start worrying over it.'

From experience she knew that no matter how hot the day had been, the ground was always cold at night, and laying down cardboard she had retrieved made a lining between her body and the cold floor. She knew that the cardboard was in great demand by the vagrants and was always on the alert. She laid some of her old clothes on the cardboard for a mattress for her bed, and settling down on her makeshift bed, and it being a warm night she had taken off the coat Shirley had given her and covered herself with it, and could feel the satin part of it against her face. It reminded her of her childhood. Just before she fell asleep she remembered she would be seeing Shirley again on Monday and decided to smarten her appearance by wearing another blouse and skirt and the coat. When she woke up in the morning she felt very sad and mournful because she had a dream of how she had lost everything she had worked so hard for.

Waiting for Shirley to appear on Monday morning, it was a lovely sunny day and she was standing by the wall near the 'Harp of Erin' pub in the clean cream blouse and black skirt that Shirley had given her. She kept touching the clothes she was wearing and hoping that she looked smart in them, and saying to herself, 'I wonder what that lady called Shirley will think of me, I do hope that I look nice and clean in them.'

She was feeling relaxed, when suddenly she remembered the dream she had the other night and of the happy time working as a nurse with her friend Helen, and she remembered the incident with Dr Cairnworth and began saying to herself, 'I wonder where that rotten sod is and what is he doing now?' It was those thoughts that persuaded her to tell Shirley about her experiences with him.

When Shirley appeared she had a big smile on her face as she said, 'Oh Margery, you do look very smart in those clothes! I'm so pleased they fit you. I was worried and my husband said that I was wrong and they wouldn't. I'm glad I was right, I can see that you look very smart and lovely.'

Exciting thoughts were going through Shirley's mind as she said, 'Let's go into the café on the corner and have a cup of tea and something to eat.' But seeing the look of panic on Margery's face, Shirley remembered what Margery had told her so she said to her, 'Now don't you worry because I'm taking you into the café and I am with you and there will not be any trouble.' Entering the café, observing that nobody was inside, Shirley said, 'Margery, go over and sit there by the window, while I get the sandwiches.'

The counter-hand who knew Margery was a vagrant who came into the Café very early every morning for a cheese roll was very surprised to see her in some smart looking clothes. He looked incredulously at Shirley, who wore a bright blue two-piece suit, and thought, 'What on earth is she doing sharing a table with a vagrant who isn't allowed to sit in the café?' But Shirley was giving him a glaring stare that seemed to say, 'Open your mouth young man and you will get the biggest wigging of your life.' Seeing that look he recklessly thought, 'I don't care what my boss says about vagrants being in his café, there's no way I'm going to upset this beauty.'

Shirley ordered two ham and tomato sandwiches and two teas and she carried them to the table. Settling into her seat she discreetly pulled the tape recorder out of her pocket, ensuring it was completely out of Margery's sight. When Margery had finished her sandwich, Shirley said to her, 'Margery please help me out because I had breakfast this morning and I can't eat this sandwich. I am full up. I'm sure my eyes are too big for my stomach.' Looking at the inviting sandwich 'Mary' was only too pleased to accept, and while she was eating it, Shirley discreetly switched on the tape recorder.

It was while Shirley was sipping her tea that she suddenly heard Margery say, 'You know he criminally assaulted me.' The surprise on hearing those words made Shirley spill some of her tea on the table, but Margery didn't seem to notice it, because she was still talking and saying, 'It was while I was waiting for you this morning, I was remembering the dream I had the other evening and it reminded me of what a doctor did to me.'

Shirley was quietly wiping the table when she tentatively asked, 'Margery, are you sure you want to talk to me about it?'

Having finished eating the sandwich Margery said, 'Yes I do, because whatever happened to me I want you to believe, because I feel you will not repeat it to any one, and even if you did, nobody will ever believe you because they didn't believe me at the hearing.'

Mentally crossing her fingers Shirley replied, 'No, of course I wouldn't say anything.'

Margery looked around the café then carried on speaking. 'You see I haven't spoken to anyone about this from the time I left the GMC hearing where I had made a complaint against a doctor and failed, and I was forced to leave the hospital.'

Looking at Shirley, Margery paused for a moment then she said, 'I came to London and went to the Charing Cross Hospital because I had worked there before, but they wouldn't employ me. I tried other hospitals but I couldn't get a position in any of them, and I've often wondered where that doctor is now.' Shirley made an involuntary whisper of 'GMC hearing and hospital', and on hearing those words Margery replied, 'Yes that's right, it was a GMC hearing, and I haven't worked in a hospital since because at that hearing they stopped me.'

Margery stopped talking and looked at Shirley before she spoke again. 'I feel I should start at the beginning and before the GMC hearing and why I made the complaint to them. It all happened just after the end of the war in Europe in 1945, where I was a ward sister in a hospital in the Midlands, near to the aerodrome where my husband had been stationed. With the war in Europe being over, it was in 1946 that the nurses had arranged for a Christmas party, but someone must have told the doctors because quite a number of them were present and I noticed that one of the doctors was a Dr Nigel Cairnworth. He was a good looking doctor and a number of nurses had a crush on him, however I knew what his behaviour was like because at the VE Night party everyone was out celebrating and there had been dancing in the streets. It was during that night he somehow managed to dance with me and his hands were going all over my body and he was making lewd suggestions. I could smell his breath and knew he had been drinking and as he tried to grab me he fell over and I managed to escape and get away back to my room. A few days later I had a shock because he was the ward doctor and as I accompanied him on his visits to the patients he was whispering lewd remarks and suggestions. Through my talks with nurses who knew of him I found out that he was a ruthless and depraved womaniser. When I saw him at the Christmas party, I kept him in sight and I began to say to the nurses it was time for me to leave.'

While Margery was talking, Shirley was imagining how smart she must have looked in her blue starched uniform with her petite attractive figure and with that air of mystique she still seems to carry with her, and thought of the doctors wanting to date her. The name of Cairnworth came to her mind and suddenly she realised that there had been a recent court trial concerning a Dr Cairnworth, but she stopped thinking about that because now Margery was saying, 'I very rarely drank in those days, certainly not since my Kevin was missing, and it was while I was eating some nuts, talking to some nurses that I felt a tap on my shoulder and there was Dr Cairnworth standing before me with a large drink in his hand. Someone walked behind him and the doctor lurched forward as though he had been pushed, but I knew hadn't because there was plenty of space behind him and he was grinning like a Cheshire cat as he spilt his glass of beer down the front of my dress.'

Margery had a blank expression on her face and had stopped talking to have a sip of tea. Shirley was saying to herself, 'Margery wants me to know this because it is like a cancerous growth bursting within her, but I must find out about the trial of Dr Cairnworth and whether it is related to Margery.'

Margery began speaking again. 'As my dress was very wet the doctor quickly drew his handkerchief from his pocket and started to pat the front part of my dress and was tweaking my breasts. I tried to stop him and push his hands away, but I had a mouthful of nuts and started coughing at the shock of what he was doing, and then someone handed me glass of what I thought was water. I took a big gulp, but I didn't know it was one of Dr Cairnworth's friends who handed me the drink, which contained neat gin. As the fluid went down my throat, the taste of the strong gin and nuts made me choke even more and I felt very ill. I heard him say to someone that he was taking me outside, and I tried to stop him but he held my arm very firmly and led me outside to the corridor where I was still coughing very badly. He opened a door of a consulting room and seated me in a chair, I had my hands over my face to try and stop myself from coughing and therefore I didn't hear him close the door. I heard him unlock a cupboard and then I felt him near me because he took my hands away and put a cloth to my face, telling me to take a deep breath because it would help me. When I took the deep breath I could smell a strong sweet fragrance then I felt a tingling go through my body and I passed out.'

Shirley could see from the glazed look on Margery's face that she was back in that hospital reliving the whole scene. Soon Margery was speaking again. 'When I recovered consciousness I was lying naked on the examination couch, and although my eyes were blurred I could see Dr Cairnworth putting on his trousers. Then the door opened and Matron and the Senior House Doctor entered the room. I can't remember the words they said to me but they repeated them to me at the hospital Board of Enquiry, and at the end of that enquiry I was told that the hospital was referring the case to the GMC. At the GMC hearing the doctor said I was drunk and I had encouraged him to have intercourse with me, and because I couldn't produce any evidence of the lint with lotion on it, nobody would believe me and I was expelled from the hospital. Some time later I was shown a headed letter paper with the words GMC on it that had been signed by the secretary of the GMC and sent to most hospitals informing them not to employ me. I also found out that Dr Cairnworth's father was a professor who at that time of my GMC enquiry, was its Chairman, so what chance did I have?'

Margery burst into tears and cried profusely. Shirley quickly handed her a handkerchief and suggested they leave the café. Outside Margery had regained her composure and Shirley said, 'I must go back to work now, otherwise my boss will wonder where I've been, do you think we could meet here tomorrow about the same time?'

Wiping the tears from her eyes Margery replied, 'Yes.'

Being very excited hearing Margery's story and disgusted and sad at what had happened to her, Shirley went straight to the firm's library to enquire if there was a file in the name of Cairnworth. After a good search the librarian gave Shirley a file relating to a trial that had taken place only 18 months ago. Back in her office, Shirley began reading. It concerned a Mrs Forsythe-Brown, who was at that time 45 years old and a well known London socialite, and married to one of the sons of the wealthy banking family company of Harding & Forsythe-Brown. She had accused a Harley Street consultant, Dr Nigel Cairnworth, of serious professional misconduct. It was alleged that whilst visiting the consultant as a patient at his surgery, he had sexual intercourse with Mrs Forsythe-Brown without her consent. As Shirley was reading she began to remember the trial because it had been front page news in all the tabloid newspapers.

While Shirley was reading the file, she remembered Margery telling her how ornate the room at the GMC had been, and began to imagine the scenario of the room at the time of Margery's meeting with all the people there, and when Dr Cairnworth's solicitors had employed a QC, how shocked and lonely Margery must have felt trying to defend herself against a legal person of that standard.

Reading the reports of the trial Shirley found that Mrs Forsythe-Brown, being extremely rich, had on the day of the alleged offence telephoned two solicitor friends of hers to meet her at her home, and had straightaway informed them of what had taken place. The following day they visited her again and informed her they had contacted Mr Jeremy de-Haan QC, a man well known throughout the legal profession for his tenaciousness and determination for unveiling the truth, as well as the high fees he charged. They also informed her that she would have to a sign an affidavit in his presence.

At the trial, Dr Cairnworth was represented by Mr Robert Raeburn QC, who began the defence by informing the jury that Dr Cairnworth's submissions would be that sexual intercourse had taken place between the two parties and Mrs Forsythe-Brown had consented, because how could sexual intercourse have taken place without the consent of the woman, unless it was rape, and rape has not been pleaded by Mrs Forsythe-Brown.

Shirley read in the next paper that Dr Cairnworth and Mrs Forsythe-Brown had, unbeknown to their respective partners, been lovers for some time. A few months before the alleged offence Dr Cairnworth decided to end their relationship and Mr Raeburn stated the allegations made by Mrs Forsythe-Brown were made by a woman rejected by her lover who felt she had been scorned.

Shirley's interest grew and as she read that Mrs Forsythe-Brown appeared very uncomfortable with Mr de-Haan because of the manner he was speaking about Dr Cairnworth's private life and of his medical career, but Mrs Forsythe-Brown appeared more relaxed when Mr de-Haan said that at GMC committee meetings held on two separate occasions, Dr Cairnworth had been accused of serious sexual misconduct, and on both occasions the victims had alleged that rape had occurred. Shirley read it was at this point in the proceedings that Mr Raeburn rose to object on a point of law, however producing some papers Mr de-Haan gave them to the Judge and also to Mr Raeburn, who rescinded his objections. Shirley became very excited as she read that Mr de-Haan then proceeded to outline the first case, that happened in 1946 and concerned Mrs Margery Hopkins, a ward sister, where at a Christmas party she had suffered a severe choking and coughing fit and was escorted to a consulting room by Dr Cairnworth, where it was alleged that he administered a drug substance and when Mrs Hopkins recovered consciousness she found herself lying naked on an examination couch with Dr Cairnworth putting on his trousers.

Mr de-Haan referred to the second case that involved a 19-year-old woman called Miss Joanna Lee. He said Miss Lee had twice before attended Dr Cairnworth's surgery with her mother, but on the third visit, her mother was not with her. It was during Dr Cairnworth's consultation with Miss Lee that he made an excuse for the nurse not to be present and in the absence of the nurse, Miss Lee was administered with a drug that rendered her unconscious. When she recovered from her unconsciousness she found herself lying naked on a the examination couch. Mr de-Haan stated that up to that time Miss Lee had been a virgin and he said that in both the 1946 case and the 1961 case, even though Dr Cairnworth was legally represented, both of these women were not legally represented at the GMC hearings.

Reading further, Shirley saw that Mr de-Haan had said that in the 1946 case, from the transcripts recorded at the GMC meetings the committee appeared to be in favour of Mrs Hopkins until Dr Cairnworth's father, Professor Cairnworth, gave his evidence, and then the GMC committee found Dr Cairnworth not guilty. And in the 1961 case Professor Cairnworth again gave evidence for his son, as well as Mrs Phillippa Cairnworth, the wife of Dr Cairnworth, and the committee again found Dr Cairnworth not guilty, because both of those women could not substantiate their evidence by submitting the drug. But Mr de-Haan said he could in the case of Mrs Forsythe-Brown, and he produced an affidavit of Mrs Broadribb, the nurse who assisted Dr Cairnworth in the surgery and who cleaned the consulting room of all medical items by putting them in a plastic bag ready for disposal. Mr de-Haan said the solicitors for Mrs Forsythe-Brown went to that consulting room, retrieved the plastic bag and showed the bag to the jury. It contained a bottle and cloth.

Mr de-Haan told the jury that it had to be proved beyond any shadow of a doubt what was on that cloth and in that bottle, and he said that the substance in the bottle and on the cloth had been analysed by Professor Colin Holding, a very senior Forensic Scientist, who in his affidavit has sworn that the substance on the cloth and in the bottle is Ethyl Chloride, which renders a person unconscious.

With that evidence the defence case collapsed, and reading the verdict of the jury, Shirley became excited and could felt her pulse racing because the jury found Dr Cairnworth guilty of rape, and the Judge had sentenced him to five years in jail.

Shirley read a few more papers in the file, and found that after the trial, the GMC committee had met and Dr Cairnworth was barred from practising as a doctor for life. Dr Cairnworth's wife, Phillippa, in a very expensive divorce action, had been given a divorce on the grounds of his insatiable sexual demands and his infidelity with other women, and had been awarded substantial costs against him.

Putting all the papers back in the file and returning the file to the library, Shirley quickly ran up the stairs and into John's office and breathlessly said to him, 'John, it's all in the file, Margery was a nurse and she was raped. Oh boy this is going to be some story!' She gave a big sigh of relief and because of her feelings for Margery tears began to run down her face. John rose from his chair and went to Shirley and lifted her face and very gently he lightly closed her eyelids with his fingers and then kissed her fully on her lips. For a brief moment Shirley responded to his kissing, but with a look of surprise on her face she broke away from him.

John immediately said, 'I do apologise, but I could see that you were emotionally upset and I thought I would shake you by kissing you.' Shirley was wiping her eyes with the handkerchief John had given her as she said, 'I feel that I should tell Margery what I have discovered, and perhaps this will help her to get over her troubles.'

While Shirley was talking, John was thinking how fortuitous the kissing had been, and suddenly he said, 'I think it would help if I took you out for meal right now.' Seeing the look of amazement on her face he countered it with, 'I agree with you that you should tell Margery, and I know how anxious you are to get this story finished, but I am concerned with the libel aspects, so I think it better if we could discuss the outline of your story, I'm sure it would help both of us.'

Understanding the logic of what John was saying and realising that Robert was going to be home late, she replied, 'All right John, but I mustn't be home late because I have so many things to do.'

Shirley was surprised by the speed at which John reacted, instantly picking the telephone up, telephoning Simpsons in the Strand, and booking a table for two. Over the meal they discussed the story at quite some length, and consumed a large amount of wine. After the meal John ordered liqueurs and was sitting quite close to her with his arm resting on the back of her chair. Just then Shirley looked at her watch, and seeing that it was very late she said, 'John I'm sorry, I must hurry, otherwise I'll miss the last train home.'

On leaving Simpsons and in a taxi taking them to Victoria Station, John had his arms around her and was kissing her, thanking her for a lovely evening. Having consumed more alcohol than usual and feeling a little intoxicated Shirley began to respond to his demanding kisses. This blissful feeling was shattered by the taxi coming to halt and the voice of the taxi driver informing them that they were at Victoria.

Hurriedly kissing John goodnight she rather unsteadily hurried off, and on the train she took off her shoes and, aware that she was slightly inebriated, closed her eyes and fell asleep. It was only the sudden jolting of the train coming to halt that awoke her, and through her blurred eyes she managed to see the name of her station. Panicking and grabbing her shoes and things she stumbled off the train on to the platform. Leaving the station she hurriedly tried to tidy herself, and as she walked ungainly down the road to her house she fell over. When she got up she could hardly walk because of the pain in her ankle, then looking at herself she began to worry what Robert would think of her appearance.

Inside the house she felt the full impact of his pent up emotions as, looking at her dishevelled appearance, he began shouting at her, 'Where the hell have you been? I've been worried out of my mind wondering what had happened to you, and from the state you are in it looks as though you been with that chap in your office you are always prattling on about.' He was still very upset as he looked at her again, saying, 'Look at you! You are tipsy, and your lipstick is smeared, and it's past midnight. What do you want me to think, eh?' Shirley however was now feeling very sick and the pain in her ankle was so severe she began to cry. This was too much for Robert, and he stormed off into the bedroom, slamming the door behind him.

A few moments later he re-emerged, and seeing her still crying, and noticing her torn stockings and very badly swollen ankle, asked what had happened. When she told him she had fallen over, he immediately took her to the local hospital, where they diagnosed a broken bone. With her ankle in plaster Shirley was told that it would be six weeks before she could resume work. Being immobile she knew it would be sometime before she could tell Margery the news she had found.

Margery did not know of Shirley's accident and had waited two days for Shirley to appear. Exasperated, she said to herself, 'My trust in people is all wrong because now that I have told her all she wants to know, she doesn't want to see me any more,' and she decided never to go near Shornfield House again.

It was nearly eight weeks before Shirley returned to work from her sick leave, and having found the file on Dr Cairnworth, the first thing she wanted to do was to look for Margery. But she was not to be found, despite asking around whether people had seen her or knew where she was, and Shirley felt totally frustrated.

Time passed, and the days had rolled into weeks and the weeks into summer and autumn, and it was on one of those cold wet autumn days when the autumn leaves were falling from the trees and lying on the wet ground, making a golden slippery carpet, she was walking through the Embankment Gardens when another of those severe pains in her chest caused her to fall to the ground. Gasping for breath, she lay there stunned until the pain had subsided, then rolling over on to her side she managed to pick herself up from the ground and stand. It was then she noticed the blood coming from a wound on her forehead.

While she was standing there in her somewhat dazed condition, she realised that all the time she had been on the ground, and even when she was trying to stand up, many people had walked by and not one of them had offered to help her. But then as she was thinking that, a very smartly dressed and well spoken elderly lady stopped and said to her, 'Are you all right my dear, and do you need any help?', and seeing blood coming from a wound on Margery's head said, 'Oh my dear you are bleeding. I have some tissues here, there you are, put them on your forehead and try and stop the bleeding.'

Margery took the tissues and the lady said, 'Now, are you sure you feel all right?' Margery replied, 'Yes thank you, except for a sore forehead, and I do thank you for the tissues.' When the lady went to leave she said, 'Bless you, and may God and peace be with you always my child.'

With the tissues on her forehead Margery put a tattered tartan woollen scarf around her head to keep them in place, but some of the tissues were standing up above the scarf and it made Margery look like an Indian squaw. When the other vagrants eventually saw her they began laughing at her and making Indian sounding noises. She felt so miserable that she didn't care what they said and went to her place in the bombed ruins near St Paul's. When evening came, her head was sore and bruised and she had a bad headache and took a while to get to sleep that night. As she was drifting in her sleeplessness a great warmth drifted over her body and she thought she could feel Kevin's hands upon her, shivering with pleasure when the warmth appeared to go over her head. A lovely contented feeling came over her and she fell fast asleep and dreamed of her family, her childhood and all of her troubles right up to the present time.

Shirley had still not been able to trace Margery and she felt anxious at not being able to tell her everything that had happened to Nigel Cairnworth, because she knew she was pregnant and would soon be leaving Fleet Street.

After her dream, Margery awake from her deep sleep in a bemused and confused state and put a hand to her head to see if her forehead was bleeding or bruised. She lay there thinking about the dream, and also thinking of Shirley and how much she had trusted her and wondering whether Shirley ever thought of her, when her attention was drawn to the snowflakes falling all around. She began thinking how beautiful they were and gradually she looked around and saw where she was lying, and began to comprehend where she was, and that it was the day before Christmas Eve, and said rather mockingly, 'With the snow falling I had better find myself a dry spot to sleep, and as it's Christmas I think I will be near my Kevin at the RAF Church in Fleet Street. I wonder what bad luck Father Christmas is going to bring me this year.'

She slowly made her way to Fleet Street and was standing outside a baker's shop in her bedraggled clothes, with a heavy long tattered overcoat with badly torn stockings and on her feet boots tied with string. She was looking in amazement at the way the baker had decorated his shop window. There were small electric twinkling lights flashing all round the edge of the window, and he had made a large loaf of bread look like a cowshed and had placed within it a small doll-like figurine of a crib with three small figurines standing on straw beside the crib. At the base of the window was cotton wool representing snow. She stood there enchanted with this Nativity scene and was thinking of the three wise men and amazed at its simple, alluring and enchanting effect.

Within the shop she saw on the shelves many decorated Christmas cakes and beautiful cream scones, which made her stomach ache with yearning because it had been a long time since she had eaten anything as nice as those looked.

Two ladies came along and stood close to her and were looking at the shop window when suddenly one of those ladies said to her companion in a supercilious voice, 'These vagrants who stand around shop windows are a bloody nuisance. All they do is make it bad for shop business because besides being dirty and scruffy they also smell to the highest heavens. Oh I do wish the authorities could do something about them and get rid of them.'

Margery shrank back in fear and anger hearing those words, and immediately stopped looking into the shop and turned to face the women, at the same time giving them a look of intense dislike. Without saying anything she picked up her bags and shuffled her way along Fleet Street, but as she went on her way she heard one of the women say in a very loud pretentious voice, 'Did you see how that horrible old hag looked at me? If she has said anything I was ready to give her a piece of my mind, but I suppose those horrible vagrant people are not really worth bothering about, they ought to be locked up and the key thrown away.'

When Margery heard those words she began to inwardly cry with deep frustration and said out loud to herself, 'How could that woman be so ignorant, if she only knew that people like me are not always as bad as we look, and I wonder what she would say if she knew that I had been a nurse during the war and had come along to tend to the sick and the dying in the bombed ruins.' Then she began to feel sorry for those women because she felt that anyone who could be so venomous couldn't have any feelings for their fellow human beings, and again she cried out, 'Those women who think so badly about homeless people like me and think that we are not human cannot believe in a Supreme Being.' Ever since the death of her husband and from the time working as a nurse and all her other troubles and traumas, her belief in the deity, the supernatural and life after death had grown stronger within Margery.

Making her way up Fleet Street she could feel the cold wind blowing as she stood in the entrance of a doorway opposite the church that she knew was connected to the RAF and therefore to Kevin, and settled herself in the doorway. She felt it would be a suitable place to stay, and she would be hidden and wouldn't be troubled from vagrants like 'Puffer Phil' and 'Turpsy Ted'. After laying cardboard on the floor, and as she was making her bed, the book she used as her diary fell out of one of the bags. Making herself comfortable she began to read it from the beginning. Having finished reading she snuggled down beneath the clothes and began to reminisce over the details of what she had written in the book and was thinking how lucky she had been to marry Kevin and how she had borne the sorrow of his death, and of and all the events that had happened to her afterwards. The thought of the abortion made her feel very bad, because she felt she had done wrong in killing an unborn baby. With those thoughts going through her mind she snuggled deeper under her tattered clothing and could feel the cold wind and because it was snowing heavily she could also feel the damp and the cold. Lying there she began thinking of Kevin and the life they might have had together, and it made her feel a little better.

While huddling there she was clutching in her hands and getting great comfort from the piece of silk that had come from the coat Shirley had given her. She heard the church clock strike ten times and the chimes ringing out, and she began to hum the nursery rhyme to herself, and suddenly began to sing it out loud:

Oranges and lemons, said the bells of St Clements
You owe me five farthings said the bells of St Martin
When will you pay me said the bell of Old Bailey
When I grow rich, said the bells of Shoreditch

When she had finished singing the nursery rhyme, she remembered how she had struggled along Fleet Street and had stood by a shop listening to Bing Crosby singing 'I'm dreaming of a White Christmas' and how she had eventually struggled along the road with pains in her chest and arms, feeling very tired and cold, and how she had settled herself comfortably in the doorway near to the church of St Clement Danes.

When the clock had stopped ringing out the tune, Margery felt quite pleased with herself and began to snuggle herself down even further under the clothing, watching the snow flakes falling, and she began to think of her parents and how happy they had been at Christmas time, then she remembered her Christmas with Kevin and how it had snowed and Kevin was unable to fly, and how they had spent Christmas together and they made love and afterwards they sang the tune they both liked, and she began to sing quietly 'I'm dreaming of a White Christmas'. After singing that song she was thinking of Kevin and she remembered the poem of 'Phantom of Delight' and how Kevin had told her the title of it had reminded him of her, and how he had managed to convince Mark to have the name painted on the side of their plane.

As she watched the snow falling she was again humming that tune, and thinking of the children she and Kevin may have had, and how lucky she had been to have found a dry place away from the wind, and she began to feel warm and said her evening prayers.

9

DEATH ITSELF

Suddenly a great pain struck her very hard in her chest and she felt it go right through her body, down her arms, shuddered and was very still. Even though she had been feeling very cold, she now felt a lovely warm feeling come over her and the pain that had been troubling her in her chest and arms had gone.

She felt herself floating through very thick clouds and she was experiencing a pulling sensation in her back, but then as the clouds began to become less dense a peculiar feeling came upon her, because the pulling sensation which seemed to be caused by something connecting her from behind, eased and as she wondered what it could be, then it suddenly snapped causing her to float along more quickly through the thinning clouds, and she could hear voices in the distance calling her name. She felt she was getting nearer to the sound of the voices because they seemed louder than before, but she still couldn't quite recognise whose voices they were.

She felt that she was floating along through the clouds and couldn't quite make sense of what was happening to her and why she felt so at ease, except she knew that she didn't feel afraid, because somehow she felt that the snapping sensation in her back was the cord of life which had connected her to earth and it had now been cut and severed. With the clouds getting thinner and thinner and the voices getting louder and louder, she floated along feeling very calm, and then she began to get excited because she recognised the voices of her mother and father calling her name.

While floating along through the clouds she began to look at herself and she noticed that she was now wearing the peach coloured two piece suit she had worn on her wedding day, then she looked around again and she felt elated when a joyous sight reached her eyes, because there in the distance she could see Kevin's aircrew members forming an arch, and suddenly right beside her she felt Kevin, who was holding out his hand to escort her through the arch to meet her mother, father and grandparents.

Putting his hand in hers he said, 'It's all right sweetheart, it's all over now. There will no more heartaches, pain or sorrow. I think you now realise that I have been with you most of the time you were on Earth, and when you saw that lady and had the abortion you did the right thing and you should not be upset. We are now together for always and we will never be apart again.'

Holding tightly onto his hand she felt a great feeling of joy and contentment come over her as they went through the arch made by Kevin's airforce friends.

10

BACK TO REALITY

PC Howsted was still in a foul mood over his car being broken into and damaged on reaching Snow Hill Police Station to begin his night shift, because he was thinking of how much it would cost him to get it repaired. He was just about to start his duties when his dark mood was further heightened at being told that his colleagues were telephoning in saying that they were unable to come to work due to sickness, and he was going to have an extra patrol to do, which included Fleet Street and its surrounding areas.

Later that evening with the snow still falling, he passed the Royal Courts of Justice and had just reached the church of St Clement Danes, when he noticed on the other side of the road something lying in a doorway, which from its position looked very ominous to him. With his foul mood still with him, he crossed the road and on taking a much closer look, he could see it was one the vagrants that roamed around the area. He was about to walk away, when the position of the body struck him as peculiar and he bent down to take a closer look.

Whilst he was looking at the body, Shirley and Robert who had been to the Aldwych theatre to see *Me and my Girl* were coming along the road on their way to collect their car from a street nearby. They reached the doorway just as Robin Howsted exclaimed out loud, 'Oh shit! It's not my bloody lucky day. Not another dead one?'

Stopping out of curiosity, they watched him carefully lift the partially snow-covered coat from off the body and shine his torch on to its face. On seeing the face, Shirley gave a stifled gasp as she exclaimed out loud, 'Oh my goodness, it's Margery!' Robert immediately put his arm around her to give her some support.

Quickly dropping the coat back on to the body and looking at them, Robin Howsted gruffly asked her, 'Do you know her, then? Who are you?' Shirley, having partially recovered from the shock, replied, 'Yes I do. I work for the *Daily Tribune* – I'm on maternity leave at the moment, but a short while ago I was writing a story about her.'

Robin laconically remarked, 'I bet that was some story. Then would you happen to know her proper name?' Shirley replied rather proudly, 'Yes, it's Margery Hopkins.'

Robin Howsted began talking on his two-way radio asking for an ambulance to take the body away. When he had finished, he picked up one of Margery's bags and feeling inside found a wartime ration book, and birth and marriage certificates, which confirmed the name Shirley had given him. Then he came across a bible with a wedding ring stuck to a page of the Book of St Luke. Putting the bible and certificates back in the bag, he then picked up another bag, which rattled.

Carefully fumbling around inside the bag he retrieved a badly torn handbag, a very dirty, tattered, ragged knitted doll and then, wrapped in old newspapers and clothing, a porcelain clock, which he handed to Shirley to hold.

Shirley was admiring the small porcelain clock, while he was still rummaging around inside the bag, when suddenly he exclaimed, 'My God! What a lot of rubbish and junk this old hag carried with her. I don't know why they do this, because they cause so much trouble and are a pain to society.'

Robin's words struck Shirley hard and made her cringe with rage, and she shouted at him, 'Don't you dare say things like that about her. And for your benefit I can tell you the reasons why she was a vagrant. That woman was a nurse during World War II, and performed many brave deeds. Her husband was in the Royal Air Force in Bomber Command and was killed on a bombing raid over Germany, fighting to make this a safer place for the likes of you and me to live peacefully in. After the war, that lady, who you just called a hag, was hoping to make a career in nursing, but she was raped by a doctor whose father was an eminent surgeon and a very senior member of the General Medical Council, and because of that connection the doctor was found not guilty of the rape. Fortunately, years later he was found guilty of rape against another woman, was jailed for five years and struck off the medical register and barred for life from practising as a doctor.'

Pointing to the body, Shirley said, 'Unfortunately for that poor soul, she had no-one to help her during her lifetime, or to inform her of the demise of her rapist. So you can see she was not the old hag as you called her, but a person who deserved our respect and sympathy.'

Robin Howsted was completely taken back by Shirley's outburst and could sense by the vehemence in her voice how strongly she had meant everything she had said. Then seeing her holding the porcelain clock in her hand and trying to redeem some form of respect from her, he said, 'Look if you want something to remember her by, why don't you take that clock you are holding, and anything else you like, because all the things in these will only be thrown away.'

Still feeling antagonistic towards him she asked him with a hostile voice, 'Isn't that stealing?'

Noting the hostility in her voice he replied in an apologetic tone of voice, 'No not if you sign for it and leave your address, because I doubt if there are any relatives around, and unless there's money involved, and in this case I would be very surprised if there was, I doubt if they will turn up and claim anything. She will most likely end up being cremated, or buried in a pauper's grave and all these belongings burnt, or thrown away.'

Having calmed down, and after leaving her address and signing for the porcelain clock, Shirley asked, 'If I was to give you £20, do you think you could arrange for some flowers to be at her funeral?'

Robin replied, 'I'm sure I could do that for you and I will send you the floral receipt to your address.'

When the ambulance men had finished their task of removing the body into the ambulance, PC Howsted left for Snow Hill Police station to complete all his paper work. Finding the body and hearing from Shirley of why Margery had become a vagrant made the damage that had been made to his car seem somewhat trivial in comparison, and his inner anger subsided. He began to think of Margery and the solitary life she must have endured and of her lonely death at Christmas time, and somehow he felt a great compassion arise within him and he felt a more chastened person.

Looking out of the window and seeing the snow gently falling, he thought how very lucky he was to have a wife like Michelle and two lovely children to go home to, and he began to look forward to his leave. Somehow he knew that this Christmas was going to be a very old-fashioned one, full of joy and thanksgiving.

Robert and Shirley walked slowly away from the scene. Back in the car Robert switched the radio on, and they heard Perry Como singing 'I may never pass this way again'. Hearing that tune and thinking of Margery brought tears to Shirley's eyes, but as she put her hand in her pocket and felt the porcelain clock, she felt a stirring in her womb, and an inner glow came over her and somehow she felt very contented.

She knew, somehow, that having the clock of Margery's as a keepsake would prove to be a lucky omen for her. She also knew that the title of the tune Perry Como was singing was not true, because she knew she was going to have a little girl, and that the name she would call her baby would begin with the letter M. And Margery would pass this way again.